D0845383

Becoming Modern

Becoming Modern

Willa Cather's Journalism

M. Catherine Downs

SUP

Selinsgrove: Susquehanna University Press
London: Associated University Presses

Associated University Presses
440 Forsgate Drive
Cranbury, NJ 08512

Associated University Presses
16 Barter Street
London WC1A 2AH, England

Associated University Presses
P.O. Box 338, Port Credit
Mississauga, Ontario
Canada L5G 4L8

The paper used in this publication meets the requirements of the American National Standard for Permanence of Paper for Printed Library Materials Z39.48-1984.

Library of Congress Cataloging-in-Publication Data

Downs, M. Catherine.
    Becoming modern : Willa Cather's journalism / M. Catherine Downs.
        p.   cm.
    Includes bibliographical references and index.
    ISBN 1-57591-023-3 (alk. paper)
    1. Cather, Willa, 1873–1947—Knowledge—Journalism.   2. Women and journalism—United States—History—20th century.   3. Reportage literature, American—History and criticism.   I. Title.
PS3505.A87Z625   1999
813'.52—DC21   98-55337
                                                                          CIP

PS 3505
.A 872625
1999

To Michael Hess. He knows why.

Contents

Illustrations

Preface

Writing has to be gone at like any other trade.[1]

—Willa Cather

It is a very grave question whether women have any place in poetry at all. Certainly they have only been successful in poetry of the most highly subjective nature. If a woman writes any poetry at all worth reading, it must be emotional in the extreme, self-centered, self-absorbed, centrifugal.[2]

—Willa Cather

He [Stephen Crane] gave me to understand that he led a double literary life: writing in the first place the matter that pleased himself, and doing it very slowly; in the second place, any sort of stuff that would sell.[3]

—Willa Cather

Illustration for *My Ántonia* by W. T. Benda

There are no extensive treatments of how Willa Cather's years as a journalist shaped her fiction and poems, although James Woodress, one of her primary biographers, has said of those years: "When she died in 1947 her public was virtually unaware of this long foreground as a newspaper and magazine writer . . . it is the long apprenticeship that led to her mature artistry."[4] My concern is with Cather's long apprenticeship—nearly twenty years—from the time in 1893 when she began to write theater reviews for the *Nebraska State Journal* in Lincoln until the day in 1912 when she finally quit *McClure's* magazine, in New York. During that time, Cather herself read or "consumed" journalism, wrote it, was employed by journalists, and came to hire writers herself as she earned managerial titles and power. This study asks what being a woman in an office, writing journalism, editing journalism, did to Willa Cather the author. It must have done a lot, because Sharon O'Brien's biography of Cather ends exactly where the journalism ends—as if to say that Cather's "emerging voice" was nurtured and matured by those years in newspapers and magazines. Although O'Brien's biography does not address the effect of Cather's journalism on her prose, clearly, O'Brien believes Cather's years as a journalist were years of becoming, and their end was Cather's jumping-off place.

The scant attention paid to Cather's journalism is surprising, considering how much of it there is. Cather's most voluminous output— her 500–600 reviews and columns from 1893 to 1902 or so—forced her to form opinions about good and bad art, and to think about what it meant to be a woman artist. Finally, as she determined to become an artist herself, writing about the stage showed her how the actor controlled and manipulated her self-advertising gestures; writing in the popular form of gossip about famous authors and actors led her to examine their marriages and divorces and make some decisions about the shape of her own life; signing her name—Willa Sibert Cather—or an invented name—such as the flowery Gilberta S. Whipple—to her reviews made her public, advertised, a writer herself. The writing Cather-the-journalist did is part of her oeuvre, as surely as is *My Ántonia;* and it is of a piece with the novels and short stories that came later.

Of previous studies of Willa Cather's journalism, the essays and headnotes in Bernice Slote's *The Kingdom of Art* (1967) and the introduction and headnotes in William Curtin's *The World and the Parish* (1970) are the most thorough studies to date. *Chrysalis* (1980), Kathleen Byrne's and Richard Snyder's study of Cather's years in Pittsburgh, includes a chapter about Cather as a journalist on the *Home Monthly* magazine and the *Pittsburgh Leader* newspaper. Mildred Bennett's *The World of Willa Cather* (1961) describes the people and places that would have surrounded Cather during her apprentice years and remains the basis for all later studies. James Woodress and Sharon O'Brien each offer chapters about Cather's life during her years as a newspaper and magazine writer, but they do not trace in depth to what extent those experiences shaped Cather's later work.[5]

What constitutes journalistic "influence?" First, there is the obvious: by working as a journalist, Cather established connections with those who could help her gain jobs and advance in them, as well as connections that led later to long and fulfilling friendships. Because she worked for Charles Gere's newspaper in Nebraska, for instance, Gere may have introduced Willa Cather to James Axtell, who employed her at the *Home Monthly*. Because of the *Home Monthly*, she met George and Helen Seibel. George, a journalist, introduced her to W. A. McGee, owner of the *Pittsburgh Leader*, landing her a much-needed job.[6] Will Owens Jones, her boss at the *Nebraska State Journal*, put in a good word for her when a representative of the McClure, Phillips syndicate came through Lincoln, looking for talent. This connection got her hired at *McClure's* in New York City. Cather's co-worker at *McClure's*, Edith Lewis, became Cather's lifelong companion. Once hired at *McClure's* magazine, Cather went on assignment to Boston, where she met Ferris Greenslet, who passed the manuscript of her first novel around at Houghton, where he was an editor. Houghton published Cather's first three novels, as well as the Autograph Edition of her published works, which she prepared during the 1930s. In Boston, doing research, Cather met Sarah Orne Jewett, who told her that it was time to leave the office, letting office dramas fade into the background so that Cather's unwritten novels could become her central concern.[7] Journalism, then, placed Cather in a network of publishers, writers, and editors. Such a network did not lead inevitably to publishing contracts, but in Cather's case it did.

The influence of journalism upon Cather is more subtle than this, however. Cather wrote about a good many things, changing her mind whenever she saw fit. However, occasionally she settled into an opinion in her public prose and identified wholeheartedly with the subject of her writing. One of her earliest reviews provides an example. In that review for the *Nebraska State Journal*, dated 23 November 1893, she praises the actress Clara Morris for her emotional performance in *Camille*. This performance became a touchstone of Cather's writerly aesthetic. In defending Clara Morris, she defended one use of theatrical art: to mirror publicly an audience's most private passion. In *My Ántonia* she has Jim Burden and Lena Lingard see Clara Morris in just this performance. Clara Morris as the dying courtesan rends her gown and tears her hair, while Jim, watching, keeps his soul-rending desires—to go east to school and to love Lena—hidden and silent.[8]

What was happening to journalism in America happened to Cather and molded her. She was not part of the first wave of women journalists, such as Sarah Josepha Hale, Sarah Payson Willis, and Margaret Fuller were, but in 1893 she was part of the second wave, and certainly an oddity in the office.[9] The concept of women's sphere/men's sphere was outdated, but it still influenced what Cather could say in her public writings. As Linda Wagner-Martin notes in her study of modernism, "the economics question and the woman question were new and central sources for subjects."[10] Cather began to use male pseudonyms when she wrote about work and finance and about sociological conditions in the United States (for instance, immigration); and when she wrote about experiences (swimming in a swimming hole, getting a job) that were then typed "male." Under female pseudonyms, Cather discussed children, the home, and women's occupations. In these cases, Cather begins to "story" a young man's or a young woman's coming of age—situations later thematized in her novels. Journalism forced Cather to create the male voice that would later be the voice of Jim Burden. Cather's Jim experienced moments that were more appropriate for a male: he went to college, he watched women and thought about dancing with them or taking them on dates, he became a successful New York railroad man caught in a bad marriage. Cather's pseudonymous females, who raised children, cooked and cleaned, became characters like Marie Shabata in *O Pioneers!*

Finally, in becoming a reviewer of arts and letters, Cather entered an old argument that had heated up anew in the 1890s: whether realism or sentimentalism was appropriate for artistic expression. Publishers were excited about realism because it was a hot property. It was new—and in these first days of consumer capitalism, driven by advertising, the words New! Improved! were used just as they are used today. Consumers bought for the same reason they buy today— it was their way of expressing status. Cather had to develop a way to be excited about realism while still practicing an art built upon older, more sentimental forms. Cather's first novel shows the influence of both realism and sentimentalism: it is a love story—the sentimental's plot—in which the male protagonist is a bridge-builder—realism's character. *Alexander's Bridge* retains some of the characteristics of novels written by nineteenth-century "lady writers" while at the same time enticing publishers with its "newness," so that Cather later became a best seller.

Cather evinced a profound uneasiness with the idea of an artist making a living by her art. Her squeamishness about earning money comes out when she damns such writers as Francis Marion Crawford for frankly owning up to writing by a formula which pleases his public.[11] Yet Blanche Gelfant has rightly pointed out that in Cather's novels, her characters' harmony or lack of it can be predicted by what the character thinks about money.[12] Money, getting money, and self-advertisement are important themes in Cather's fiction, as they were in Cather's life. Her preoccupation with the money theme stems from her employment—and her heritage. As a nineteenth-century woman, Cather, by tradition, should have been home by the fire. In fact, she was in her office, performing an activity that was not well-defined for a woman—earning money, holding power.

Yet Cather was a shrewd businesswoman. The first literary agent in America was Paul Revere Reynolds, and Cather became one of his clients in 1915. She hustled to get the facts for each article she wrote and was pleased when she scooped the competition.[13] Her office-honed efficiency and concern with the details of typography, advertisement, and illustration led her to abandon Houghton for Alfred K. Knopf's new publishing house, because she felt that Houghton did not give her enough control, that it did not push her works vigorously in the marketplace. The portrait of Cather the writer at her desk slowly, carefully revising a sentence while Edith Lewis pours tea must be tempered by the portrait of Cather negotiating a salary instead of a space rate with McClure, or Cather lining up an illustrator for a hot story. And for that matter, Edith Lewis was not pouring tea. She worked for *McClure's* at first reading proof, and later was an assistant manager.

Journalism's greatest change during Cather's tenure was how it did things—its new technology. In the 1890s, Cather, a journalist doing both newspaper and magazine work, had seen the coming of new machines for making paper, of typewriters, of half-tone machines for reproducing photographs, of linotype machines for typesetting, and of bigger and bigger rotary presses for printing. Cather worked in this world of increasing automation, yet she disliked it. In 1917, with *My Ántonia* accepted at Houghton, she lodged a quiet protest against technology and made that protest a part of her text. To her publisher, she insisted that a certain illustrator—W. T. Benda—be used. Cather had first met Benda when as managing editor of *McClure's* magazine, she hired him to illustrate various short stories and serialized novels. Now she wanted Houghton to commission him to work on her novel. Although Benda lived and worked in the twentieth century, with all of its technological wonders, his illustrations *looked* like the old woodcuts which had been used for illustration before the advent of half-tone reproduction, the newer, and much cheaper, way to print illustrations alongside text.[14]

Cather's new book included illustrations by Benda, illustrations which became a kind of narrator, just as Jim Burden and the Widow Steavens are. In choosing her illustrator, Cather chose the appearance of an older technology, even while Houghton used modern technology to strike off the first copies of her novel. Benda's illustrations spoke to Cather's audience, insisting that *My Ántonia* was an expensive product, a high-quality product that employed older methods to get its message across. The illustrations counterpointed Jim Burden's bad marriage, Ántonia's lower-class status and immigrant beginnings, and Ántonia's becoming a single mother—all issues which were "modern" and "disturbing" in Cather's time, and which, combined with the illustrations, created a most modern irony. Thus even technologies with which Cather came into contact during her years as a journalist became knit into the substance of her novels and a subject of them.

Cather frequently praised artists who seemed to care nothing for the commercial success of their work. Her public praise of art that seems magically free from commercial ties identifies her with the *art pour l'art* school that was popular near the turn of the century. However, Cather, like all artists, presents only part of Cather for public consumption. This book considers that other part and the way that early "other part" of Cather's life fitted her to become, for a time, one of the most successful modernist writers.

I would like to acknowledge the help of many. This study is about currency, production, and value. I would like first to acknowledge those who gave me their intellectual currency, which is the nation's only renewable resource; and their time, which is precious, and quickly exhausted. Linda Wagner-Martin's name goes first. The writer's thoughts must be urged into form; if thought were clay, then her hands knew well the potter's art. At a planning session early on, Margaret Anne O'Connor discussed my ideas with me: I would like to acknowledge that session's shaping influence, and the influence, as well, of O'Connor's queries and ideas in the margins of an early draft. Susan Rosowski, on our first meeting, said a few deft words which changed my thinking. I felt, in addition, that it was her hand which opened many doors in Nebraska. Meridith Thomson's friendship has been the embodiment of the term "collegiality." How often she entered my world and changed it is recorded upon these pages.

Kathleen Rutledge, Gilbert Savery, and Dale Griffing, Nebraska journalists, talked with me about their profession; Barbara Rippey shared her thoughts about how journalism shaped the thought of Nebraska writer Mari Sandoz. Because these Nebraska scholars and professionals took time to discuss their concerns with me, I can say to myself, and to readers, that my observations concerning journalism have some grounding in fact, although I myself never practiced that art.

The scholar depends upon many to make clear the way to knowing: at the University of Nebraska, the curator of the University's Special Collections, Lynn Beideck-Porn, offered invaluable research assistance. In addition, it was a pleasure, both intellectual and emotional, to talk with her. As the curator who spent much time with Cather and Bernice Slote's papers, she had insightful comments for my questions.

I acknowledge the gift of that other currency: the Alein Mcleod McLaurin Fellowship for dissertation research, generously granted me by the University of North Carolina's Department of English, enabled me to research Cather's journalism in Nebraska; the Bahr grant, given also by the English Department, allowed me to travel to Nebraska to deliver a paper and discuss my ideas with other Cather scholars.

Finally, I must thank those who nourished me, body and soul, as I wrote and before. I acknowledge Michael Hess's support during the years it took me to write this book by dedicating it to him. These small words seem pitiful compared with the debt that I owe this friend and companion, but I set them down here nevertheless. I acknowledge the faith of my parents—Blanquieta Joy Hogue Downs and Robert John Downs—in my endeavors. Without their early and constant encouragement, I think that even my native stubbornness must have fallen prey to doubt.

List of Abbreviations

Note: A newspaper or magazine with no page number given in *The World and the Parish* or in *The Kingdom of Art* may be read in microfilm at the Nebraska State Historical Society's archives, in Lincoln. Since this is a study of Willa Cather's journalism, KA and WP citations often contain a page reference to the volume from which they were taken; but also the periodical in which Cather originally published is often mentioned so that the reader may place Cather's journalism in the context of her life history.

Courier	*Lincoln Courier*
Journal	*Nebraska State Journal*
J	*American Journalism,* by Frank Luther Mott
KA	*The Kingdom of Art,* by Willa Catha
NSHA	Nebraska State Historical Society archives, Lincoln, Nebraska
LOVE	Slote Collection, Love Library, the University of Nebraska, Lincoln
M	*History of American Magazines,* by Frank Luther Mott
WCPM	Willa Cather Pioneer Memorial, Red Cloud, Nebraska
WCSF	*Willa Cather's Collected Short Fiction,* by Willa Cather
WP	*The World and the Parish: Willa Cather's Articles and Reviews, 1893–1902,* by Willa Cather

Becoming Modern

1
Introduction: Back Creek, Virginia and Red Cloud, Nebraska

Design has the capacity to cast myths into an enduring, solid, and tangible form, so that they seem to be reality itself.[1]

—Adrian Forty

Journalism is the vandalism of literature. It has brought to it endless harm and no real good. It has made art a trade. The great American newspaper takes in intellect, promise, talent; it gives out only colloquial gossip. It is written by machines, set by machines, and read by machines.[2]

—Willa Cather

Clara Morris in *Camille*

23

In 1923, book reviewers for newspapers and magazines across the country opened their copies of a new novel, *A Lost Lady*, by Willa Cather, the famous Pulitzer-prize-winning author. When they closed its covers and lifted their pens to write their reviews, they felt that Cather had once more written exactly what they expected: once more, some of them loved her work, and some of them hated it.

To some, Marian Forrester, the protagonist of *A Lost Lady*—who, during her husband's loss of health, youth, and wealth, takes a young lover—seemed a true character study:

> Mrs. Forrester, pagan, tippler, lover of men, possesses many of the virtues and principles of her time. . . . She takes the best care of . . . [Mr. Forrester], endures a sort of banishment for his sake, . . . she saves her face, being freed by her husband's absence to take the earthy lover who renews her sense of youth. So runs the hidden Victorian code . . .[3]

Others, however, agreed with J. B. Edwards of the *Sewanee Review*, when he noted that Cather had produced one more tasteless novel:[4]

> A study . . . of an imaginary lost woman, no matter how pretty the style may be, is apt to take more of the nature of malicious gossip than of the quality of literature . . . The author seems to regard morality as a matter of taste, but this is not realism, for taste is rather a matter of morality.

And so the reviews of *A Lost Lady* went: there were good ones and bad ones. The critics' opinions mirrored those of the home folks. Cather reported in a letter that, in Nebraska, people liked either her novels or those of Dorothy Canfield Fisher, her friend as a schoolgirl. Cather's novels were considered risqué, while Fisher's were safe.[5]

The two kinds of readers and reviewers reacted to Cather's complex, modernist structuring of the novel to feel two different responses. They read about Marian Forrester, whose husband's financial entanglements slowly reduce her circumstances. The couple's downhill slide, Marian's attempts to form liaisons with younger men on the make, and, in her more desperate moments, to take solace in alcohol, are the details of a "realistic" story, a story about unheroic characters, about climbing down the social ladder instead of up. The whole is presented via a limited omniscient narrator who looks over the shoulder of Niel Herbert, a romantic young man who deifies Marian as his goddess. The ironic juxtaposition of the worshipful young man and the ideal who slowly reveals herself to be human and caught in the most un-Olympian of circumstances is Cather's plot and theme. Critics who recognized Cather's crafted irony wrote sympathetic reviews. Those who locked themselves into Niel's limited consciousness wrote negative ones.

Where did Cather learn to write a novel like *A Lost Lady?* Her abilities were certainly native, since her earliest writings reveal a prodigal mind. But also the mind met a cultural moment, was strained through it, and Cather-the-novelist emerged. The strainer, her long apprenticeship as a journalist, shaped especially her early novels.

What Was News in the 1890s

In the 1890s, in Lincoln, Nebraska, where Cather practiced journalism and attended the University of Nebraska, the major daily newspaper sported a masthead across the top of the first page: *Daily Nebraska State Journal*—and that was the only "visual," the only illustrative material there. The rest was small type, seven columns across. If a headline said MURDERED FOR MONEY, as one did 1 September 1890 just as Cather arrived in Lincoln to begin school, it said so with relative quiet, modestly heading only one column, one-seventh of a page across. In many late nineteenth-century papers, murder went cheek-by-jowl with Benjamin Henry Harrison's doings, since these types of stories had not yet been segregated in city/state and national sections. There were just eight pages (sixteen on Sunday), one story after another.

During Cather's tenure at the *Journal,* however, events were rapidly changing the publishing industry. In 1883 Joseph Pulitzer founded his newspaper, the *New York World.* Pulitzer, who had arrived in America an impoverished immigrant, set out to publish a newspaper for "the people" instead of for the upper classes, who read Charles A. Dana's *New York Sun.*[6] Because Pulitzer's paper appealed to the less educated, it used more visuals: it inaugurated such practices as printing photographs, cartoons, and banner headlines that spanned seven columns—attributes that have since become common. Pulitzer's paper openly aligned itself with the working class by exposing corruption among elected officials and publishing anti-trust articles.[7] Since the price was cheaper, too, owners of upper-class papers shook their heads at Pulitzer's innovations—and checked their sales figures. Pulitzer's idea of printing a "Sunday supplement"—printing an extra number of pages on Sunday—was especially bad. The supplement featured novels (reading novels on Sunday!) and a new cartoon, "The Yellow Kid." The Kid, as his name suggests, was dressed in a yellow nightshirt. Speaking in the accented English of an immigrant New Yorker, he represented a new, multicultural America. Upper-class readers sniffed and called Pulitzer's paper "yellow journalism," for the Yellow Kid's nightshirt.[8] Sidney Kobrey terms the increasing use of visuals in the news "pictorial journalism."[9] Cather's first attempts at short-story writing and publication, as well as her obtaining a job on the Lincoln paper, took place as Pulitzer's innovations began to catch on.

America was moving toward consumer capitalism during this same period, and advertisements changed to reflect sellers' new strategies. First, advertising itself became a business, when, from 1870 to 1880 advertising space doubled, and then from 1880 to 1890 it doubled again.[10] No longer could sellers list their product and places of business and wait for customers to walk in. Instead, sellers employed ad agencies, and ad agencies sought new ways to create a need in buyers for the product.[11] One strategy was Joseph Pulitzer's: ad writers used more visuals, taking more and more space, to dramatize the importance of products to customers. "Bargains in Everything" shouts the six-columns-across ad for the Racket store, in Auburn, Nebraska, on 26 August 1894. EVERY LADY VISITING OUR STORE WILL GET A PATENT KNIFE SHARPENER FREE, the ad continues. As this ad writer knew, consumers in Nebraska in 1894 were still suffering from the Depression of '93. Anything free was tantalizing. The big type attempted to display, by sheer size, the size of the bargains at Racket Store.

Ad writers utilized another strategy as well, exactly the opposite of the "dramatic": a strategy of reticence. A reticent ad used a headline and small type, just like the newspaper's type, one column wide. The ad pretended to break a story (New York's drinking water was the breeding place of many diseases), then offered a solution (drink Duffey's Pure Malt Whiskey instead).[12]

Ad design was new, but the idea of designing consumer goods had been around for a long time. Adrian Forty in *Objects of Desire* writes that designers went to great lengths to make designs palatable to the public. They used three tactics to sell to niche markets, the small submarkets that advertising creates. One, they designed practical objects to look like something else. For instance, Isaac Singer made his home model Singer sewing machine fold down into a wooden cabinet that looked like a piece of fine furniture rather than suggest a machine in a sweat shop. Two, designers made new products look old, antique, and valuable. Forty tells how radios were housed in neoclassically styled cabinets, a casing which conferred age, grandeur, and dignity upon the troubling mess of wires and tubes. Three, designers made their products look futuristic, a tactic that equated newness, strangeness, and otherness with superior value and modernity, a marketing technique (New! Improved!) with which we are all familiar.[13]

Thus, when Cather landed her first job as a reviewer in 1893, the newspaper's daily offering was a mix of politics, sports, news, and gossip. Fledgling ad writers and publicity managers were beginning to manipulate newspaper makers so that the news would function as both content and advertisement. As for the ads themselves, they ran the gamut, shouting and whispering.

Women Journalists near the Turn of the Century

Pulitzer himself used Forty's third design strategy, making the newspaper look like no newspaper ever had. One of his innovations was to hire a woman, Nellie Bly, to write exposés of New York's social problems.[14] By working ·for Pulitzer, Nellie Bly became a New Woman, and she helped "Improve!" Pulitzer's paper. A typical example of her journalism was this: Nellie Bly faked a kind of epileptic fit and had herself committed to New York's infamous insane asylum, Blackwell's Island. Once inside, she gained information about the abuse of patients. The resulting study was called *Ten Days in a Mad House* (1887). Bly was herself a courageous crusader and a brilliant journalist. However, the way she was "packaged"—lots of visuals, her pseudonym printed in her column itself a "visual"—was Pulitzer's contribution, and her packaging made her a *dramatic* success, a *spectacular* success, watched, ogled, applauded because she was a woman, and because the newspaper, and especially an insane asylum, were not woman's sphere.

Writing for the newspaper or magazine was the way out of woman's sphere for many, starting back with Sarah Josepha Hale, Margaret Fuller, and Fanny Fern. Mott notes that by 1886 there were five hundred women journalists; in fact, journalism was a major employer of women professionals.[15] However, women reporters were spread unevenly through the newspaper staff, and the society page became a ghetto for women. Wrote Anne McCormick, foreign correspondent at the *New York Times,* about those early days[16]:

> Women writers languish over the society column of the daily newspaper. They give advice to the lovelorn. They edit household departments. Clubs, cooking, and clothes are recognized as subjects particularly fitting to their intelligence.

A woman who worked elsewhere was watched. Maurine Watkins, a reporter on the city beat for the *Chicago Tribune,* was fired for her beauty. Male reporters were so fascinated by her that they lingered near her desk and missed deadlines.[17] Robertson reports that one owner of the *New York Times* refused to employ women full time for as long as he owned the paper, from 1896 until 1935.[18]

Women journalists worked in Nebraska from the early days, but, as Arthur J. Riedesel reports, they were often anonymous:

> In most cases, she was the drudge in the ink-smeared smock, balanced on one of the high stools that survive in most shops from those long-gone decades, clawing the hand-set straight matter from the oversize upper, lower, and small-cap cases, all under the most abysmal lighting conditions. Or perhaps she was distributing type after the forms were killed, or feeding a treadle press.[19]

Only a few Nebraska women journalists have left their names and their histories. One was Elia Peattie (1862–1935), the *Omaha World-Herald* reporter with whom Cather enjoyed a long friendship. Peattie left Omaha in part because her male colleagues grew jealous of her successes as a reporter.[20] Being a newspaperwoman had other drawbacks as well. In Peattie's unpublished memoirs, she reports that she loved her career and wanted to be a careerwoman. Nevertheless, the reporter felt that she had to apologize constantly for her ambitions, saying that she did it only for the children, only for her husband.[21]

Willa Cather as a Journalist

Willa Cather became a journalist when Nellie Bly was still making headlines, when Elia Peattie left Nebraska to escape her colleagues' jealousy, when the editors of highbrow monthly magazines like *Harper's* tsk-tsked marketing strategies like those of Joseph Pulitzer.[22] Cather's later work expressed all of the journalistic postures of the decade. When she wished, she staunchly sided with The People, writing of new immigrants and their problems in novels like *My Ántonia*. But in her newspaper reviews of just a decade before, she had looked down her nose at novels which were "timely."[23] At last, when she became a full-time novelist, her novels told the stories of immigrant lives (a "timely" subject) in the lofty, controlled, "timeless" prose of *Harper's*. Yet the creation of the highbrow, with its positive distaste for the middlebrow, was itself "timely"; its covert subject was the new marketing techniques employed by journalists in the nineties. Cather's writing about the tensions between the two was one way she expressed her modernity.

Cather's politics came from her newspaper years. Early American newspapers were party organs, existing largely to advertise a candidate's platform and urge his election. By Cather's time, another kind of newspaper began to compete with the party organ—the independent. The editorial page consequently shrank, news grew to fill the lacuna—and the reporter became important. The paper, freed from party bias, expressed a greater interest in printing the Truth Unvarnished.[24] The paper became a place where readers expected to see "realistic" writing, where party or ideological bias was not forced upon the reader, a place that reported the most gruesome murders without blinking.

Cather, writing for the *Nebraska State Journal,* was not compelled to produce adulatory praise for this year's political candidate. When the *Nebraska State Journal* allowed its writers their own opinions, it espoused *personal journalism.*[25] Writing for the *Journal,* Cather had the freedom to write on many subjects, and she expressed her modernity and freedom from party control by doing so. Cather would have known what personal journalism meant and what past practices had been. Cather herself gave a speech about the issue of personal journalism at the first meeting of the women's auxiliary of the Nebraska Press Association in 1896.[26]

Political independence was not the same as political indifference. The paper for which Cather wrote was full of political commentary. Its editor, Will Owens Jones, was a Republican. In the 1890s in Lincoln, the Republican party was still Lincoln's party, although its credibility was slipping and Populism would soon drain off adherents to both parties. Very conservative Republicans were nativist and prohibitionist. Most Nebraska Republicans, however, were more liberal—antinativist and antiprohibitionist. Cather expressed her own political leanings when she fictionalized political clashes that her newspaper had reported. One such clash had occurred in 1892 over the issue of temperance.[27] Cather, creating drinking or teetotaling characters and the cast of their friends and enemies, remembered—subtly— the complex issues that the temperance battle spun off.

Robert E. Wenger reports that temperance was about class and immigration. Pro-temperance people attempted to reduce the influx of German and Czechoslovakian immigrants by prohibiting alcohol for both religious ritual and in the beer hall.[28] The *Nebraska State Journal* employed at least one anti-temperance, anti-nativist writer, who noted that the newspaper wished that it could endorse Ada M. Bittenbender for the position of judge, but she was such a prohibitionist that the paper couldn't, in good countenance, urge its readers to support her. Prohibitionists in turn considered Republican liberals, such as the editor of the *Nebraska State Journal,* a threat.[29]

Closely linked to Prohibition was women's suffrage. Historian Anne L. Wiegman Wilhite notes that the suffrage issue came to a head in Nebraska in 1856 and again in 1887, when Susan B. Anthony spoke in the area.[30] Many men held a pro-suffrage stance—and the reason they did so is connected to the temperance issue. Some pro-suffrage men believed that giving women the vote would give Prohibition the strength it needed to pass the legislature.[31] In short, the suffrage vote in Nebraska was not just an equal-rights vote. Instead, it was nativist (anti-Catholic, anti–immigrant) and conservative. Women who wished to express their equality with men, yet who espoused liberal politics, had to express their equality in ways other than the vote—by getting a "man's" job, as Cather did, or by playing "men's" sports or taking up "masculine" studies, as did Cather's friend Louise Pound when she became a champion athlete and gained a doctorate in the then-elite field of philology. Cather herself expressed her liberalism and espoused equal rights for women by—ironically— sneering at the women's suffrage campaign, and by writing, over and over, the sympathetic story of the drinking man, the drinking woman, often immigrant, one of The People, who was shunned or despised.[32]

The drinker, then, in Cather's fiction illustrated her political engagement, her modernity, as did her choice not to write directly about politics and to remain an "independent." Cather's symbols of her engagement and modernity seem idiosyncratic, but they are no more so than, say, those of Ezra Pound, who borrowed the alliterative stave of first-millennium Anglo-Saxons in order to make it new.

Becoming Modern

Certainly contemporary readers' inability to "read" Cather's subtext in such novels as *A Lost Lady* is exacerbated by early twentieth-century modernists, such as Pound, who, eager to leave behind their literary ancestors, damned nineteenth-century writing—especially women's writing—with such vigor that seeing around the modernists into the more distant past is difficult. But the fact is, while twentieth-century modernism tried to break with its past, it dragged the past with it into the future. *My Ántonia* is illustrative: Mrs. Harling, who employs Ántonia, scolds her in Victorian terms of morality and propriety for dancing in public. Mrs. Harling's old-fashioned morals and Jim's complicity with them were Cather's nineteenth-century scaffolding. Upon this she erected the disturbingly modern scenes of Antonia's elopement, her birthing a child, her plowing. Cather did embrace the present, but her modern novels may sometimes wear yesterday's fashions.

One more obvious protest of the *fin de siècle* against older sets of mores was its fascination with sex. Tabooed, and therefore modern, subjects were the extramarital affair, visits with prostitutes, contracting syphilis. The latter two plots came to America via de Maupassant, Alexandre Dumas *fils,* and Henrik Ibsen. Thus, *fin de siècle* writers expanded the list of topics about which one could write and it brought outsider characters such as unmarried lovers and French *grisettes* into the literary limelight. Those who objected to the new cast of literary characters, the *fin de siècle* labeled *prudes,* and aimed witty satires at them.[33] When Cather praised de Maupassant, Dumas, and Ibsen's works—and she did so fulsomely—she admired European openness concerning the tabooed subject of sex. Thus her espousing European works at all was a badge of modernity, one she displayed to all her friends in Lincoln. For instance, in 1892 Cather wrote a letter to a friend begging the return of her copy of Daudet's *Sapho*[34]; and in 1900, Cather's two old friends, Frances and Mariel Gere, were still writing each other letters remembering how Cather had so admired Verlaine, that "degenerate Frenchman" during her college years.[35]

The way in which a writer structured a work also signified modernity. Novels and plays with obviously complex plots came to be denigrated as melodramas. By contrast, new novels evinced an increasing concern with the interior drama of the mind (which became the basis for the new science of psychology); the interior drama, with its simpler exterior plot (Stephen Dedelus grows up) gave greater importance to character development, and the *Bildungsroman,* or coming-of-age story, became an accepted form for the modern novel.

Technology and Journalism

Cather became a newspaper writer partly because new discoveries and technologies created new jobs in the media. Because of technological advances, the forty-four hundred periodicals in the United States in 1890 grew to fifty-one hundred by 1895.[36] More periodicals required more writers, editors, and printers, thus Cather and many other writers could find employment. The circumstances that created her employment, however, later found a place in her fiction. For instance, a woodcut engraving might cost three hundred dollars, whereas the new half-tone method, instituted in 1884, could reproduce a photographic image for twenty dollars.[37] Woodcuts were such a large expense that Beadle's Dime Novels hired writers to create stories for already existing woodcuts.[38] The cheaper half-tone process allowed both newspapers and magazines to cut their prices for the first time. The photo's text and the newspaper's text supported each other and created a whole story that was different from all the stories that came before. If the medium was the message, its import was its urgency and its astonishing details of seeming reality.[39] It is no surprise that Cather, who began her career in the nineties, should mature into an author with two great strengths: one, her ability to describe a scene or a person in a few deft sentences, and two, her ability to plumb the unphotographable interior of the psyche. Once the photograph came to be set beside the text—even in a newspaper—the text could no longer just be about description; it had to turn inward, to the less visible.

The new half-tone process, bigger presses that could make more impressions an hour than ever before, and a new wood pulp process for making paper led publishers to reduce their prices and expand their audiences. In addition, electricity came to replace steam generators, and big presses sprang up and began turning in San Francisco and in Chicago, turning out pages of printed matter for a public that relied on print for entertainment and knowledge.

Cather's Childhood in Virginia and Red Cloud

At the same time that the wheels of the presses rolled faster and faster, a young girl was growing up in an almost idyllic pastoral setting. Cather was born in Virginia in 1873, in the Shenandoah Valley town of Back Creek. Her place of birth, which is still standing, was a sheep farm called Willow Shade. Thus, the earliest work with which Cather had contact was farming, a labor that knew no desks and whose time-clock was the sun.

As O'Brien relates, the women in Cather's family showed young Willa what a woman was supposed to do. Sidney Cather Gore, Cather's great-aunt, became a major landholder, postmistress, and boarding-house owner near Back Creek. Her townspeople felt her presence so keenly that they named their locality "Gore, Virginia."[40] However closely she lived with her mother, a homemaker, Cather must have heard and occasionally seen the busy Aunt Sidney around whom a town revolved.

Cather's paternal grandmother, Caroline Smith Cather, followed her husband dutifully from Virginia to the Nebraska Divide. Her motto, "A change of work is a rest," must have fallen on young Cather's ears from time to time.[41] Her grandmother's character must have nourished both Cather's fears and her determination, for Cather thought enough of her to model Grandma Burden in *My Ántonia* after this grandmother. Perhaps thinking of her grandmother, Cather always worried that an "artist" was a person who did no "sanctioned" work. Cather insistently made her writing not just an avocation, but a profession, with regular hours and duties.

Cather's Aunt Franc showed Cather one way of living one's love for learning. Frances Smith Cather, wife of Willa's uncle, George Cather, had attended Mt. Holyoke.[42] A learned woman, she impressed Cather with her breadth of learning and her love for literature. Cather writes of sitting by Aunt Franc while the older woman recited Byron.[43] However, as a young woman, Cather saw Frances Cather as one whose avocation conflicted with her duties as a Nebraska farm wife. Cather's short story, "A Wagner Matinée" (1905), displays with brutal clarity how Frances Cather's literary and musical ambitions were overwhelmed by the necessity of milking the cows and cooking. The story gives a clear picture of what Cather thought—at least during one time in her life—of the vocation of homemaking on the Nebraska plains.

After Cather and her immediate family followed her grandparents to the Nebraska Divide in 1883, Cather met another kind of homemaker: the Czechoslovakian, German, and Scandinavian pioneer women who farmed and told stories and made bread. Because they came from a different culture, they were not bound by the late nineteenth-century Anglo-American notion of women's sphere (which was the home). Thus while new immigrant women could cook and sew, American ideals had not yet barred them from plowing. The immigrant women's difference fascinated Cather, and she wrote of them in two kinds of scenes. In "The Bohemian Girl," for instance, Nils marvels at the cooking and sewing skills of the immigrant women.[44] In *My Ántonia,* however, Jim Burden is disgusted when he finds Ántonia in the unwomanly attitude of plowing. Cather was a good enough ironist to allow Ántonia to speak for herself, defending her vocation and the breadth of her "job description" to Jim.

After living on the prairie for eighteen months, Cather's family moved to town, where her father worked for Security Investment Company, an insurance and loan business. Cather's first encounters with work had been with farming and housework. Now, in Red Cloud, Cather moved into another story, the story of American business. Cather revered her businessman-father and as a girl had played in her father's office, where she had her own desk, where the hum of

business being transacted entered her consciousness.[45] When her father would stroll down to the courthouse, he would leave his daughter to take messages. Visitors would tell her their grown-up plans, as
if she were someone important.[46] If at home she was "child," and
"daughter," defined by her position in the family and by her gender,
in the office she was defined by what she could do, or so it must have
felt to the young girl.

Horatio Alger's Ragged Dick had been plying the pages of the
nation's magazines since 1867; his story included the story of businesses, offices, and work. Cather readily absorbed the idea that Ragged Dick always got ahead if he worked hard. Tommy, in Cather's
short story "Tommy, the Unsentimental" (1896), was a banker on
the make, a character that Cather must have drawn from her early
impressions of workaday Red Cloud. Perhaps Tommy is a partial
portrait of Cather's real neighbor, Carrie Miner, a businesswoman
who clerked in her father's store. Later, Cather would model Frances
Harling of *My Ántonia* on this businesswoman. Wick Cutter, the
unethical lender in *My Ántonia,* was also a town character, as were
the two businessmen, on whom were modeled the title characters of
her late short story "Two Friends" (1932).

If going to the office with her father made her feel important, her
small-town Nebraska upbringing may have made her feel deprived
after living in the fine big home in Virginia. Because her grandfather,
William Cather, owner and builder of Willow Shade, had been a
Union man during the Civil War, he remained prosperous after the
conflict.[47] Woodress describes the kitchen at Willow Shade as having
three tables: one for making bread, one for rolling out pastry, and
one for cutting meat.[48] Food was cooked in a cavernous fireplace.
Moving from the spacious Back Creek farm to the Nebraska Divide
and then to Red Cloud was a comedown, at least regarding the
kitchen. Because housing was scarce in Red Cloud, Charles and Virginia Cather rented a one and one-half story frame house and moved
in with four children, Rachel Boak (Virginia's mother), a cousin, and
a servant. In the kitchen, there was room for only one work table
and an iron stove. There was a formal dining room and a parlor,
although Grandma Boak's bedroom both housed the servant and
served as a passageway to the kitchen. Infant children slept in their
parents' bedroom, and the older children initially all shared the un-
heated attic.

Once in Red Cloud, Cather occasionally visited ex-governor Silas
Garber and his wife Lyra in their grand home.[49] She fictionalized her
visits to the Garber home in *A Lost Lady,* when she has Niel compare
the magnificence of the Forrester home to his own: "their [Niel's]

house was usually full of washing in various stages of incompletion,—tubs sitting about with linen soaking,—and the beds "aired" until any hour. . . . Having lost his own property, [Niel's father] . . . invested other people's money for them. He was a gentle, agreeable man, young, good-looking, with nice manners, but Niel felt there was an air of failure and defeat about his family."[50] Although Cather wrote many loving remembrances of her family and her home, this portrait and one in *Song of the Lark* show another way of looking at her childhood days and explain why, perhaps, she was so eager to escape to the University of Nebraska when she graduated high school.

The drama of have and have-nots made it into her fiction: the martyred hero of "Peter" commits suicide because his son, a budding businessman, opposes Peter's impractical artistic values. Cather's works are also about ethics and money—she portrays selfish capitalists as well as generous ones. Thus vicious Wick Cutter is set against generous Doctor Archie, and Ivy Peters's destruction must be measured against Alexandra Bergson's creation. In "Tommy, the Unsentimental," the title character and hero is a girl who is dedicated to the banking business.[51] Tommy saves the day when there is a run on the bank.

The American business ethic, combined with values imparted to her during her earliest childhood, may have given Cather an important model to follow. If, for Cather's grandmother, "real work" had to take precedence in her life, and Cather at this age found housework worthless toil, could not one's art be considered "real" work? America's work ethic, as preached through Horatio Alger's fiction, said that if one worked hard enough, starting at the bottom, one could make it to the top. Cather expressed her admiration for this ethic throughout her journalistic career and discovered how it might be applied to "art work." In one review, she praised the singer Lillian Nordica (1859–1914) for her ability to work, even under great strain, and even among people who did not understand her art.[52] In small towns like Red Cloud, Nebraska, "hard work" was something one did in the field or at the bank. Among the local wags, Cather must have heard that art was frivolous, not work at all. In the persons of Nordica and others, Cather saw how one might do that soul-saving labor preached by Alger, yet create her own artistic vision. When she began her career in journalism, she found a way to work and to write at the same time.

Work was what one did, and Cather learned to pattern her doings after those of family members and townspeople. But Cather also began, at this time (the late 1880s) to pattern how she looked. During her years in Red Cloud, Cather began to create personae for herself.

Family photographs show her taking part in amateur theatricals—dressed as a man. Around 1885, when she was twelve, Cather created a persona whom she called William Cather, M.D. She masked as William Cather, with her hair cut short, until after she began college. "In a sense," O'Brien wrote, "her male impersonation was her first major work of fiction."[53] As O'Brien has shown, one cause of Cather's masking was her old trouble with homemaking as a career. She saw the lives of the male physicians in town as vastly preferable to the life of an Aunt Franc, or of her mother, and made her choice by changing her clothes, her hair, and her name.

Hermione Lee, in her biography of Cather called *Double Lives,* noted Cather's actual surroundings and role models—her grandmother Boak, whom Cather portrayed in "Old Mrs. Harris" as cooking unceasingly; her mother, who was often pregnant or nursing; the town gossips, whom Cather described in *Song of the Lark* as being especially harsh on creative, individualistic people. They magnified the difference between her surroundings and her desired worlds—the rural cycle of time in Back Creek, the land given a romantic history by having been deeded to the family by Lord Fairfax, the stately mansion of the Garbers, those who escaped Red Cloud and returned on the iron horse only to leave again. Says Lee of these differing worlds: "Cather's writing would always arbitrate between realism and romance, and her move from early childhood experiences (vivid encounters, strongly felt landscapes, first-hand narratives) to adolescent fantasy, escapism, and play acting look forward to that negotiation."[54] Lee's biography proposes that tensions and contrasts shaped Cather as an author.

One more such tension stretched Cather between two futures—male and female. The contrast became apparent in Cather's clothing. From the age of twelve until after she went away to college, Cather dressed in boy's clothes and bobbed her hair. Specifically in her role as William Cather, M.D., she transformed her increasingly female form into the shape of a male, whose job was to do "real work," not "housework." In 1895, long after Cather had quit her William Cather disguise, she still admired actresses who played men's roles. "Her dancing in boy's clothes," Cather says of Cecil Spooner, "is easy and graceful. In skirts she is sometimes a little jerky in her movements."[55] In her short story, "Flavia and Her Artists" (1905), the character Jimmy Broadwood, an actress, according to the narrator, resembles nothing so much as a rosy boy. Sarah Bernhardt, a favorite actress, played the title role in *Hamlet.* The cross-dressing girl made Shakespeare's *As You Like It* (Roselind, played by Julia Marlowe) and *The Merchant of Venice* (Portia, played by Helena Modjeska) enormously popular at the turn of the century.[56] The cross-dressing girl had it all: the admiration of men because she was pretty, and the admiration of women because she was publicly successful.

The young girl Willa Cather continued to style herself "William" and to ride with Dr. Damerel, a Red Cloud physician, on his rounds. She "crossdressed" in her clothing and in her career choice: she would become a doctor, she thought. However, Cather had already slipped into her career as a journalist: she wrote high school news for the *Webster County Argus*, a newspaper—Cather became a journalist very early indeed.[57] She did not see journalism as her career, and her early contributions do not stand out. Instead, when, in 1890 she prepared to enter the University of Nebraska, she signed up for science classes in order to begin the serious study of medicine, and she walked into her first classes with her hair bobbed short and wearing "men's" clothing.

2

The Waltz and the Real: Lincoln, Nebraska

The newspapers are supposed to represent, if not discrimination in art, at least self-respecting intelligence . . . [1]

—Willa Cather

The world went very well then, before electrical appliances were born, . . . when the hiss of steam and the glow of arc-lights had not yet frightened away romance . . . .[2]

—Willa Cather

Cather could sneer at the "realists of the everyday" but she became one after all.[3]

—Loretta Wasserman

Sketch of the Episcopal Church in Brownville, Nebraska, from the *Nebraska State Journal*, 12 August 1894

On 26 November 1893, an unsigned column by Willa Cather ran in the *Nebraska State Journal*, one of Lincoln's daily papers.[4] Cather had just started her first real job (her first piece had run 5 November), and she didn't quite know how to be a newspaper columnist. Instead of the five *W*s, her columns were character sketches, worthy efforts for a budding novelist. Indeed, she seems to have copied the form from herself: it was a style she used in the University of Nebraska student newspaper, of which she was an editor. No other *Nebraska State Journal* columns were quite like Cather's early efforts. Perhaps Will Owens Jones, who was her managing editor at the *Journal* as well as her journalism professor at the University of Nebraska, where Cather was a junior, set her straight, or perhaps Julius Tyndale, the drama editor of the *Evening News* (a rival paper), gave her a few pointers[5]: after 17 December, she began writing more traditional reviews of theater and opera. Until then, however, these first special columns, titled "One Way of Putting It" by Cather and called *vignettes* by the critic William Curtin, offer a glimpse into young Cather's mind.[6]

Her 26 November vignette, for instance, is about an act of communication between an artist and the consumers of her art. Cather describes a pianist playing in a dance hall. In the vignette, the pianist has been playing all evening, and she is tired. She feels old as well: the dance floor dramas of love given and withheld seem stale, but she keeps her jaded feelings hidden because she is a professional. On the dance floor, partners embrace and move. The pianist's music commands the dancers' tread and rhythm; the pianist chooses the script, old sentimental songs, which shape the dancers' love. The pianist's private cynicism, however, is a true story. It is real, the stuff of small tragedies. Yet the dancers' passion is real, too: once more they dance as if they were newly in love.

Cather's column is not about a dance-hall pianist wearing a facile mask, but rather about two realities that exist side by side. The pianist's cynicism is one reality; with the dancers, she creates the other reality by making music. Newspaper readers, the piano player, and the author know both stories. The dancers just keep on dancing. Their story hangs upon the piano's notes in a rented hall: to continue this story, they must remain ignorant of the pianist's point of view. Newspaper readers keep both stories in their minds, for it is the tension between the two that creates the dramatic irony which is Cather's point. From the lovers' deep involvement in their own story to the lofty distance of the newspaper reader is Cather's juxtaposition of sentimentality and realism, the waltz and the real.

Cather's time as a Nebraska journalist was spent, in part, deciding with which school of literature she would align herself. During her various explorations of sentimentalism and realism, Cather sought not just the proper word choice for her work, not just which narrator, not just which story. Realism in the nineties connoted the brash and new, the farmer and office worker struggling against weather and capitalism, narrated by the male author, and appreciated by the male critic. Sentimentalism connoted love lost and won, cheap books and magazine fluff, the old and passé, confided by the female author and consumed by the female reader. In the nineties in Nebraska, Cather's writing meanders, first to one, then to the other, her allegiances signalled by her choice of subject. When she discussed the French writer Zola or the actress Eleanora Duse, she was Cather the realist, appreciating French forthrightness about the perils of sexual stereotyping, or appreciating the Italian actress's ability to evoke emotion without exaggerating it (a "realistic" actress). When she gushed about actresses Clara Morris or Sarah Bernhardt, Cather was reacting as a sentimental "reader," displaying the depth of her feeling about the emotions evoked. For Cather these actual people and things were vessels which contained the characteristics either of realism or of the sentimental. By the time that she left Nebraska in June 1896, she had completed three short stories in the realistic style. However, she had also determined that there were reasons to be loyal to aspects of the older sentimental school as well. Cather appears to vacillate between the two schools, her vacillations bearing no pattern and making no sense. But the fact of vacillation was itself the pattern, a pattern formed precisely because Cather was a college girl in the 1890s.

Cather's College Years

Cather the columnist was first Cather the co-ed. She had matriculated at the University of Nebraska in Lincoln, an egalitarian, co-educational, land-grant school.[7] But before college she had entered the university's Latin school, a preparatory course, thus spending a total of five years at school. Cather's coming to the university in the fall of 1890 was the logical step for the profession that she had chosen for herself: to be a doctor. At sixteen she placed herself in the hero's story: she wanted to work and see the products of her work. She wanted money for her labor—she did not want to fall prey to Nebraska shysters.[8]

Medicine was Cather's choice of profession perhaps because it enabled one to actively cure, to remedy passive suffering. Cather's mother was prone to illness—which perhaps had been brought on by childbearing. On two occasions, Red Cloud physician Dr. McKeeby had only to look into the sick woman's eyes to affect a cure (O'Brien 1987, 91). Between the helpless, sick, frequently pregnant Virginia Cather and the miracle-working doctor, the choice was clear. If Cather had read the papers, she would have had more reason to fear "woman's lot." The *Nebraska State Journal* of 28 June 1896 reports the suicide of a farm wife who drank carbolic acid to end the pain of illness brought on by childbearing.[9]

Cather entered the university, fully intent on becoming a doctor; however, by March of 1891, the spring of her first year, her resolution began to waver. Woodress tells how one of her English professors, Ebenezer Hunt, assigned the theme "The Personal Characteristics of Thomas Carlyle" to his class. He was so impressed by Cather's performance that he published it in the *Nebraska State Journal* on 1 March 1891. Thirty-six years later, Cather reported that this event— seeing her work in print—caused her to consider the profession of authorship.[10]

After finishing her year as a prep, Cather matriculated as a freshman in the fall of 1891 and quickly put her interest in and talent for literature to work: she helped begin a new campus magazine, the *Lasso*. In the spring of her freshman year, she also became associate editor of the *Hesperian,* a semimonthly campus literary magazine which became the first real venue for publishing her own work. During her editorship, she published her earliest poetry, translations, short stories, and plays.

Cather's earliest short stories tell with what schools of literature she identified as she entered the university. "Peter" (1892), "The Clemency of the Court" (1893), "The Elopement of Allen Poole" (1894), and "On the Divide" (1896) are starkly realistic; that is, they treat male characters who are poor, and whose lives are attenuated, in some fashion, by their environment. Because they attempt to portray actual details of people's lives, they are also "local color."[11] Cather's first story, "Peter," is a perfect example of her early writing style. Quick of plot and unsparing of character, she seems to have been copying Hamlin Garland's revolt from the village.

By 1892, when Cather wrote "Peter," a war of words was in full swing in the magazines, with William Dean Howells of *Harper's* and his realist defenders and literary progeny (such as Hamlin Garland, writing for the *Arena*) squaring off against old-guard Thomas Baily Aldrich of the *Atlantic* and Richard Watson Gilder of the *Century*.[12] Literature needed to be about real human beings, asserted the realists, not about swashbucklers in haunted castles and not about the woes of ladies in love. Searching for a convenient scapegoat on whom to blame American literature's seeming desertion of reality as a subject, realists lit on women writers. Their scorn was withering. Bliss Perry painted a picture of the harm wreaked on civilization by "The Amateur Spirit": "the lady amateur . . . writes verse without knowing prosody, and paints pictures without learning to draw."[13] The wording of such an attack was not accidental. Until the 1850s and 1860s women's writing, associated with the literature of sentiment, had held a healthy share of the book market.[14] Daniel H. Borus, in his study on realism, notes that its most vocal proponents (Dreiser, Norris, Crane) attempted to take some of the market from women by their "aggressively masculine" rhetoric.[15] The lady writer was also ignorant, asserted her critics; to become worthy of being read, she had to hasten to repair her ignorance in a time when women were still not allowed to enter or graduate from the nation's more prestigious universities. "As critics from Leslie Fiedler to Carolyn Heilbrun to Nina Baym have demonstrated," says Judith Fetterley, "American literature as defined by the literary establishment whom Cather intended to impress, is a male preserve; the woman who would make her mark in that territory must perforce write like a man."[16] By aligning herself with male critics and authors, such as Iowa-born Hamlin Garland (1860–1940), and by going to school, Cather gave herself a profession, removing herself from the round of housekeeping, pregnancy, and illness that she saw as limiting a woman's life.

Realistic literature was the new kid on the block, and because it was new, it was the darling of publishers (who could market it New! Improved!) and the *enfant terrible* of the old guard. Romance writers hastened to attack the realists as vulgar. To counter, publishers said of idealists that they liked their "fine writing" too much; and since the new literary magazines, such as *McClure's* and the *Arena* paid by the word (one-half cent or more per word), they set their editors to trim the fine writing, to trim both page and budget. Cather jumped on the realists' bandwagon early, embracing their less florid style. She says, praising George du Maurier, who published his best-selling novel *Trilby* when he was 60: "There is nothing so fatal as that habit in young authors of seeing things in a 'literary' way"—and by "literary" here, Cather means steeped in fine writing.[17] The paradigmatic three-volume novel bit the dust, and modernist compactness gained a foothold.[18]

Realism of the 1890s depended on careful psychological development of each main character to set up the novel's class conflict.[19] Such characters differed from those of a traditional nineteenth-century novel, such as E.D.E.N. Southworth's *The Hidden Hand* (1859).

Southworth's villains are villains from page 1 to the end. The story of how the villains became villainous is the realist's story. The realist's plot was also simple, driven by the characters' natures. Such a plot was "organic," as opposed to the "artificial" plot of a traditional novel.[20] Cather cared to fashion new organic plots: in her very early story "A Son of the Celestial" (1893), characters Yung Lee Ho and Old Ponter argue about literature. Yung likes Longfellow's *Hiawatha,* with its stilted and "artificial" structure: "we cut our trees into shape, we bind our women into shape," he says. The American takes up for *Hamlet,* with its organic development.[21] Cather also stood up for realism's plain language (as opposed to the ornate rhetorical style, called "fine writing," of traditional writers) in her earliest journalism, written for the school paper. In her editor's statement for the University of Nebraska fortnightly *Hesperian,* she asserts that, under her editorship, the paper will be written in language that was "plain" and "unornamented."[22] She was enamored of Flaubert's *mot juste,* especially preferring *Madame Bovary.*[23]

Cather wrote "Peter" in the realistic style. The plot is stark and simple: far from his home in Czechoslovakia, where he had been a respected musician, Old Peter tries to stay warm in his prairie dugout throughout the cold winter. His son, who has adapted well to life in America, tells his father that they must sell his violin in order to raise money. Rather than do so, Peter smashes his violin, then shoots himself. In Cather's hands, Peter is ground down by age, homesickness, poverty, and the lack of an appreciative audience. Peter's son is heartless; his only desire is to make money.

Cather made "Peter" realistic by choosing a plot and themes that "storied" Peter's life on the farm, but actually commented on the citizens of Red Cloud and Lincoln. Cather got her plot from the death of a neighbor, who was the father of the real-life heroine who appeared later in *My Ántonia.*[24] "Peter" describes two ways in which immigrants viewed the native-born: Peter's view was that the old country held all that was good. His son's view, however, accepted an extreme form of American capitalism as the best way of life.[25] "Peter" holds special resonance for another reason. The two conflicting immigrant views mimic a conflict among artists living in America at the turn of the century: should art's work be the making of money, i.e., the creation of a saleable commodity? Or should art be made as an end in itself, i.e., because it is intrinsically valuable? Although "Peter" is about immigrant views of Americans and is true to the immigrant story, "Peter" is true to the artist's story as well.

Strangely enough, "Peter" tells the story of prohibition. Old Peter drinks whenever he can. Anything that is not nailed down, he pawns for a pint. In the early 1890s, politicians were stumping for prohibition. In Nebraska, the prohibition vote was nativist; that is, it sought to drive out the Germans, with their beer halls, and the Bohemian Catholics, whose liturgy required wine.[26] Prohibitionists welcomed female suffrage, because at that time, female politicians often campaigned on the prohibition plank. Women's suffrage, the prohibitionists thought, would double the prohibition vote and send the Germans and Bohemians packing.[27] In her sympathetic picture of homesick Peter the inebriated musician and his grasping, artless son, Cather casts her vote with the antiprohibitionists—a vote which welcomed immigrants but denied suffrage to women.

By choosing to write "Peter" in the realistic style, Cather sided with market forces, publishers, professional writers, and the "new" while at the same time her plot ironically cautioned against measuring worth only with money. "Peter" was new and shocking. Its subtext, antinativist and antiprohibition, defied Nebraska's most conservative elements. Cather's authorial persona in her short story flaunts its newness and openly embraces immigration and unfamiliar immigrant lifestyles. Like a reporter, Cather's persona refuses to blink at the squalor of Peter's dugout or at his death.

Cather wrote "Peter" at the university, and once more a teacher noticed the force of Cather's writing, sent the manuscript away, and got it published—this time in the May 1892 *Mahogany Tree* of Boston. If "Carlyle's" publication did not cause Cather to turn author, then surely receiving a copy of the *Mahogany Tree* with her story published inside must have cemented her decision. Her work, which had received such high praise and the honor of getting published, was realist. Realism, it seemed to young Cather, must be the formula for success.

Student Life in the 1890s

At the university, Cather received an education, but she also entered an elite brother- and sisterhood not shared by many in the state of Nebraska: she could read Latin and Greek, she had read Browning and Shakespeare, all under the tutelage of scholars.[28] As Helen Horowitz has shown, universities, at which only 3% of Americans matriculated in the 1890s, created and maintained several undergraduate cultures which shaped how Cather viewed herself.[29] For instance, college women in Cather's day could belong to a sorority, which preserved itself as an upper-class, ultra-feminine organization.[30] But women who did not have the correct social standing, reports Horowitz, were excluded from sororities and became strikingly independent. College women who could not pledge a Greek letter society entered a male culture and became, to the extent that this was possible, "one of the boys."

Such girls were not of the upper crust. They went to college to train their minds for a well-paying job. Once they gained employment, reports Horowitz, they found work to be more important than marriage. More than half the female college graduates of the 1880s and 1890s did not marry.[31] Such women joined literary societies, calling themselves "barbarians" to distinguish themselves from the "Greeks." Literary societies, based on the activities of debating and criticizing student work, existed outside the classroom and had their own programs, separate from course syllabi.[32] As a member of the Union literary society, Cather may have debated such issues as "Realism versus sentimentalism in literature." She certainly identified with Union ideals, taking the trouble to write a spoof of sorority conversation in the school literary magazine, *Hesperian*. In the spoof, which ran 15 February 1893, Cather has "Psyclonia" say, "By the way Lavvy [short for "Lavender"], I hear you attended one of those antiquated literary societies last Friday. How in the world did you stand it, to meet *all sorts* of people. You know, they aren't a bit *exclusive*."

Cather's college allegiances color her earliest writing, which paradoxically both warmly embraces the democratic and flaunts its snobbery. If Cather did indeed fall into Horowitz's "independent woman" pattern—and her friendship with Louise Pound, another independent woman who never married, supports this—then Cather's early experience with the university was one of belonging to a sector of college life that required of its members intellectual rigor and independence of thought. She was the member, if not of a sorority, then of another exclusive club. Although being a "barb" put Cather among "the people"—the elite Greeks would have snubbed her—her membership in a literary society made Cather careful to display her adoption and understanding of "correct" and high literary ideals.

Cather's affectations were most likely fed by another gestaldt: Edith Lewis reports Cather's intense shame because of her origins in "the provinces." Being sent to Latin school instead of being allowed to matriculate directly probably reinforced Cather's feelings that she had come from the provinces, and that they were inferior places. The conflicting desires and abilities—talent, inferior feelings, loyalty toward the tough and kindly immigrant women of Red Cloud, memories of the more capacious and gracious home of her childhood, dislike of the shallow sorority crowd—fed her earliest attempts at journalism. Often, these took the form of the Jeremiad and were directed against those who were not as educated as she. One example is her ongoing criticism of the local theater's recently painted drop curtain. It shows naked maidens and youths disporting themselves in a pool. The legend, "Somnium Fons Vitales" appears beneath the scene:

> I have been suffering acutely from [the Lansing Theater's new drop curtain] . . . for two long years, and sometimes I have longed for artistic knowledge that I might understand and appreciate it better, but recently an artist told me that I was enviable because of my ignorance, that art could not help one with that curtain . . . I begin to believe his statement, for I have found art books as powerless to help me with the anatomy [of the nude figures on the curtain] as classical lexicons are to throw light upon that abominable Latin [motto printed on the curtain]. "Somnium Fons Vitales." I wonder how many people have been able to translate it? Lincoln is full of colleges and ought to contain a good deal of classical learning, but the lore of this generation has not got as far as "Vitales."[33]

Of a piece with her Lansing Drop Curtain invective (Cather wrote on the subject for years) is her criticism of women's clubs. She said of the Robert Browning Club in particular, "Sordello doesn't seem to mix well with tea and muffins."[34] Her sophomoric barbs here are consistent with the high seriousness with which the literary club might have held Browning and her own feelings of self-importance: what sixteen-year-old would want to associate with a group that others scornfully called "universities for middle-aged women?"[35] Cather continued to distance herself from a culture of women, who, out of necessity or desire, did not seek employment outside of their homes. Cather felt that domesticity undermined her career—she certainly did not see women's clubs in any historical context. Cathy Davidson tells the history of women, who, barred from men's clubs, founded women's clubs and created their own sort of coterie publishing by discussing literature at length in their letters and diaries, and by lending books to each other.[36] Says Elizabeth Ammons, in her recent study, "the explosion of women's clubs at the turn of the century was a visible manifestation of middle-class women's widespread determination to value the power felt in a public realm."[37] Women's clubs were often effective tools for education, but at this point, Cather could only celebrate her intellect by her inclusion in a college culture, and by her difference from the ladies who went to Robert Browning club.[38]

In her classes Cather entered a culture of letters, two cultures in fact, because members of English departments near the turn of the century were experiencing upheaval and choosing sides. On one side were Cather's more traditional professors, such as Herbert Bates. In

Bates's class, Cather may have heard statements like those he would make later in his translation of Homer's *Odyssey*. Throughout the introduction to his translation, Bates sighs for a place [ancient Greece] that was gone, "a grace, a beauty—one might say, a loveliness—that the world has lost."[39] What is best about this ancient lost time is that there were no crass businessmen, there was not even any currency. Although people had leisure, they did not indulge in idleness; even the princesses did their own washing, and thus the society in which they lived was, according to Bates, classless: the only honors given were honors earned by merit. Says Bates, "The Odyssey exceeds too in another quality—the power of the poet to enter heart and soul into the scene he sets before us . . . what intensity of human feeling Homer throws into each [scene]!"[40] Of teaching the Odyssey (Bate's translation was a classroom edition), Bates wrote in the introduction that students should not be made to study figures of speech. To him, "the play of the imagination is most important."[41]

Bates is important because Cather admired him.[42] Bates's teachings told Cather that her feelings were the best judge; that the act of reading was first an act of feeling—enjoying—the poem, and then an act of entering Homer's world through her deep feeling. In addition, Bates ennobled the figure of the author as being the bearer of a supreme imagination. The author Homer seemed to have fashioned his world by his writing, as if by writing of the deeds of heroes, he had single-handedly made a perfect democracy, still untarnished by greed, whose prerogatives were enforced by glittering demigods.

Bates was a belletrist, an early kind of reader-response critic. The belletrists, according to Daniel H. Borus, came from the upper classes in colonial America. As members of the upper class, they sought the fame of publishing, but not remuneration—gaining money by such work would remove them from the class of gentlemen. To suit their needs of self-expression, they formed literary clubs, like the Bread and Cheese Club in New York City, to which James Fenimore Cooper belonged. At club meetings, exclusively male, members would bring their manuscripts for criticism by other members—having read a manuscript before the members constituted its "publication." Such writing was often political satire, or witty exposés of the foibles of others—it was the work of insiders, all of whom understood each other well. Such small groups of writers with common tastes and goals engaged in *coterie publishing,* creating writing only for their group.[43] Borus notes that it is no wonder that such clubs praised social order, commerce, and strong government—they were, in fact, praising themselves.

By Cather's time, the coterie as arbiter of taste and the center of publishing had long dissolved. Commercial publishing houses had become the venue through which literature was dispersed, and newspapers, magazines, and classrooms, the theater for the critic. However, the ideal that art has no market value—and also that it is the plaything of the wealthy, not work—comes from the old coteries and is clear in Bates's comments.

After Bates's class Cather learned about Shakespeare in the fall of 1891 from a professor trained in German philology, the "new" method that set traditional professors on their ears. Lucius Sherman, the professor, made the members of his class scan poetry according to his new "scientific method" for teaching literature. Universities hired the new philologists for their ideas and their impressive credentials, gained from prestigious German graduate schools, and thus began the war between professors. On one side was Herbert Bates, who asked his students to memorize and recite passages of literature. On the other side, Lucius Sherman, who asked his students to "experiment" with assigned passages of literature. In an "experiment," students would make hypotheses about poetry such as, "Homer was a more metaphorical poet than Shakespeare."[44] The student would prove such an assertion by counting metaphors. Such a classroom technique essentially teaches reading skills; Cather, an impressive reader who enjoyed reciting poetry, hated the scientific method.

Cather did not accept Sherman's dicta with any grace; instead she was the class cut-up.[45] But Cather had other venues in which to attack her enemy—first, the *Hesperian,* and after October 1893, the *Nebraska State Journal.* The epigram she penned on the subject and published in the *Hesperian,* which she was then editing, is typical:

> I am dying, Egypt, dying
> Ebbs the crimson life-tide fast;
> And the dark Plutonian shadows
> Gather on the evening blast;
> Ah, I counted, Queen, and counted,
> And rows of figures massed
> Till e'en my days are numbered,
> And I'm counted out at last.[46]

The incident of the fighting professors may seem silly, but Cather ground her ax against Sherman publicly for years. She praised the actor Joseph Jefferson as late as 1899, for instance, in an open letter to him, "You seem not to belong to the quibbling world of analytical criticisms and conflicting estimates and hairbreadth distinctions, but to the common world of all of us."[47] A Frank Norris character was "a big splendid girl who had never gone to college,"[48] and she reported that, sitting in the audience listening to the very successful composer Ethelbert Nevin were his math teachers, who had written him off as a dunce.[49] Thus although Cather's realist writing, which avoided using emotional language elements like adjectives, had gained her publication, she admired a teaching method which espoused a sentimental, non-ironic, emotion-filled response to literature.

Cather at the *Nebraska State Journal*

When Willa Cather became a newspaperwoman for the *Nebraska State Journal,* her professors were at intellectual loggerheads, and Cather was a published realist author, entering a field where editors trimmed "fine writing" to save money on printing and make-up costs. Because she did not fit in with the sorority crowd, she allied herself—at least on paper—with "the people," while at the same time holding herself aloof from the ladies of Lincoln to prove her intellectual superiority. Her models for writing may have been realists, but her model for criticism, Herbert Bates, was a belletrist who emphasized the traditional over the timely and the genteel over shock value. Cather probably would not have been able to articulate these many conflicting influences on her first paid writing; nevertheless she carried them with her to the office.

Cather became a professional journalist in the fall of 1893, and her first positively attributable works appeared in November.[50] It could be that Will Owens Jones, managing editor of the *Nebraska State Journal* and founder of the journalism club at the university, where Cather had recently become the managing editor of the *Hesperian,* gave Cather her position as drama critic.

Woodress suggests that Cather became a journalist because of the severe depression that hit in 1893. Previously, her father had financed her education; with the beginning of the depression, Cather's brother Roscoe was not sent to college, but began earning money to ease the family's financial burden.[51] Willa Cather went to work out of necessity. Except for short periods in which she explored such other professions as grade-school teaching, journalism became Cather's profession and support for nearly twenty years, from 1893 to 1912. During that period, in addition to her college journalism, she was a columnist at the *Nebraska State Journal;* held the positions of contributor and editor at the *Lincoln Courier,* a weekly; contributed to the *News,* Lincoln's other newspaper; was managing editor of the *Home Monthly,* a women's magazine in Pittsburgh; worked the telegraph desk for and submitted columns to the *Pittsburgh Leader,* a newspaper; contributed to the *Library,* an art magazine in Pittsburgh; was Washington correspondent for the *Pittsburgh Index,* a weekly; contributed articles to the *Pittsburgh Gazette,* a "yellow" newspaper; and became the managing editor at *McClure's,* a muckraking magazine of national standing, with home offices in New York City. When *McClure's* reorganized under new management in 1912 and Cather took a leave of absence—in fact she never returned—she started her second career, applying all her knowledge about authors and audiences, narrative voice and disguise, to writing novels.

Kathy Rutledge, who is, at this writing, editor of the editorial page of the *Lincoln Journal,* says that writing a Sunday column like Cather's was more creative than daily news reporting, because a column gives journalists the power of expressing their opinion. Nebraska journalist Dale Griffing remarks that journalists sought out the privilege of writing regular columns, especially those with bylines, even though they had to take another job to support themselves. Cather's job, in short, was a plum, but not a highly remunerative one. She often wrote theater reviews, as well as "human interest" news reports during the week, which would have brought in a little extra money. Cather was paid one dollar for a newspaper column.[52] For shorter reviews written during the week, that amounted to one dollar, but for her Sunday column, which could span four physical newspaper columns, she could earn four dollars.

Cather's career of newspaperwoman was a flamboyant choice, in the way that William Cather, M.D., vivisectionist of the prairies, was an early, flamboyant persona that Cather created for herself. For one thing, in August 1890 Elizabeth Stuart Phelps's article in the *Forum* had just condemned the theater as immoral—by implication, perhaps the drama critic was slightly tainted as well. As a woman journalist, Cather took up the career of Nellie Bly, whose journey around the world for the Pulitzer chain had been completed in 1890.[53] If Cather had known of Nellie Bly then, she would have viewed her as theatrical and self-advertising. The critic John Jakes reports that, by 1890, journalism was still considered unladylike, although change was in the air. To disguise their public selves, many women journalists signed a pseudonym or hid behind the serviceable name, "anon."[54] Cather's early, anonymous contributions to the *Nebraska State Journal* are what one would expect from a young female journalist[55]: the grating outrageousness of some of her contributions advertised her Nellie Bly willingness to work and her readiness to hold the realistic pen, while her anonymity coyly reflected the passing idea that women were not public.

Being a woman and being a professional were still issues in Cather's Lincoln. A rival paper, the *Nebraska State Democrat*, regularly featured squibs that ridiculed women. On 27 April 1895, for instance, a woman comes out of her house, bent on making a small repair with a hammer and nail. A grocery boy, seeing a woman with a hammer, falls into guffaws so loud that the woman is driven inside, her repair unmade.

Cather's days at the office are hard to glimpse; the routine of her professional life is hidden—as Dana Gioia has shown, what happens in the office is just not the subject for poetry. Once she had become a drama critic, she must have finished classes and then dressed for the theater—there were two in town, the Lansing with its awful drop curtain, and the Funke. After the show she would go to the office to write her review. The late hours and long days must have been heady but tiring. Stephen Crane, reporting the disastrous winter of 1894 for the Bachellor syndicate, remembers seeing a young girl at the newspaper office asleep standing up.[56] Somehow Cather found time to read rival papers and magazines: *Harper's,* the *Critic,* the *Independent* and *Outlook,* two Protestant magazines, the scandalous *Town Topics,* and the papers from New York and Chicago.

Cather wrote her reviews by hand as the typewriter was still an expensive, new-fangled invention (the telephone, however, interrupted office routine—the newspaper advertised a telephone number during Cather's years there). Cather would turn in her copy, then the copy-boy would escort her home. Her reviews, reports Curtin, were part her own material and part rehash written by other journalists, as was common in the days before wire services.

Woodress maintains that Cather's copy was not edited by her boss[57]; instead, it went straight to the composing room, where one of four or five compositors made their way through Cather's scrawl and corrected her spelling errors. Compositors loaded type, one letter at a time, into their composing sticks and from there into long galleys. The miraculous Merganthaler Linotypes—machines which could set whole lines of type at once—did not come to Lincoln until after Cather left. The writers of the WPA volume, *Printing Comes to Lincoln,* mourn the passing of handsetting techniques, noting that the *Journal's* old nonpareil type font had a crispness that the Linotype obliterated. The same volume documents the rise of the "art" book—whose publishers, ignoring the linotype, meticulously typeset by hand in lovely handmade fonts such as Caslon.[58] Much later, Cather would choose Alfred K. Knopf for her publisher. Knopf, a young man at the time, was a leader of the "art" book school of book design in New York, and in choosing him, Cather remembered the technological changes that had overwhelmed the former way of doing things. Although Knopf and printers who worked for him did not necessarily go back to composing by hand, they did use special type fonts which had been lovingly designed and cut, and frequently handmade papers or special imported papers, whose names were lovingly remembered in colophons, appeared in Knopf works. In choosing Knopf, Cather chose an older, seemingly handmade technology.

Indeed, Cather's journalism in Lincoln is the beginning of so many characteristics that formed Cather the writer, it is worth scrutiny. In her hands, the lives and works of dramatists, actors, novelists, and poets became the putty out of which she fashioned her author-self. Writers such as Zola, actresses such as Clara Morris, and even Caslon type become no longer themselves, but icons which stood for Cather's developing sensibilities and taste. Some major milestones of the late nineteenth century—the invention of electric lights, for instance— Cather left to others to discuss. But some concepts and images— realism, the French, Sarah Bernhardt—she defined, shuffled, and re-made throughout the rest of her Nebraska years. These subjects were important to her, and she couldn't seem to let them alone, manipulating them on some invisible chessboard until she won.

Inventing Realism: Cather's Brownville Story

By the beginning of 1894 Cather's ironic vignettes of her "One Way of Putting It" column gave way to theater reviews and even regular newspaper stories. How Cather the reporter worked can be inferred from correspondence regarding a trip to Brownville, Nebraska, to gather material for a human interest story.[59] Mariel Gere told the story of Cather's and her trip to Brownville in a letter dated 6 February 1956, though the trip itself had taken place in August 1894.[60] Brownville, once the territorial capital of Nebraska, had been a shipping center on the Missouri. In her article, which ran 12 August 1894, Cather attributed Brownville's later decline to the untrustworthiness of the Missouri's currents, but very probably, rail had something to do with reducing shipping on the river.

As Gere relates, during their Brownville visit, she was surprised at Cather's interest only in the dilapidated buildings of Brownville, at the way Cather ignored the still-living town. Cather even created some dilapidation of her own. She went with Gere, who was her photographer, into the Episcopal church. There she pulled out the kneeling benches from between the pews and piled them roughly at the front of the church, so as to suggest its disuse. Gere snapped away, and later, as it was done then, an illustrator drew, from the photographs that Gere had made, the visuals that would adorn Cather's story.

"The ruin and neglect of [the Episcopal church] . . . is pitiful," Cather wrote in her article. "The stained glass windows are broken in, the walls black with the litter of mould, the carpet white with plaster fallen from the ceiling, the prayer benches broken."[61] We do not know how the citizens of Lincoln reacted when they read Cather's "realistic" human interest story, but we do know how one Brownville citizen, who was the editor of the *Auburn Granger,* felt about the article. The *Granger* writer was incensed that Cather would publish an article about decay; that writer saw Brownville in the hero's story instead. "If downright lying with malice aforethought makes interesting reading, then the article in the State Journal of the 12th . . . must have been treacle to the palates of the patrons of that stale sheet," the Auburn writer editorialized on 24 August 1894.

Cather was delighted at the brou-ha-ha that she had raised. She sent a copy of the *Granger* to her friend Grace and wrote her that they probably should postpone all travel to Brownville lest they meet with an unkind reception.[62] Shocking readers was exactly what realist reporting was meant to do. In her negative reporting on Brownville, she had seemed not to blink in the face of a sad decay, while in fact, feeding the pride of Lincoln citizens at their own city's contrasting bustling efficiency. Cather had scored big, and she bragged of her success to her friend.[63] Years later Cather noted that newspapers printed nothing but lies, but as a young reporter, she was eager to get—or make—a story.[64]

As a teenager Cather had sought the publicity and challenge of high-profile positions: her masking as William Cather and choosing to become a woman doctor is ample evidence for that. Becoming the employee of the managing editor of the *Journal,* Will Owens Jones, may have exacerbated that tendency as Cather grew into her late teens. What we know of Cather's feelings comes from her letters written to him after she had left Nebraska for Pittsburgh—and the letters show a kind of desperation to prove her worth. In her letters, Cather brags lustily about her salary while employed at the *Pittsburgh Leader:* $75 a month.[65] The owner of the *Leader,* millionaire W. A. McGee, hired Cather even though a long queue of out-of-work reporters waited in the lobby.[66] On 7 May 1903, Cather wrote Mr. Jones (always it was "Mr. Jones") about how careful she was of herself, now that S. S. McClure had pronounced her a worthy writer. Yet on 29 September 1900, after a letter describing her mother's illness and the necessity of Cather's coming to Lincoln to care for her, Cather ended by asking, very quietly, for work.[67]

Another incident reveals tensions that may have existed between worker and boss: on 27 February 1904, shortly after she published "A Wagner Matinée" in 1904, Jones roasted Cather thoroughly and publicly in the *Journal*. He felt that Cather had done to her own what she had earlier done to the citizens of Brownville. Yet in the teens, when Cather was a publishing novelist, she was still writing him about her novels, and he was reading them and asking questions about style in letters to her. It is easy to speculate about why Cather was so desperate to please her boss. The depression could have made the need for money particularly real to her. Perhaps Jones had felt compelled to hire her because the paper's owner, Gere, was a friend of the Cather family. At any rate, this dynamic—a boss she could not completely please, a need within herself to please completely—may have driven Cather during her first years as a reporter and critic to write copy that was shocking. Larzer Ziff notes that realist writers sprang directly from the newsroom, citing realists' fact gathering techniques in particular.[68] Cather's dynamic with her boss shows another way in which realist writing can be said to come directly from the newsroom: it sprung from the interpersonal tensions of the office.

Trilby and the Literary Sentimental

By the time she became a drama critic in 1893, Cather had sat through a full year of Sherman's Shakespeare. How she molded her personal grouches into public stances—and how these stances became crystallized into an aesthetic—can be seen from Cather's relations with Sherman. When Sherman, a columnist at the *News*, criticized George du Maurier's best-selling novel *Trilby* (serialized January–August 1894 in *Harper's*) for its immorality, Cather let Sherman have it with both barrels in her own *Journal* column.

Trilby took the country, including Nebraska, by storm.[69] *Trilby* is essentially an Anglicized *Camille*. The plot, like any sentimental one, is convoluted. Little Billee, the Laird, and Taffy are English artists living in the famed *Quartier Latin*. Trilby, a model who has posed in the nude, occasionally sits for the artists. Their most famous portrait is of—her foot. A brilliant musician, Svengali, sometimes accompanies Trilby, and the five have a good time. Then disaster intervenes. Little Billee falls in love with Trilby; and, as in *Camille*, his family is horrified, and they extricate their innocent boy from his engagement with the lowly model.

Trilby becomes the mistress of Svengali, who, it turns out, has a past. He is part Jewish, and to gentile American audiences still frightened by the otherness of new Jewish immigrants, Svengali's Jewishness is explanation for what he has done with Trilby. By herself, Trilby cannot sing. Hypnotized by Svengali (who directs her from the balcony with his hand), she has become one of the most famous concert sopranos in all Europe.[70] The greedy Svengali forces Trilby to sing one engagement after another. When Svengali suddenly has a heart attack during a concert, Trilby, freed from his hypnotic power, falters in her song before an audience that includes Little Billee. Her exhaustion is complete, and Little Billee sees her once more before both she and Little Billee die.

For Cather the bad-girl realist, *Trilby* was a feast. Set in France, it wafts just whiff enough of the *Quartier Latin* to be titillating, since, for Cather's audience, anything French, and in particular the nude artist's model, was obscene.[71] Said Cather, regarding the French, "The French are full of Oriental feeling. Those hot winds that blow up from Provence carry the odor of citron and orange groves ever to Paris."[72] At the same time, *Trilby* is full of sentimental tropes. Since in Cather's mind Lucius Sherman's classes robbed literature of its emotional value, Cather defended *Trilby* not because it was titillating (new), but because of its sentiment.

In the late nineteenth century sentimentalism was revived when Emmanuel Swedenborg's ideas, popularized in America by Theophilus Parsons, began to find literary form.[73] By the time that Cather was at work on her *Trilby* articles, novels which espoused Swedenborgian sentimental philosophy evinced several characteristics: the Doctrine of Uses, wise children, and the Doctrine of Correspondences. The Doctrine of Uses states that every earthly happening was planned by God. Novels most often illustrated the Doctrine of Uses by having something evil befall a beloved character—and for that reason, in Harriet Beecher Stowe's *Uncle Tom's Cabin,* Little Eva and Uncle Tom die, their deaths becoming occasions for survivors to mull over the use or worth of dying and to give special strength to Stowe's message to readers. The idea behind "wise children" is as follows: In Swedenborg's thought, poor and uneducated characters, children and rural dwellers, were seen as closer to God—school and city dwelling got in the way of Higher Knowledge, it seems—so Stowe (and other sentimental writers) chose a child and a slave to impart her most serious truths.[74]

To make sure that they aired their didactic messages frequently, authors engineered convoluted plots with many partings of lovers, near-disasters, and drawn-out deathbed scenes (they rhetoricized parting). According to Susan Sontag, tuberculosis was such a favored way of carrying off literary characters because the slow pace of the disease gave dying characters ample time to leave their loved ones again and again, imparting Higher Truths each time. Of course, tuberculosis—and many other illnesses in those days before antibiotics—were *real,* and the sentimental novel, at its heart, was *real,* too. It did real work, reassuring survivors and the lonely that they had not endured parting in vain.

Sentimental authors believed in the Doctrine of Correspondences, in which earthly objects pointed to heavenly truths. Such a belief led easily to a symbol-laden literature, each symbol standing for a "higher," or religious, truth. Swedenborgian sentimentalism asked readers to discover religious truths by "reading" symbols. The act of reading, for them, was an act of becoming more human because more right-feeling.[75] Cather appreciated the direct shorthand of symbol-making in the French Symbolists, who, Josephine Donovan has noted, were also influenced by Swedenborg but did not insist on religious messages.[76] Like the symbolists, Cather wrote Swedenborgian symbols into her novels, but without insisting upon religious messages. Cather's sun-behind-the-plow symbol in *My Ántonia,* the white mulberry in *O Pioneers!,* and Bartley Alexander's great bridge reflect just this sort of inheritance.[77]

In her 16 September and 28 October 1894 *Nebraska State Journal* columns, Cather defended *Trilby* on sentimental grounds, according to Swedenborgian philosophy. For one thing, it made her cry. *Trilby* was a great novel because of the emotional response that it evoked in Cather and the way those responses moved her heart to feel kindness and sympathy toward her fellow human beings (this was Trilby's "Use")—Cather didn't feel compelled to count one metaphor. Sherman's method short-circuited the flow of passion from artist to reader or viewer. Using that method, one consumed art by first thinking about it, analyzing it. And while Sherman's method created critical distance, effective art was, according to young Cather, about feeling: therefore *Trilby* had reached the uttermost ends of art. Thus Cather began to erect in her mind a series of oppositions. There was Sherman the scholar—a prude and a nativist who counted literary tropes without feeling them. Against him, Cather declared herself to be one of "the people," not a scholar, who felt literature intensely, who was a francophile and celebrated literature's ability to explore subjects then considered immoral, such as the lives of women who for one reason or another fell outside the accepted social fabric.

In supporting *Trilby* in terms of the emotional response it evoked, Cather displayed her alignment with the sentimental novelists, in spite of her many assertions that she belonged to the realist school. Sentimentalism was another mask that Cather could wear to indicate her political, social, and emotional alignments, which were deeply felt and "true." Cather could celebrate *Trilby* because it was both realist-shocking, which affirmed her alignment with her newspaper trade, with the "new" American novelists, and with French realists, such as de Maupassant and Dumas; but she could also celebrate *Trilby* because its deathbed scene, like Little Eva's, was a real tearjerker.

Cather as a Drama Critic

Cather's work as a drama critic reinforced both her feelings about the power and worth of emotional responses over and above the worth of the analyst, and, paradoxically, her alliances with the clear-eyed realist as well. As a columnist, she watched a play, then went straight to the newspaper offices, where she wrote her story. Her critical tenet in 1894 was that she must write criticism instantly, while her emotions were still engaged. The critic's job was not "judgment, but sympathy."[78] She said that art itself was an idealistic project: it should present lofty types, define lofty conceptions, and win viewers or consumers by telling of love.[79] However, Cather castigated Ouida in the terms of a realist critic, scolding her for her "mawkish" sentiment, complaining that all women writers know is "adjectives and sentiment."[80] To Cather in Lincoln, the emotions dramatized on stage called forth her sympathy, her humanity, and her antipathy toward Sherman. Her ability to appreciate and understand the language of emotion suppressed in a subtle, ironic realist text made her the sophisticated critic, under fire by the plebeians. In fact, an actress of the emotional school acting in a French realist play and making theater of a parting invigorated Cather the critic. Such a moment was both old and new, real and sentimental—it was complete.

Camille, Willa Cather's favorite play in the 1890s, like *Trilby*, combines trappings of both sentimentalism and realism. *Camille* draws out the slow death by tuberculosis of the courtesan Mdm. Gautier (Camille); her lover's doomed attempts to save her; and the machinations of M. Duval, the lover's father, who places himself repeatedly between his son and the courtesan, parting them often before death finally claims Camille. Camille's noble renunciation of her love for

Armand Duval shows others how to be so brave and how to love without possession.

Camille, France, and the demi-monde were worlds unexplored by Lucius Sherman. *Camille's* sentimental themes, its appeal to feeling, mixed with France's frank discussions of prostitution (Cather felt that discussing "lower" characters instead of "higher" ones was proof of a work's realism) were anodyne enough against Sherman's excesses.

One of Cather's favorite actresses—Clara Morris—acted in *Camille* in November 1893. William Curtin notes that Morris acted using the emotional method: her stage business was exaggerated. She did not just cry, she wept copiously. She did not just display sorrow, she fell on her knees.[81] Cather calls her actions "natural." Morris made her character's sufferings obvious and drew them out, inviting the house to participate. Morris's style of acting—as well as the plays she acted in and the critics who appreciated her—created the sentimental on stage. *Camille* also imitated the day's dramatic advertising, with its big display type.[82] The French emotional school was a style of wordplay that had work to do—enlisting the sympathy of an audience, moving it to pity—and it made manifest the difficulty of its labor.[83]

Clara Morris had reached the end of her career at the time that Cather had become a reviewer: her Madame Gautier was a swansong. A younger actress, Eleanora Duse, was then making headlines with her new type of "realistic" acting called "suppression." Duse's style was so affecting that she came to rival the old-school emotional actresses such as Clara Morris and Sarah Bernhardt. Duse fascinated Cather, who seems to have admired both kinds of acting simultaneously—emotion and suppression of emotion. Duse displayed fewer histrionics on stage—the "work" she did was hidden, and she did not make immediately clear to her audience what its reaction should be. To feel the catharsis that the tragedy is said to grant an audience, the audience watching a "suppressed" characterization had to participate, and participate more individualistically as well. An audience watching Duse had to perform the same "work" as a reader reading a realistic or protomodernist novel: the reader had to read symbols whose message was not obvious.[84]

Just writing about the drama did not necessarily force Cather to become a modern novelist twenty years later. However, Cather not only wrote about plays; she also defended them. In her reviews, Cather argued down both Lucius Sherman and Reverend Harmon D. Jenkins, minister to the First Presbyterian Church of Sioux City, Iowa, a minister who had sermonized his prudish dislike of an actress.[85] The weapons in Cather's arsenal of invective which she wielded repeatedly against such foes became the tools of her trade as she began to write fiction; thus her fictional works are symbol-laden, realist and sentimental, full of wise children, rural and uneducated folk, and fallen women. Cather assembled her defenses for public consumption in the newspaper. It is possible that she saw her most eloquent defenses as raising her worth in the eyes of her boss—and whether tensions between her and her boss existed during her Lincoln years or not, she saw her income as keeping her safe from the depression and as relieving her family of much of the burden of her support. In a way, her self-worth was tied to how barbed, outrageous, and dramatic her public writing could be.

The *Courier* and Art as Work

Cather graduated from the University of Nebraska in June 1895. Upon her graduation, she needed to work full time, and although her job at the *Nebraska State Journal* continued sporadically until 1902, it did not support her fully. She was still dependent upon her parents for part of her income, a dependency which, she wrote to Mariel Gere, her parents could not continue.[86] Because she had to find another situation, she initiated efforts to become an English teacher at the University of Nebraska and enlisted the help of Charles Gere. She knew that her sex was a drawback. Mentioning this in a letter to Gere, she asked to be appointed to an instructorship instead of an adjunct professorship. That way, she reasoned, the university could pay her five hundred dollars less per year.[87] As Woodress reports, Lucius Sherman, head of the English department, foiled her efforts.[88]

In August 1895 the *Lincoln Courier,* an arts and entertainment weekly, was reorganized, with W. Morton Smith as its owner, Sarah B. Harris with an interest and the associate editorship, and Cather with the post of associate editor. Cather moved her column, "The Passing Show," to the *Courier* during her tenure there, which lasted until November. Curtin notes that the *Courier* gave Cather another, longer, format, and a more gracious deadline as well.[89] As a result, Cather's writing in the *Courier* became more considered, less passionate. The short term of employment at the *Courier* was her first foray into magazine writing, a type of writing that she would soon begin in earnest. At the end of her tenure at the *Courier*—which, for unknown reasons, was short—Cather went back to Red Cloud.[90]

Bernice Slote notices a darkening of Cather's columns at this point, one year before she left Nebraska for good. Many of Cather's reviews comment almost nakedly on her monetary and career situation. Says

Slote, "the problems of the artist's life and work narrow to her own particular questions,"[91] and of those the most important question was how to be a woman, an artist, and still find work.

When Cather became frustrated with women as artists, she was unable to see how the weight of tradition worked against them. After all, a major paradigm in Cather's time was Charles Darwin's *Origin of the Species* (1859), which told, not the stories of individual adaptations, but rather how groups fit their environments. Whole groups acting as one fell into an evolutionary paradigm: they lay along a "chain" from higher to lower animals, with the highest being man, the artist. Women attended women's clubs. "Has any woman really had the art instinct," Cather wrote, after learning of actress Mary Anderson's marriage[92]; the word "instinct" is proof here of with which paradigm Cather works. The fatal flaw of women artists, according to Cather, was that they thought only of marriage. "I have not much faith in women in fiction," Cather says of Ouida. "They have a sort of sex consciousness that is abominable. They are so limited to one string and they lie so about that."[93]

In the late 1800s, when divorce was so rare that William Dean Howells could coyly call his novel about divorce *A Modern Instance* (1882) and the *Nebraska State Journal* announced divorces as it did marriages, births, deaths, and society gatherings, Cather was celebrating in print actress Marie Burroughs's divorce, saying that she (having miraculously escaped the evolutionary tug) was married to the stage.[94] At this point in her life, Cather believed that if women were to be artists they must not marry, and they should only write/act about love. Says Cather of the female characters in David Belasco's plays, "a woman has but one [stage] business, to be in love, and to have it mighty hard."[95] Perhaps it was early in her career that she began to construct a possible life for herself, a life for writing, not for matrimony. Her subject could be love and art, and in the short stories of *The Troll Garden,* her second book, which was published in 1903, love, art—and work—were her subjects.

Again and again during her last days at the *Journal,* Cather felt compelled to fit art into her world's concept of what constituted work. Her desire was shared by most of the realists, who insisted that they were writing for the common man.[96] In the 1890s, the common man or woman in America had to work and did not see art as labor, but play. Besides the physical act of taking up journalism and thereby making her writing into work which paid, Cather used her newspaper pulpit to teach her readers just how hard writing was—to professionalize it and make it into a career which one earned by study and hard work.

For instance, Ruskin, she told her readers, took ten years to write *Modern Painters*.[97] Cather idolized honest labor and honest gain, which was the only honest way of living.[98] Her other exemplar of the artistic work ethic was Robert Louis Stevenson. Her definition of how he worked was precisely that of the gentleman writer: Stevenson, says Cather, never wanted fame; he was modest. He turned out very little work, and he did so after having polished it to perfection. As a result, his writing would live forever.[99] Stevenson's evil opposite in Cather's literary criminal lineup was F. Marion Crawford, who turned out one book after another for money. Crawford's frank commercial zeal was the antithesis of a gentleman artist. Another evil-doer was Ouida, who, Cather claimed, "scarcely deserves great credit for a passionate pursuit of what, to her, is not labor, but indulgence, not gestation, travail, but relief, a pleasurable exercise."[100] Writing had to be birth, the event that led her mother to illness. In her last Lincoln writing, Cather advertised her availability as a worker, and told just how hard she would work.

As Cather looked hard for a position, she joined a new professional group. In January 1896, the Lincoln Press Association created a ladies' auxiliary, and Cather and five other women joined the annual meeting. Thus, at age twenty, ready to leave Nebraska, she became a clubwoman at last. Cather's cohorts included Sarah Harris, the *Courier* editor. Harris would continue to print Cather's columns in her weekly until August 1901. When Cather's novel *Song of the Lark* came out in 1915 and many in Lincoln found it, to their chagrin, realistic and distasteful, Sarah Harris stood by her friend. Elia Peattie also was elected to the press association. A novelist herself and a friend of Cather's during the years to come, Peattie praised Cather in the fall 1895 edition of the *Nebraska Editor* as one of the state's chief newspaperwomen. It was during the meeting of the press association that Cather gave her speech, "How to Make a Newspaper Interesting." In her speech, she asserted that "a neutral newspaper is an abomination. The newspaper should be personal."[101] Cather had taken her stand from her own newspaper's style of personal journalism, in which the editor and the writers expressed their opinions in the newspaper pages. And so by joining the press association, by making a speech, by writing letters asking for work, by accepting invitations to the Gere's dinners and meeting their important guests and making business contacts, Cather advertised her professionalism and availability.

She was professionalizing herself in other ways, too; however, these did not show. She was trying on new paradigms for *woman, work, artist*. In her late *Journal* article on women and poetry—the same article, written in January 1895, in which she stated that she had little hope for women as poets—she mentioned her admiration for Barrett Browning, Christina Rossetti, and Sappho. Cassandra Laity has pointed out that early modernist women poets took Sappho as their poetic foremother.[102] Sappho fit young Cather's limited paradigm about successful women: their one subject was love. According to Cather, Sappho was the greatest love poet of them all.[103]

Sappho of Lesbos, unmarried, writing of love (that Swedenborgian bond), admired by all Greece and all time, was the perfect signal to Cather's readers that Cather was a new kind of poet. The Greek then connoted a very high level of education. Greek, in the 1890s, was like high IQ and SAT scores one hundred years later: ability to understand Greek meant that one belonged to the educated elite. The Greek also connoted excess Eastern passion so intense that "Greece" equaled "France" as the code word for the frankly sexual. Herbert Bates had made of the ancient Greeks a perfect democracy, with no threatening monopolies, sexual inequalities, or "frenzied finance." In praising Sappho, Cather praised passion and rejected economies based upon money. Freed from household duties, Sappho became the best poet that ever lived. Cather advertised her "Sapphic modernism" by reading Daudet's *Sapho* (1884) and writing about her book to her friends.[104] As Laity notes, women writers, such as H. D., looked to the poets Sappho, Dante Gabriel Rossetti, and Algernon Charles Swinburne, and the painter Burne-Jones, as artistic predecessors. Cather herself wrote after Tennyson's death that Swinburne ("the author of 'Atalanta in Calydon,'" and the poet who had composed in the difficult sapphic meter) should be the next English poet laureate.[105] Cather wrote about Burne-Jones in a poem ("like a Burne-Jones vision of despair," from "White Birch in Winter," in *April Twilights* [1903]) and in one of the short stories of *The Troll Garden,* "The Marriage of Phaedra."[106]

As Cather gave birth to her professional self, she asserted her femaleness and the worth of female authors by praising Sappho. Ironically, she expressed her belonging to the world of critics and editors by damning "fine writing" and women's clubs ("unprofessional"). She asserted her independence from the university by characterizing those within its walls as pedantic, and those without its walls as "the people" who felt, rather than counted; nevertheless, she trumpeted her Latin and Greek, her Shakespeare and her Browning. Cather's assessments and allegiances are paradoxical and conflicting. The newspaper oeuvre is of a piece, however; it shows her accepting pieces of her world and knitting them together to suit (to clothe) herself.

Perhaps it was at Sarah B. Harris's home, or at a dinner given at the Charles Geres, or at her parents' home where Cather met James Axtell, of the publishing firm Axtell, Rush, and Company in Pittsburgh. Wherever she met him, he hired her in the spring of 1896 to start a new magazine in Pittsburgh, that was to be called *The Home Monthly*. Cather finally had a self-supporting job. She left Lincoln—for good—in July of that year.

3

Selves and Others: Pittsburgh, Pennsylvania

Though love be cold, do not despair, / there's Ypsilanti Underwear.[1]

—Jingle

Now, Miss Lewis does not think that anything Willa did in Pittsburgh was important—her writing and so on. I violently disagree.[2]

—Mildred Bennett

. . . the magazines, which are . . . the best means of living, . . . they are both bread and fame to [the author].[3]

—William Dean Howells

Richard Harding Davis and Gibson's Girl by Gibson, from *Scribner's,* **August 1890**

Cather arrived in Pittsburgh by train 3 July 1896. Stepping down from the platform, she stepped into a new self. Free from college and away from home, she was independent at last, the new employee of Axtell, Orr, and Associates, publisher of Pittsburgh's *Home Monthly,* a women's magazine.[4] Axtell had grand plans to expand his business dealings. Originally the publisher of the *National Stockman and Farmer,* he bought the *Home Monthly* with hopes of encroaching on the *Ladies' Home Journal's* fabulous circulation.[5] Axtell's idea—from farm to suburban home—was not so far-fetched as it might seem: the *Ladies' Home Journal* began as *The Tribune and Farmer* in 1879,[6] and it was selling to a national audience from Philadelphia. Magazines were following people from farmhouses to cities as the population shifted from agriculture to urban life.

Cather was essentially the managing editor of her magazine. She had a secretary, but she had to secure manuscripts, write stories and poems, line up illustrators, and even supervise the typesetters from time to time. She was still young, she was on her own and supporting herself for the first time, and she was enormously pleased. In addition, her enthusiasm was large enough to drive both her short-story writing (which she did after coming home from work) and her work itself. Editing requires attention to detail, and so her work needed all that she could give it. Frequently she found herself in a comedy of errors. Once she hired an illustrator with whom she was pleased—except the artist always drew the eyes too far apart. Cather had the solution: she gave the illustrator a photograph to copy and impressed upon her the need to copy faithfully. Finishing her task, the illustrator commented to Cather that the photograph was of a very beautiful model, but the eyes were too close together, so she had corrected the problem in her own rendering.[7] Another time Cather telephoned her friend George Seibel (a Pittsburgh journalist) in the middle of the day. Talk to me about Nietzsche for five minutes, slowly and distinctly, she commanded Seibel, a German-American. Later, Seibel, as he reported in his 1949 article "Miss Willa Cather from Nebraska," wormed out of Cather the reason for her telephone call: upon interviewing pianist Harold Bauer, the musician had discussed mainly Nietzsche, but so rapidly that Cather could not take notes fast enough. Seibel's synopsis helped Cather fill in the gaps in her story. Cather's work habits reveal a creative woman, determined to succeed.

Cather could even make copy out of her living circumstances. She lived in a series of boarding houses in Pittsburgh. Her first boarding house was close to the *Home Monthly's* offices, and Cather biked to work, riding the trolley to visit friends.[8] On 23 February 1902, she published an article in the *Pittsburgh Gazette* entitled "Boarding, not

Living: Some of the Types One Meets in the Game of Progressive Eating." Cather's short story, "The Count of Crow's Nest," (1896) opens by describing boarding-house types. Cather, using her Henry Nicklemann pseudonym, mentions one newly arrived boarding house couple who think that the husband's salary is princely until they move to Pittsburgh, try to buy a house, and end up in boarding houses, just like Cather. Her salary—one hundred dollars a month—may not have been princely enough to finance a house, but it did grant her independence. In addition to her *Home Monthly* salary, she may have been paid extra for the articles, stories, and poems that she wrote. However, if the pay was anything like that she gave to George Seibel—six dollars for the story, "A Higher Critic"—it wasn't much.[9]

During her stint at the *Home Monthly,* Cather continued to sell her work to the *Nebraska State Journal* and to the *Lincoln Courier.* Often this material was reworked to fit the pages of the *Home Monthly* and vice versa. Cather did not consider the *Home Monthly* her sole support in Pittsburgh, and immediately upon arrival set out to find other outlets for her work. She wrote Will Owens Jones, her previous employer at the *Nebraska State Journal,* about interviewing with the owner of the *Pittsburgh Leader* for a job with his paper.[10] Her first columns appeared in the *Leader* beginning in September 1896, even though she had just arrived in July.

Pittsburgh and the *Home Monthly* presented Cather with a new problem: how could a single working woman who lived in a boarding house give advice to women who, ideally, according to the notions of "women's sphere," were darning socks by their suburban firesides? It seems amazing that the outspoken, realist author of "Peter" should find herself the editor of a traditional woman's magazine. "It was a curious place," writes Edith Lewis, "for a young, rebellious mind, impatient of all camouflage, to find itself in.[11] Indeed, after she became famous, Cather would gloss over the *Home Monthly* year as she told her life story in many interviews.[12] Cather hid her rebellion by dividing her opinions among several male and female pseudonyms, each of which mouthed gender-appropriate sentiments and published in appropriate venues.[13] Cather had played at being William Cather, M.D., as an adolescent, and as she grew into young adulthood, her ability to manufacture pseudonyms and play parts served her well. As a journalist in Nebraska, Cather had left unsigned her early, often pointed newspaper columns—this was her first public self, anonymous, fierce-penned Billy Cather. Now, as a Pittsburgh journalist, Cather adopted several pseudonyms. Her pseudonyms were not the troubled halves of a sick personality: Cather chose pseudonymous voices to articulate and explore her world and to sell her columns.[14]

Pittsburgh was the first place where Cather had written extensively under pseudonyms; most of her Nebraska columns were unsigned. Not until Cather moved to Pittsburgh in 1896 did she begin signing her *Nebraska Journal* contributions "Willa Cather"; the same relocation made Cather create additional personae behind which she could render her opinions in Pittsburgh. Thus, living in Pittsburgh, she became Willa Cather in the Lincoln papers. Pittsburgh audiences were familiar with Willa Cather, too—but mainly as a writer of short stories and poems. As a reporter or reviewer, she appeared under pseudonyms such as "Helen Delay" or "Henry Nicklemann," or she wrote anonymously in the Pittsburgh press. The scholar can only imagine how many anonymous writings by Cather must exist in back issues of weeklies like the Pittsburgh *Index* and the *Library*, and newspapers like the Pittsburgh *Gazette* and the *Leader*.[15]

Cather's first job in Pittsburgh was a challenge. She had published her enmity toward the *Ladies' Home Journal* in a 12 January 1896 *Nebraska State Journal* article—just six months before she was to leave for Pittsburgh. "Above all," Cather had written, "the *Ladies' Home Journal* covets articles from actresses, prima donnas, and eminent divines. We all know what pure and exquisite prose English prima donnas write."[16] Cather's last concern before leaving Nebraska had been making herself and her work professional, that is, insisting that her work was laboriously crafted and polished by a writer trained, schooled, to be a writer. Her graduation from college "certified" her worth. Suddenly, Cather found herself working for a *Ladies' Home* lookalike, and she had to hide her dislike for its lack of intellectual tone.

Despite whatever reservations she may have had about embracing women's culture, in 1896 Cather's Pittsburgh life was financed by her editorial position at the *Home Monthly*. Signing different names to the different pieces that she wrote, Cather addressed the very audience she had dismissed as unworthy to appreciate her talent as a writer. About women readers Cather had once written: "Ladies' literary clubs are particularly funny. Family matters mix so strangely with Kant's philosophy or Ruskin's theories of art."[17] To write for a market which embraced the literary club, Cather would either have to avoid "serious" discussions of art, or find a way for art and family matters to mix.

As editor of a magazine which targeted the hearth-and-home market, Cather had to disguise those parts of her character that did not fit in with the hearth-and-home ideology, the ideology of women's sphere, and of the home as the ideal retreat from the business world. Cather disguised, fit, and hid her ideas under such pseudonyms as "Helen Delay," "Elizabeth Seymour," "Charles Douglass," "John Esten," and "Mary K. Hawley." As Cather became in turn each of her pseudonyms and produced articles, reviews, and poems to fill the *Home Monthly,* she had to adopt, at least temporarily, the sentimental ideals—and a special language in which to couch them—that created readers for such journals.[18]

Her feelings on joining such a magazine were complex, a combination of smirking superiority to it all and a kind of wholehearted commitment whose effects were profound. She is most revealing in her letters. In one letter to Mrs. Gere she asks for photographs and anecdotes of Mary Baird (Mrs. William Jennings) Bryan. Cather could not wait to finish her article on the wives of the presidential candidates: she was certain that she would "scoop" the competition.[19] In the same letter Cather defined success as working on a project whether it was congenial or not. Cather wrote that she enjoyed the feeling of importance that she gained in Pittsburgh—the feeling that no one else could do what she was doing as well as she did. This one letter to Mrs. Gere is about conquering, about the benefits of her work, about being on top of things. The next month, she wrote Mariel Gere, Mrs. Gere's daughter. The magazine, she asserted, was trash. Indeed, in a later interview, she would manage not to mention the *Home Monthly* at all when asked about her work history.[20] Whatever compromises she might have made, writing for the magazine and editing it caused Cather to have more and more ideas for her own work. Cather wrote that she was happy about the way her two professions urged her on.[21]

In January 1897, six months after moving to Pittsburgh, Cather gave birth to the pseudonym Helen Delay, who was one of those terrible beings, a female author. As Helen Delay, Cather was a book reviewer who gave advice to her *Home Monthly* audience about which books they should read. Her Helen Delay, measured against the *Home Monthly's* audience, is only partly successful in projecting the image of a warm, motherly type who loved home and fireside. Cather defined Helen's audience in the *Home Monthly's* policy statement:

> The *Home Monthly* is not ambitious of becoming a dignified review, nor is it to be used only as a vehicle for the dissemination of fashion gossip and culinary recipes. It is equally certain that it should not be made a mere purveyor of sensational and unwholesome fiction . . . every phase of home needs will receive attention . . . while the best story writers in the country will furnish entertainment for the idle hour . . . these pages will be kept clean and pure in tone . . . to entertain, to educate, to elevate.[22]

Helen Delay's pronouncements, however, belied Cather's own ethics and experiences. Due in part to the rapid increase in magazines and newspapers, women's sphere was collapsing like an old balloon.[23] Those same office buildings that created downtowns and suburbs and created a "woman's sphere" in the first place also meant more jobs for both sexes. Cather wrote her "Helen Delay" column from an office where she employed a private secretary.[24] One year after she moved to Pittsburgh, Cather was working the telegraph desk at the *Pittsburgh Leader,* a job that earlier had been held only by men. Cather—delighted to be working, and to be independent—saw work precisely as the way to make her mark on the world.[25] Yet in a review Cather wrote, "The commercial idea allowed to reign is an insanity, is the destruction of art and reduces life to a monomania!"[26] Her conflicting loyalties were similar to those she had felt in Lincoln, where she both enjoyed the notoriety and power of being a reporter and resented how much of her story-writing time that it took. Home and fireside were for Helen, but not for Willa Cather.

Cather had termed the *Home Monthly* "trashy"; later acquaintances remember that Cather found other freedoms of expression during her Pittsburgh years: her boss at the *Pittsburgh Leader* in 1897 introduced her as "Bill Cather." She still looked unconventional, in a skirt that was far too short.[27] Taking freedoms of dress and self-naming may have cost her her job. Cather's stay at the *Home Monthly* was short, approximately one year; she invented Helen Delay in January 1897 and left the magazine in July of that year. Cather probably left under pressure: Edwin Stanton Bayard, editor of the *Home Monthly's* sister publication, the *National Stockman and Farmer* (housed in the same offices), didn't like her at all—and he was James Axtell's next-door neighbor. Her leavetaking must not have been too violent, however, since she continued to author her "Old Books and New" column, signing it Helen Delay until February 1898.[28]

Cather did temper her voice while employed by the *Home Monthly* by adopting, for the first time, a deliberately "feminine" voice. It was a good exercise, verbally dressing up as Helen. Cather as Helen had to elaborate feminine ideologies and obligations and for the first time perhaps, to create meaning from these for herself. Sharon O'Brien writes that Cather's meeting with Sarah Orne Jewett in 1908 helped Cather realize that "woman" and "artist" were not incompatible terms. O'Brien's assertion is true; however, the seeds of Cather's accepting herself as a woman artist lie, too in Pittsburgh, with Helen, because Helen's story was Cather's first *Künstlerroman.* Ann Romines notes that some of Cather's most important works have at their heart an encounter in which "an original mind wrestles with the double loyalties to the life of the household, the stuff of home plots, and the impulse to run away," a plot that was perhaps Cather's life-plot in Pittsburgh.[29]

Helen Delay's Place Is in the Home

In her columns, Cather, disguised as Helen Delay, had to project the image of the ideal home with its chaste woman inside. Toward the end of the century the home separate from the business world had taken on additional metaphorical power. The business world became the social-Darwinist stage upon which the stronger vanquished the weaker. The home became an anti-Darwinist space, where people's actions were still governed by religious laws.[30]

It is appropriate that Cather inaugurated her "Old Books and New" column in January 1897 by mentioning the most sacred domestic setting: Helen Delay shared a few of her favorite books while sitting by the fireside. The hearth signaled buyers of such books as Longfellow's *The Seaside and the Fireside:* the fire tempered Cather into a Helen Delay and made her column safe reading. Cather/Delay further sanitizes the column by urging tired housewives to sit and read with her. "Helen" was one of them.[31]

In her first column "Helen Delay" placed herself in the moral, law-governed sphere of the home by creating a story within her "Old Books and New" column. In her enthusiastic review of Edna Lyall's *Donovan* (1882),[32] Delay wrote about her minister friend who stayed up all night to read Lyall's book. Lyall was not like author Mrs. Humphrey Ward, who had written a book in which a minister-character loses faith (*Robert Elsmere* [1888]). Instead, according to Delay, Lyall's books "help us through this trying life," an echo of the biblical phrase, "this vale of tears."[33] Delay earnestly wrote to her readers, whereas Cather actually respected Mrs. Humphrey Ward, who had "the power to write a really important novel";[34] but for this audience, she criticized the British novelist. Cather constructed a Helen Delay who sat by the fire, reading a book about one minister, telling an anecdote about another. Cather had her Helen broadcast a soothing and popular story, the same story told by the then-best-selling author Charles M. Sheldon (*In His Steps* [1896]), who imagined Jesus in modern-day America. Cather herself sent negative comments back home concerning the church: "the Presbyterian church of Pittsburgh objects to enjoyment of all kinds, particularly aesthetic enjoyment."[35]

Helen Delay assured her readers that Edna Lyall's books showed charming pictures of family life,[36] and that they were perfect for young girls. Delay, using the euphemisms of the day, assured readers that Lyall's books were free from discussions of sex. Delay always wrote to readers of the safety of the books she recommended: Mark Twain's *The Prince and the Pauper* (1882) was written for his little daughters.[37] *The Mill on the Floss* treated family life fully.[38] The words "family life" and "young girl" communicated to Delay's audience the books' freedom from overt sexual misconduct that goes unpunished, and from stories in which marriageable women fail to do their duty and find husbands at each story's end. Delay's assertions about "young girls" echoed Howells's—an assertion that Cather deplored in public.[39]

From January 1897 to February 1898, Cather placed Helen in sentimental poses, in the enclosed spaces of home, reading to the children. April 1897 found Helen on a porch whose posts had been carved upon by boys. Birds announced the spring at Helen's mythical suburban home, so different from Cather's actual boarding house, near downtown. Helen wrote to her readers about Jean Valjean, protagonist of Hugo's *Les Misérables,* who was poor and starving, and therefore, in the sentimental tradition, closer to God and able to deliver the didactic message of forgiveness and generosity.[40]

Helen embraced other tenets of the sentimental. Eschewing realism, for instance, she rhetoricized partings. In May 1897, she wept with her readers over *David Copperfield.* She especially liked the scene where David's mother dies, holding the infant David on her breast.[41] In September 1897, Helen assured her readers that Sidney Carton's death in Charles Dickens's *A Tale of Two Cities* was peaceful because he thought of others before himself.[42] Helen Delay, at her most conventional, allowed Cather to identify and explore sentimental tropes. In these, Helen adopted the posture of the sentimental consumer: she remained still by her fireside, yet through weeping, she participated in the deaths and sufferings of others.

The age's fascination with childhood, its treatment of childhood as the golden moment of life—the moment when imagination was especially alive and when the human creature's play was innocent of sexuality and of atavistic competition—was an especially strong remnant of the sentimental ideal, one that still informed people's actions. The publication (and popularity among adults) of such works as *Little Lord Fauntleroy, Tom Sawyer, Huckleberry Finn,* and *Ragged Dick* attested to this ideal's strength. In these works, the bond between child and adult was special; it was not that the adult taught the child, but rather that the child had come to school the adult. Sigmund Freud did not destroy his century's notions about childhood; he appropriated them for the next century. Delay frequently discussed children, childrearing, and books for children.

Cather's discussing books that told about boys' adventures both undercut and supported the messages that Helen Delay was trying to send. As Marcia Jacobson has shown, the boy book is not for boys at all, but for adults.[43] Boy stories, notes Jacobson, quoting Frank Norris, were antisentimental. Indeed, most boy books show boys acting contrary to society's rules, like little savages, running away, telling lies, and dressing as a girl like Huck Finn. The boy abjures domestic space and escapes civilization.[44] One of the chief architects of the boy-myth was Ernest Thompson-Seton, the author of the boy scout handbook. Cather ate dinner with Thompson-Seton and made copy out of her discussion with him in a review. The boy story did support Helen Delay's preference for stories which avoided discussions of sexuality. Boy books idealized boyhood in an age when manhood, especially a highly sexed manhood, was considered the norm. Boy books were to "juvenalize" a developing boy and make him sexless.[45]

At the end of her first Helen Delay column, Cather turned to the popular and sentimental topic of children and discussed their proper literary upbringing. However, Helen Delay hid Willa Cather with her "unconventional" Nebraska childhood. Delay advised mothers to choose books that were for both boy and girl children so that the sexes would be socialized alike for as long as possible. Cultural distinctions between the sexes, advised Delay, were "hateful."[46] Cather herself had had a childhood in which the "hateful" distinctions had not been heavily imposed.

One of the unisex books Helen Delay recommended was *Little Women* (1868–69). Louisa May Alcott's book tells of the coming-of-age of four sisters and their neighbor, a boy. One of the girls, Beth, dies in a cloud of sentimental tropes. The other three girls marry. The boy grows up to be a businessman. Between the beginning and the end, however, one of the girls, Jo, becomes a published author, and her parents praise her for doing so. Jo is an educated "bluestocking" who defies the conventions of women's sphere and seeks publication (without publicity, however; she does not sign her name to her work). The other daughters enter men's sphere and work as well, even though the positions they hold—governess, nurse, and amanuensis—cause them to use only those "female talents" of caring for, cleaning, and nurturing others. There are role reversals and cross-namings as well: Jo and Laurie could both be boy's or girl's names; Jo begins working even as a young girl, while Laurie, a boy, lives a "girl's" life of being tutored in the home. It is easy to see why *Little Women* made

Cather/Delay's list of unisex books. While most boys probably would not have read Alcott's book, Cather could see in Jo an alternative socialization of girls which emphasized their abilities as workers and thinkers, and not just their clothing and their futures as wives.[47]

Helen gave advice to the mothers in her audience about what to read to their little boys. By writing about adventure stories, Cather could write about the other world outside the home, worlds forbidden to proper Helens. Helen, although seated by her fireside, voyaged to foreign lands in the books she discussed. Says O'Brien: "The woman reader who identified with the genre's heroic protagonists could enter Emily Dickinson's House of Possibility—a Utopian realm beyond existing social arrangements—and hope that she could achieve their victories herself."[48] Helen could also remain properly feminine by adventuring in books alone. For instance, in February 1897, Helen extolled the virtues of Anthony Hope's *Prisoner of Zenda* (1894).[49] In Hope's book, Rudolf, the male protagonist, masquerades as a king and draws his sword against black-hearted villains. Women characters remain in the background or get rescued. Unlike the sentimental romance, *Zenda* casts aside the happy marriage ending and eschews rhetoricized partings, asserting that issues of nationhood, honor, and the pursuit of adventure are valid theaters of human endeavor. Adventurous readers of either sex could "read" themselves into Rudolf's place and embark upon a literary adventure. Conventional readers could note that women stayed at home while men swashbuckled their way through a dangerous world, setting the rightful king back on the throne at last.

In July 1897 Delay used the historical romance to voice Cather's opinions about technological advances. Ensconced in her home library, far from the dirty business world, Delay rendered her opinion on the setting of Hall Caine's novel *The Bondman* (1890). This naturalistic novel, set in Iceland, is far from the "world of railroads and telegraphs and commonplaceness."[50] The setting of the novel, like Helen Delay's home, is defined by its difference from the "commonplaceness" of an urban space defined by its technologies.

Innocent Children and French Novels

By March 1897 Cather had been in Pittsburgh nine months. She was living alone but had a busy social life. Among her closest friends were George and Helen Seibel, with whom she was reading French and German fiction and poetry. What must have been heady nights full of poetry and philosophical discussion spilled over, at last, into her days: that great evil, French fiction, seeped into the *Home Monthly*. At first, Cather tried to make it as innocuous as she could. She introduced two books, Alphonse Daudet's *Kings in Exile* (1879) and *The Crime of Sylvestre Bonnard* (1881) by Anatole France, to her *Home Monthly* audience.[51]

Cather had been reading Daudet since at least 1895, when she mentioned his name in a review.[52] He had a special significance for her: *Les Femmes d'Artists* (1874) validated her own life. To her, the novel advocated a single life for artists, since they could really be married only to their art. However, she did not inform her *Home Monthly* readers of this private belief.[53] Cather attached another significance to Daudet and perhaps to Latin authors in general: they were hot-blooded and passionate, and they felt first and considered later.[54] Cather's audience would be familiar with this stereotype. To them, French literature was about the senses. It did not teach morality.

Helen Delay, cognizant of public opinion regarding French authors, hastened to defend and excuse them. Daudet's *Kings in Exile,* for example, seemed very sentimental to Helen. By using "sentimental," Helen assured her 1890s audience that Daudet was old-fashioned, since sentimentality, according to Harriet Beecher Stowe in her novel *Pink and White Tyranny,* was passé by 1871. Next, *Kings in Exile* was appropriate to *Home Monthly* readers because it was about a mother raising her son, the prince. The mother-child relation was one that Helen Delay had been careful to mention in every issue of the magazine. Raising the children right was the main duty of women; one way they do so was by reading their children didactic literature. Cather/Delay assured her audience that *Kings in Exile,* though by a French author, was moral and didactic: "The dignity and strength of the queen alone," she said, "would make the book well worth reading."[55]

Delay defended *The Crime of Sylvestre Bonnard* in the same fashion, hastening to assure her readers that the book was not about a "crime" at all, but rather, about an old man who raised a little girl to adulthood, teaching her right from wrong, and selling his most precious possessions to raise her dowry. *Crime* was a child-teaches-adult story. The little girl caused the old scholar to become less pedantic and more humorous. Delay concludes her review, "If there is any book more pure and delicate of flavor, more rich in high sentiment than this one, I do not know it."[56]

Once the French tide was loosed, it seems that Cather could not dam it. The April 1897 issue of the *Home Monthly* saw her singing the praises of Victor Hugo's *Les Miserables* (1862), a book that she had read in her younger days. In the *Home Monthly's* pages there began a profound interchange between Cather and Delay here. Willa Cather, her hand forced by Helen's book column, began to mine her own childhood, to think about a childhood among books.[57]

Because her childhood was so different from that of Helen Delay's Pittsburgh audience, and because Cather had once been "William Cather, M.D.," Cather disguised herself as a boy for her readers. In Delay's sketch, a farm boy is reading *Les Misérables* propped up against a sheaf of wheat. Says Delay, "He worked his way through college on the strength and inspiration he got out of that book, and he is one of the fellows who will do something in the world."[58] The little farm boy reading would have been a comforting symbol to Cather's audience, as he was to Cather herself. The boy's youth made him pure; his being raised on a farm made him purer still. Cather placed the child into Horatio Alger's rags-to-riches story, but she rewrote the Alger myth, attributing success, in part, to one's having read the right books as a child.[59]

The farm-boy figure would have resonated with Cather's audience, because he was not of the city, but rather remained insulated from it. The home distant from the city protects the occupants from the evil of the city,[60] a place which could lure country boys to the dissipations pictured in *Ten Nights in a Barroom* (Timothy Shay Arthur [1854]). That story, in which the innocent farm-boy is corrupted by the evil city, was well known. To keep her writing "elevated," Helen sketched, not the farm-boy's downfall as a result of his traveling to the metropolis, but his perfect youth. Cather's own life took a shape not in the story: farm life ironically propelled her, disguised as a boy, into a position in the evil city where she/he would "do something in the world."

Cather's/Helen's ideal boyhood does not lead the young man straight to the business office. An aspiring boy must read, and thus Helen included a caution to mothers of dreamy boys. If these boys read too much, said Delay, that would not hinder their development into manhood or a future career in business. Delay informed mothers that a boy who read books would be a better person; and indeed, imaginative boys could even grow up to be authors.[61]

Cather, of course, after her "boyhood" in Red Cloud, far from those dangerous cities, grew up to aspire to authorship. By May 1897, when she published her advice to mothers in Helen Delay's column, she had already published eighteen short stories and poems. She projected her own real childhood, as well as her ideal childhood, into Helen Delay's vignette of a boy's growing up because to Willa Cather, men, not women, were serious authors. In addition, by defending the imaginative boy in corporate Pittsburgh, Cather sought to insert this figure into the rags-to-riches story. A literary education made a better man, a man who was going somewhere, doing real work. Helen Delay projected a life for the literary boy: he did things; he would be a mover and a shaker.

In June, two months later, the theme of children growing up with books was still on Willa Cather's mind, and Helen Delay then published a vignette of a girlhood filled with books. William Curtin tells us that the girlhood pictured by Helen was Cather's own.[62] Delay had played it safe in her column so far, recommending only appropriate books for young girls. But in her June 1897 column, Delay told how her aunt (modeled on Cather's Aunt Franc) introduced her to Byron, who had been the bad-boy poet of the early nineteenth century.[63]

The elderly aunt, said Delay, had first read Byron when she was a young girl and had had to hide her copy in the bottom of her closet. Ownership of Byron's poems, approval of them, meant approval of his hedonism, or at least a vicarious protest against the asexual life, the sheltered life, that women were supposed to lead. When the aunt shared Byron with Delay/Cather, she conducted Delay/Cather out of safe, unsexed little-girlhood and into a world where literature did not encode "safe" mores but instead conferred sexual knowledge. Delay, who, in telling of her aunt, became like her aunt, extended a knowing hand to *Home Monthly* readers, urging them, at least figuratively, from their firesides.

Although Delay praised Lord Byron, she disinfected him as well. First of all, she insisted that his book was "old" and thus no longer contraband which young girls must hide. Instead, the book had become an "antique," hallowed by its very age. Delay's emphasis on the book's age showed how Cather used one of Adrian Forty's design schemes: cover the troubling works of a complicated and new-fangled device with a cabinet designed in the old style. The elderly aunt conferred age and dignity on Cather's scene: she also appeared in the motherly, sentimental, and safe posture of reading to and teaching a young girl. While the imaginative boy would grow to be a successful businessman, the imaginative girl was affected by literature because she simply gained in knowledge. She did not have a future as an educated woman—she would be a bluestocking. She could not go into business, as Cather did. Therefore this little girl, one of Cather's first female protagonists, was quiet; and she listened and remembered.

Henry Nicklemann: Othered Again

When Cather quit the *Home Monthly* in June 1897, she did not sever all ties, but continued to author Helen Delay reviews and occasional articles until December 1899. When Cather quit, she repeated a pattern in her life: she largely ceased to publish poetry and fiction because she had relinquished editorial control of a vehicle for her own work. When she had had control of the *Hesperian,* her college literary magazine, she had launched her own career as a short-story writer and poet. Working for the *Nebraska State Journal,* however, she had to churn out theater and art reviews. At the same time, she was pursuing a full course of study at the University of Nebraska—there just wasn't time to find another outlet for her creative work. Coming at the end of her *Nebraska State Journal* career, the *Home Monthly* managing editorship had given her such an outlet, and she had taken full advantage of it.

After she quit the *Home Monthly,* Cather obtained a job on the telegraph desk of the *Pittsburgh Leader* in August 1897. The job paid well and was challenging; however, it left her little time to write and few vehicles in which to publish. Edith Lewis comments that these years were a low point in Cather's life. She was stuck in a paradigm she had so often damned: working as a newspaper writer, she felt her best years as a creative writer slipping away.[64]

She did not remain silent by any means. She continued her "Passing Show" column in the Lincoln *Courier.* "Old Books and New" continued to appear in the *Home Monthly,* and occasionally she sent her poems to the *Courier* to be published. Publication on 17 March 1900 of her poem "In the Night," in a new literary magazine called *The Library,* marked the end of the dry spell. She quit the *Leader* and, for a few months, she had both voice and vehicle.[65]

Cather created "Henry Nicklemann," a male pseudonym, shortly after she began work with the *Library.*[66] Cather could have invented Henry Nicklemann for purely practical reasons: during her tenure at the *Library* she could publish multiple articles under different names. For instance, on 16 June 1900, Henry Nicklemann published an article on horse racing in the *Library,* and Willa Cather published a two-part story—"The Affair at Grover Station"—under her own name. Whatever her reasons for bringing Henry to birth, he remained a rich and useful voice for her, one which she exploited during her days with the Pittsburgh press.

Given Henry's birth near the turn of the century, it is possible to construct his lineage: his fathers were the journalist Richard Harding Davis, the early muckraker Jacob Riis, author and journalist Stephen Crane, Cather's own Lincoln pseudonym *Deus Gallery,* and intellectual German immigrants, such as the Westermann family in Lincoln.

In the 1890s, the son of novelist Rebecca Harding Davis, Richard Harding had come to be regarded as America's *wunderkind,* and he can easily be credited with helping to father Henry Nicklemann, since the Cather family had his books on their shelves in Red Cloud.[67] His handsome (reassuringly "American," not "foreign") visage appeared in Charles Dana Gibson's illustrations of America's leisure time: Gibson's rendition of Richard Harding Davis squired Gibson's girl on her wheel, for a walk in the park, and for an ice cream soda. Davis was the acme of the journalistic profession, which in those days was not a TV anchor, but a foreign correspondent. Davis was flamboyant on the job, even joining the Battle of San Juan Hill during the Spanish-American War. Davis incorporated his exploits as a journalist into his many novels, which sold well. Public, successful, handsome, and lucky, Davis traveled to the world's far-flung and dangerous places and escaped unscathed. Later, a writer/journalist of the Lost Generation, Ernest Hemingway, would mimic Davis's career.

Stephen Crane, like Richard Harding Davis, was a journalist, a foreign correspondent who covered the Spanish-American War in Cuba. However, he also had the advantage of being infamous for his *Maggie, A Girl of the Streets* (1893), a tale of immigrant lives and prostitution in the city. Richard Harding Davis was dashing, but Stephen Crane had tuberculosis, the disease which had been romanticized in such works as *La Dame aux Camélias.* Davis was sunny, while Crane led the archetypal hidden and tormented fin-de-siècle existence.

Journalist and muckraker Riis published *How the Other Half Lives* in 1890. His book, which set photographs of New York's most wretched immigrants against text describing their lives, made his horror and disgust at the lives of "the other half" into good copy, an income, and ultimately, laws which changed how landlords dealt with their tenants. For Riis, immigrants' otherness, their very differences and poverty, placed his copy in demand.

These three—Davis, Crane, and Riis—were three of Nicklemann's forebears; the last was a creation of Cather's. In Lincoln Cather had invented a pseudonym which she had used only twice: *Deus Gallery*— the god of the gallery. The god of the gallery went to the theater and sat in the gallery, where the seats were cheaper: *Deus Gallery* was Cather masking as The People instead of as her very educated self, the latinate title she assumed undercut her very attempt at masking as a proletarian. Most of the gallery gods, she wrote, were boys.[68] They never analyzed; they simply felt, and they were honest in their assessment, giving hearty applause—or boos—when these were due.

When Cather went to Pittsburgh, *Deus Gallery* fathered Henry Nicklemann and published his thoughts in an article, "A Philistine in the Gallery."[69] In this case, the gallery was the art gallery, not the cheap seats in the theater: "There are thousands of people," Henry wrote, "who go to the [art] gallery in family parties, who do not stand squinting before a picture with half-closed eyes or making measurements with a lead pencil, and who do not talk about 'atmosphere' or 'color schemes,' who sincerely and genuinely enjoy the exhibit."

Henry's chief asset as *Deus Gallery* or as the Philistine was that he was not specially educated to criticize plays or art. He played a role Cather could play only if she could have uneducated herself, turned off her critical faculty. As Henry/*Deus Gallery*/The Philistine, Cather could express naked like and dislike without tempering these emotions to taste, gender, class, or to her educational status. The Philistine could join the common people. Cather created Henry the Philistine to write about "the people" and to write of the emotions that she imagined the people to have.

It was convenient that Henry Nicklemann's surname sounded German or Scandinavian—it made his childhood in German/Scandinavian populated Nebraska seem plausible, and to English/Scottish descendants in Pittsburgh, it sent a message. In Pittsburgh, Cather wrote, the Germans created and supported much of the city's culture. Presbyterian Pittsburgers were too busy working to enjoy creating beauty or consuming it, wrote Cather.[70] Nicklemann sounded natural talking about art in Pittsburgh.

Riis and Davis, Crane and *Deus Gallery:* Cather had many models on which to design Henry Nicklemann's newspaper persona. The name itself came from The Nicklemann, a spirit which appeared in Gerhart Hauptmann's play *The Sunken Bell.*[71] Reviewers of the play had written that Hauptmann's play, like Stephen Crane's *Maggie,* was scandalous; indeed, when it opened, it set off riots in New York because of its skeptical questioning of established religious values. Ultimately, the play affirmed the primacy of art and the freedom of expression, values which Cather herself had expressed: "In the kingdom of art there is no God but one God and his service is so exacting that there are few men born of women strong enough to take the vows."[72]

Henry's writing explored the city, the place that Helen's writing shunned. To Cather, writing that chose the city or technology as its subject was the most modern kind of writing. For instance, of British author Rudyard Kipling she had said, his verse is "the most modern verse that ever has been written" because it can "adequately handle the life we know and live."[73] Henry's writing fled, not to Iceland as Helen's had, but to the heart of the city itself for its subject.

The *Library's* lifespan was so short that Nicklemann could scarcely be considered to have "developed" during "his" term there, from April until August 1900. However, even after the *Library's* demise, Cather continued to sign Nicklemann's name to articles in the *Pittsburgh Gazette* from November 1901 until November 1902.[74] The pseudonym allowed her to have both a private life and a public presence. She could speak her mind disguised as Henry Nicklemann, one of the minority of Pittsburgers (according to Cather) who loved art with an unlettered passion. As Henry Cather could discuss art and its conflicts with American concepts of work and labor without having to answer to strangers for any unconventional (unwomanly) opinions. Henry was, in critic Edward Said's terms, an "other" whose foreign opinions could be excused because he was German.

Henry Nicklemann: Willa at Work

Willa Cather used her Henry Nicklemann pseudonym to discuss work, a "masculine" activity that was supposedly removed from Helen's sphere. In Nicklemann's article on Stephen Crane, Cather created a vehicle and a voice to discuss newspaper and novel-writing as work. Henry Nicklemann's article in the *Library,* "When I Knew Stephen Crane" (23 June 1900), reveals much about Cather as an author, as a shaper of a narratorial voice, and as a creator of news. Cather wrote the Stephen Crane piece to acknowledge his death: it was an obituary. However, it was disguised as an interview which Cather said took place years before, in Lincoln, when Cather was a columnist for the *Journal.* Crane actually visited Lincoln for two weeks to report on the severe winter of '94 and Nebraska's continued economic slump. Crane was working for the Bachellor-Johnson Syndicate at the time; his article "Waiting for Spring," appeared in the *Journal* on 24 February 1894. Cather could have met Crane during his time in Lincoln; it is possible that Crane noticed Cather—asleep, standing, after one of her late nights out.[75]

In an obituary an audience expected to see rehearsed the facts of the deceased's life. In the Stephen Crane article, which is highly fictionalized, Cather criticized her own double life—as a female artist and as a "male" reporter. Cather could not criticize the press herself since it was her employer. She was able, however, to express her concerns about her dual role as both columnist and artist by reporting a supposedly true meeting between Henry Nicklemann and Stephen Crane.[76]

Cather's Stephen Crane obituary-cum-interview-cum-editorial begins by describing herself—a self which she had disguised behind her pseudonym. Nicklemann is a wet-behind-the-ears student at the University of Nebraska. However, "he" has had the boyhood of which stories were then beginning to be made: a western boyhood among cattle and horses. The western as a genre was growing in popularity—it had a symbiotic relationship with the burgeoning magazine industry. The industry used the western to fill its pages, and western writers used the magazine's space rates to fill their pockets.[77] The western was a grafting of European romances onto American stock. It retained the flavor of chivalry, of civilization, without admitting titled nobility into its world. When, Nicklemann admits in his article that he knows cattle, horses, and—not so incongruously—Greek, he states succinctly that he comes from this western scene.

Cather also created in Nicklemann a modern pastoral figure; he walked out of a western Arcadia into the newsroom where he met Crane. Arcadia was Cather's code word for a place that should be changeless, antique. However, in "Winter in Arcady," a poem written about the same time as the Crane piece (1901), she described a dysfunctional pastoral to which change had come. "Winter in Arcady" mourned the passing of Pittsburgh composer Ethelbert Nevin, who, in addition to being a friend to Cather and an admired artist, also seemed to have been the embodiment of youth and power to her. The musician's study, a small building in which he composed, had been nicknamed "Arcady" by Cather.[78]

Cather had Nicklemann contrast Stephen Crane with a nameless college professor (her old bug-boo Lucius Sherman still haunted her). Earlier Cather columns had sniped at Sherman, and her Crane article, six years after she graduated, shows how deep her rancor was.[79] No longer were professors like Sherman only pedantic, although she had called him this. To Cather in 1901, Sherman had become the personification of inhuman forces that choked off art's life-blood, a kind of government entity, a powerful being who tabulated statistics and judged. Cather, disguised as Nicklemann and on the receiving end of Sherman's pedantry in the "Stephen Crane" sketch, labeled herself "the people." Henry Nicklemann, who was one of "the people," just liked a good story; he never tabulated and measured. Sherman played a kind of Monopoly of the Intellect. Henry was above such games.[80]

Nicklemann/Cather put Cather's ideas about newspaper work into Crane's mouth: it was all hack work, Crane said. According to Cather's fictionalized Crane, newspaper work debased the artist because it was written to a deadline to fill out a column. Crane's literary work was very different from his newspaper work: according to

Crane, it took him hours to write each paragraph. There was no money in it because he took pains with every detail. He did it for the joy of it.

In his supposed interview, Nicklemann posited a role for the artist that fit the archetype for the American worker: work was hard, work drained the worker, but work was a worthy pursuit for both worker and for the society in which he or she lived. Nicklemann's views on art and work are easy to trace. Before Stephen Crane, Cather had hammered away at her art-is-work theme in other columns. In a comment about Ethelbert Nevin, for example, Cather carved out a valued role for the artist, a role equal to that of the industrialist when she had Nevin beg his father to excuse him from business so that he could be an artist.[81] Cather castigated Ouida for coming to her art so easily: "It is not labor, but indulgence."[82] Cather's theme about the labor of art was a common one at the time, stemming from Ruskin's Arts and Crafts movement.[83] Cather voiced these common opinions about work and the artist in staid Pittsburgh through Henry Nicklemann because he was an appropriate voice for these opinions. Because he was male, he would have been in offices and understood the hierarchies of industry.

Finally, Cather described Crane as almost the cartoon of the starving artist. So devoted to art was he that he was desperately thin, had practically starved himself to death. He took up newspaper work only when his situation became desperate. He was a true artist, not tainted by materialism. He spoke for the old coteries, where men of letters shared their poems and essays for the joy of it. In the 1890s, selling literature still retained a stigma: commodifying literature broke the exclusive circle of the coterie; literature that was sold became gauche and middle-class because it was commodified. Women who sold their literary wares were doubly stigmatized. Not only were they barred from the coterie by their sex (though they started their own clubs), but they were supposed to be at home, a place removed from the dog-eat-dog world of buying and selling. The starving artist-genius was a fin-de-siècle pose, one that Cather also had granted Poe in an earlier review. The starving artist pose advertised its wearer's (and here, creator's) modern disdain for art-as-commodity, yet also still affirmed the woman's position as the pure (untouched by commerce) representative of the home, far from the working world.[84]

Cather's "Stephen Crane," in short, forced her to invent a history for Henry, to arrange Henry against a social and economic backdrop. Because he was a young reporter, he was engaged in a very modern business. He was interviewing Crane, one of the most famous and infamous realists—and this meant that Henry was thoroughly modern and a bit risqué. Henry believed in hard work. He participated in the American Dream. However, he retained the impossible ideal that, although art was work, artists should not profit by it; instead, they should starve, and wear the signs of their starvation like a badge.

When she wrote her Stephen Crane column, "woman" and "serious artist" remained oxymoronic: a nice woman like Cather should not have been praising the author of *Maggie, A Girl of the Streets;* a woman like Cather should not have sought payment for her art. Cather used Nicklemann to defend her role as the interviewer of Stephen Crane, the outspoken and famous realist writer. Cather was supposed to be home by her fire.

The Voyeur and the Other

Henry Nicklemann signed his name to a short story in the *Library* on 28 April 1900. "Dance at Chevalier's" is a cross between George Washington Cable's *The Grandissimes* (1880) and Anthony Hope's *Prisoner of Zenda* (1894). In "Dance at Chevalier's," Cather used her Nicklemann pseudonym to discuss one of "his" obsessions: the issue of race and class as America absorbed her enormous newly immigrant population. Characters in "Dance" personified national traits—French Creole, Mexican, Euro-American—and knit them into a complex plot. "Dance" is about a love triangle; its *dénouement* is murder. One character, a newspaper reporter, hovers at the edges of the action, watching. Henry Nicklemann, himself a journalist, watches the watcher and the actors and tells what he sees. America's melting pot, social Darwinism, newspaper reporting, a young male realistic journalist: it is no accident that these should come together in "Dance at Chevalier's." Henry was particularly prepared to watch. "He" was a young man coming of age during the rise of realist fiction.

In Cather's day realism was gendered. Realists, like the romancer Hawthorne of another generation, damned the mob of scribbling women, and precisely like Hawthorne, damned them because the literary marketplace belonged to them.[85] Whether they saw their enterprise as one of gaining "market shares" or not, male realists, such as Stephen Crane, Harold Frederic, Frank Norris, and Theodore Dreiser, chose writing strategies that insisted upon their masculinity.[86]

Masculine fiction, realist fiction, defined itself by what women's fiction was not. Because women's sphere had granted women the duty of educating children, works typed as female played out their scenes in domestic spaces and took didactic themes. Because didactic novels treated not what-is but what-should-be, didactic novels often treated ideals, heroes.[87] Realist novels aggressively adopted middle-class unheroic characters like Silas Lapham, who got obnoxiously drunk and made bad business deals. A realist novel followed Maggie through impoverished New York streets until she met her lonely death, and in the novelistic world that Stephen Crane created, her death was senseless, not didactic. It was difficult for traditional nineteenth-century readers to learn anything at all from *Maggie, A Girl of the Streets*, because she had taken a lover without marrying him, and later, in her desperation, turned to prostitution for income. Realistic novels eschewed domestic spaces and hung out in the streets, the bars, the office, where "nice girls" never went.

Realists wrote about "serious" things, class conflicts and the problem of prostitution. Social Darwinism remained a favorite realist topic because Darwinism was seen as a serious attack on the Judeo-Christian world view, therefore to write a Darwinist novel was to attack the didactic and the Swedenborgian sentimental at its heart. Social Darwinism was the naturalist's theories applied to the business world, a world which was not yet a woman's world. The Darwinist novel also assumed that characters' national traits governed their actions; thus a Darwinist novel's plot often drove characters to unheroic ends, giving a slap in the face to heroic sentimental fiction.[88]

A serious writer had to rely on "his" powers of observation to bring new topics to the novel, for instance, descriptions of New York streets in Howells's *A Hazard of New Fortunes*. Most women novelists were excluded from observing the city by tradition and ideology. Elizabeth Blackwood, America's first woman doctor, relates how, during her nighttime house calls, men would proposition her in the streets.[89] Willa Cather herself was escorted home from her nighttime jobs at newspaper offices by the copyboy, a common service extended to the first women journalists.[90] Looking was a male prerogative that Willa took as her own, but advertised (comfortingly) as Henry's.

Henry fit his role as reporter of the story of "Dance" especially because he wrote in the age of yellow journalism, that style of writing which was designed to play on the emotions.[91] Like dramatic ads, like the emotional actress, the yellow journalist made a bid for his reader's disgust, horror, shock, or joy. "Dance," with its murder plot and love triangle, was made for the yellow journalist, and Henry was there to do the job. Thus we return to our young reporter, who has come to the dance at Chevalier's.[92]

The *dramatis personae* at Chevalier's are Little Harry Burns, the reporter; old Jean Chevalier himself (he's not pure French; he's part Indian and speaks a "vile patois" not understood by "Christians" like Henry, the narrator); his lovely, single daughter, Severine; Denis, a giant Irishman, suitor to Severine; and Signor, a Mexican (a "nasty Greaser," "swarthy" and vengeful), rival to Denis. The "dance" itself is a ball, but it is also a deadly dance of class, race, and economics, a microcosm of America in the 1890s. Severine becomes the prize in lieu of money; the competitors sashay on the dance floor instead of in the office.

Cather's "Dance" describes national stereotypes and assigns to those stereotypes blame for a disaster. According to Ronald Takaki, it was American industrialization itself that led to such public stereotyping of people of color, women, Jews, Catholics, and non-English speakers in America.[93] Industrialists hired workers who could mindlessly tend machines and stand in assembly lines, doing repetitive tasks. In their need, says Takaki, the captains of industry invented ideas about the people who would take on such repetitious tasks. People who applied for blue-collar jobs must be mindless, the story went; they needed guidance and a firm managerial hand. The "others" who applied for work at America's new factories were often immigrant peoples, who, new to America, and without land or family connections, had to have money to live. Stereotypes of immigrant Americans became fossilized into national institutions: laws were enacted, wars were fought, medical diagnoses were invented to account for the cultural differences of the "others."[94] Cather had her share of stereotypes for "others," both good and bad. Henry Nicklemann himself was a "good" stereotype, a German or Scandinavian immigrant who liked art. Cather's very first forays as Nicklemann into the land of the other—however clumsy or cruel—led Cather to hone her immigrant story ideas until they become, for awhile, the central plot to her novel-writing career.

The Chevaliers themselves were French-Americans who preserved their linguistic and cultural heritage. Critics have noted Cather's admiration of French culture.[95] Cather's own culture included the French in the category "Euro-Americans" so they were not so stigmatized as people of color. However, Cather, like many of her countrymen and -women, felt that the French are far more "passionate" than Anglo-Americans (who were "cold").[96] Sarah Bernhardt was perfect for the stage because, according to Cather, her French blood made her fit the type of "emotional actress" that was popular then. By contrast Lillian Nordica, a Euro-American, should stick to stage recitals, said Cather. Her cold northern blood prevented her from becoming a great actress. On the other hand, Cather wrote, she had the greatest admiration for Nordica, a "hard worker"[97]; she would never want to know Sarah Bernhardt personally. The immortal Sarah was too filled with animal passions.[98] Severine's "animal passions" caused her to encourage two lovers instead of only one, and that was the naturalistic tragedy of "Dance."

If the French were stereotyped as passionate, Mexicans, like Signor, were even more so. The critic Ruth Miller Elson lists the stereotype as courteous and proud, but also as lazy, vengeful, and violent.[99] According to Takaki, the act of calling Mexicans ungovernable, stupid, lazy, and frivolous gave white men the right to employ them for very low wages in burgeoning western industries and the right to take California and Texas away from Mexican rule in the Mexican War (1846–48).[100] Mexicans, this myth says, could not govern or supervise themselves because their passions always got the better of them. Someone else had to do it. This was the "white man's burden."

This stereotypical Mexican is the villain in "Dance at Chevalier's." True to type, his ungovernable passions cause him to steal kisses from Severine, although she is already spoken for, and to poison her lover, Denis. "Dance" holds no surprises. Denis the Irishman, true to type, is gullible, drinks too much, and is overly passionate. Severine's womanly lack of intelligence causes her to tell Signor of her love for Denis. Signor promises not to tell old Jean Chevalier of his daughter's love for the Irishman—in exchange for a kiss. Signor's jealousy festers; he poisons a bottle of whiskey (the poison had been especially prepared by "an old Negro from the Gold Coast"). Denis, having witnessed Signor give Severine the promised kiss, drowns his sorrows in the poisoned whiskey. Denis dies, and Signor escapes. The reporter watched: Nicklemann, with his cold, passionless eye, recorded this study of immigrant Americans' "lower natures."

Henry's portraits of the "others," non-Euro-Americans, in "Dance" and in a newspaper article he wrote, a sociological study called "Out of Mulberry Street," are disturbing reminders of Cather's culture, especially of her belief that national traits are inborn, not culturally defined. However, it was through Henry's yellow journalism and realist short story that Cather explored America's immigrants and began to write about them. The form dictated content, as it did in some of Henry's other articles: "A Chinese View of the Chinese Situation," "Pittsburgh's Richest Chinaman," and "A Factory for Making Americans."[101]

In each "yellow article," something passionate happens. Although in her yellow journalism, Cather's desire may have been to shock for shock's sake, she may also have been announcing her loyalty to passion and her hatred for statistics. During her years in Pittsburgh, she continued railing against the professionalization of sociology, which asserted itself by tabulating statistics on America's new immigrant

population. Cather's passionate and titillating stories were antistatisti-
cal, a fact that she broadcast in a review.[102]

Cather never really lost the idea of inborn traits, yet she did come
back to the immigrant in her fiction, each time becoming more sympathetic and complex in her treatment: *O Pioneers!* explores the lives
of German, Swedish, Bohemian, and French immigrants, for instance. Henry was the springboard. After her Pittsburgh years, Cather
began pioneering her own literary exploration of immigrant
America.[103] Critics remind us that Cather's writing of sympathetic
immigrant characters at all was shocking in its time—and in fact her
books offer quite a multicultural reading experience.

In Pittsburgh Cather's necessity of supporting herself by her journalism made her think about how to portray female and male characters believably, sympathetically. In Pittsburgh Cather thought about
immigrant life in a jingoistic manner, but her immigrant studies later
led to novels solely about immigrants. Pittsburgh transformed
Cather's pointed character sketches into fuller, more believable portraits of individuals. Her Pittsburgh fiction, which is handled in the
following chapter, is still peopled by cardboard characters, but there
are others, as well, who are memorable. It was Helen, Henry, and
the crowd of other pseudonyms who prepared Cather to become the
author of her first books, *April Twilights* and *The Troll Garden*.

4

Pittsburgh Short Fiction: *April Twilights* and *The Troll Garden*

Business does not exist in the world of poetry, and therefore by implication, it has become everything that poetry is not—a world without imagination, enlightenment, or perception. It is a world which poetry is trying to escape.[1]

—Dana Gioia

The novel manufactured to entertain great multitudes of people must be considered exactly like a cheap soap or a cheap perfume, or cheap furniture. Fine quality is a distinct disadvantage in articles made for great numbers of people who do not want quality but quantity, who do not want a thing that wears, but who want change—a succession of new things that are quickly threadbare and can be lightly thrown away.[2]

—Willa Cather

Printing press, ca. 1895

Cather produced a great deal of fiction and poetry in Pittsburgh, driven by her deadlines and by her heady, intellectual friendships with the Seibels and Isabel McClung. She had been writing fiction and poetry to fill the pages of the *Home Monthly* and the *Library*. After she quit journalism to become a high-school teacher, however, she began to try to publish book-length manuscripts.[3] A vanity publisher, Richard C. Badger, must have sent Cather a circular advertising his firm in 1902, because by 1903, Cather had collected her poetry in a slender volume called *April Twilights*.[4] Shortly after this success, H. H. McClure, cousin to S. S. McClure of the McClure, Philips syndicate, was passing through Lincoln, Nebraska. He happened to ask Will Owens Jones if he knew of any up-and-coming authors, and Jones mentioned Cather. Shortly thereafter, Cather received an invitation to call on S. S. McClure and discuss possible publication of her short stories with his firm.[5]

On 1 May 1903, McClure gratified the vanity of the young author by offering to bring out her short stories in a collection and to place her other stories in his magazine and in others. McClure came across on most of his promises, publishing her collection *The Troll Garden* (after a two-year wait) in 1905 and placing a couple or three short stories in national publications.[6]

After she began teaching, Cather largely ceased publishing reviews or articles, and thus her reactions to cultural change become harder to trace. Up until the moment when Cather published *The Troll Garden* in 1905, Cather had been embroiled in several cultural debates, such as the realism versus sentimentalism debate of the 1890s. Her views on such subjects had been easy to trace because she had written about them so regularly. In this chapter, in the absence of many reviews by Cather, readers must look to Cather's stories and poems to chronicle her thoughts during the late Pittsburgh years. Although she had created the fictional voices of Helen and Henry for her journalism, in Pittsburgh they began to narrate and become characters in her short fiction. She also had gathered information about a new plot, the narrative of women at work.

Cather's Mask and Cather's Face

When Cather collected her first volume of short stories, she easily donned the masks of Helen Delay and Henry Nicklemann, masks she had used to write her journalism (prose). However, one of her concerns, that of the male with "female" traits or the female with "male" traits, continued in her short stories. These "mixed" personae do not strictly fit Helen or Henry's profile.

Cather is interesting when she stays within the bounds of Helen or Henry's experiences, writing their stories as if they were indeed lived by a woman or a man. Sometimes, however, Helen and Henry's voices—under whatever pseudonym—meshed. It was often in this voice, a blend, that "Willa Cather," or increasingly in Pittsburgh, "Willa Sibert Cather," wrote her short stories. "Sibert" was the middle name of her mother's brother, William Seibert Boak, killed in the Civil War. Cather's mother kept the memory of the family martyr alive, and Willa would have heard his story many times as she grew up.[7] The new middle name was important enough to Cather that she must have broadcast it to her old friends. In a letter Frances Gere wrote her sister Mariel that Cather had chosen yet another nickname—perhaps because she thought it sounded "distingué."[8]

Cather had written William Seibert Boak's story into a poem called "The Namesake" and included it in her book of poems *April Twilights*. In her poem, Cather seems to become her persona, putting on the uncle's name along with his "masculine" dedication to an idea beyond love. Her male mask took on the realities of her female life; Henry's mask became part of Willa Cather's face; she began to use her many voices fluently and interchangeably—under her own reconstituted name. This fusing of personae should be no surprise; it was a natural development from her journalism.

Early on during the reconstruction process, Cather did not have much control over which voice she was using. For instance, during Henry's tenure, Cather tried to keep her voice under Henry's control; but occasionally Henry's mask slipped off, revealing Cather's face. Nicklemann's contribution to the *Library* of 2 June 1900 is an example. In the article, Nicklemann is hanging out at the train yard when Lizzie Hudson Collier, a Pittsburgh actress, gets off the train. The young male reporter notices Collier in ways that Willa Cather cannot: as a male, Nicklemann can stare at and report Collier's handsome figure.[9] From time to time in the article, however, Cather slips into her "Helen" voice, reporting a sentimental scene between Collier and a little baby from the slums. In her article on Collier, Cather cannot seem to decide whether she wants to tell a "Henry" story about the night, the trainyard, and a beautiful woman, or a "Helen" story about hotel rooms, hovels, babies, and motherhood. In fact, the voice changes depending on whether Cather is discussing an exterior ("Henry") or interior ("Helen") space.

In later years Cather gains control of Henry's persona and voice, turning it on and off at will. For instance, in her 1912 novel *Alex-*

ander's Bridge, Cather has Lucius Wilson follow Winifred Alexander's figure just as Henry once followed Collier's. Wilson considers thoughts appropriate to his station as a middle-aged professor of philosophy. Cather easily switches voices when she wants to write about the thoughts of Winifred Alexander, the lovely woman whom Wilson watches. Winifred is thinking about the imminent arrival of her guest and hoping that she is not too late returning home to give a proper welcome.

The voice which crossed gender bounds allowed Cather to tell a story which was "new." Cather practiced working with her Willa Sibert Cather voice in a piece of journalism written for the 19 February 1898 *Courier,* under Cather's customary title, "The Passing Show." Cather's story starts like yellow journalism: a young girl runs away with an older man. It ends like a sentimental novel: a poor little girl is all alone in the world. Cather does not merely get her masks confused in her "unyellow" article. Instead, she uses the narrative of the sentimental to undermine the yellow journalist's assumptions. The story behind Cather's "unyellow" column is this: Adelaide Moned, the daughter of an actress, ran away from her mother and stepfather's acting company with the company's manager, and went to her father's Pittsburgh home. Rumor had it that Adelaide, seventeen, was engaged to someone else, and her accompanying her male manager set Pittsburgh's tongues wagging. Juicy tidbits made the Moned case even more intriguing. Moned's mother, once an actress of note, had begun to show signs of insanity. Her mother was also a divorcée, and thus, a woman with a "past." As Cather told it, her boss at the newspaper asked her to get Adelaide's story, to reveal the more sordid details of Adelaide's life and that of her mother to the public, a "yellow" way of writing. All of the best newspapermen in town had tried and failed, and if Cather could bring this story off, it would be a real "scoop" for the paper.

Cather agreed to try for Adelaide's story, but at this point in her column, she began to reveal, not Moned's love life, but an insider's view of the yellow journalist at work. Cather had known Adelaide's mother, and so she bought flowers for the girl and sent them, signing her name as her mother's friend.

As a result of her subterfuge (she came, after all, as a reporter, not as a "friend") Cather obtained her interview, but in her *Courier* column, she did not reveal the girl's closest confidences. Instead, she portrayed the seventeen-year-old as an innocent child scarcely out of convent school who missed her mother. Here, there was no fodder for the yellow journalist's cannon, but rather the plot to a sentimental story. Cather revealed how much she loathed invading the girl's privacy, but she reminded her audience that invading privacy was exactly the reporter's job: "In a book," Cather wrote, "the reporter would go in to the managing editor and say with pallid lips, 'There is no story!' and get cashiered. But in the rocky old world that is, things don't happen that way . . . the men were waiting for my copy . . . well, we 'scooped' New York." In Cather's account, Henry the reporter set out to get his story, no matter what, but it was Helen the sentimental who wrote the story and pictured the girl's embarrassment about all the publicity that her actions had caused. Cather's Moned article reveals the less savory truth behind what a newspaper reporter did, and how a newspaper reporter worked. In 1894, when she had still been a cub reporter and written her "yellow" story about Brownville, Nebraska, she had been delighted at achieving a scoop and upsetting the upright citizens of Brownville. By 1898, she had begun to erect a wall between what was properly public (and newsworthy) and Moned's private (censored from the news and safe from the competitive business world) business. By 1906, Cather was thoroughly tired of the newspaper industry, and she was writing her friend Carrie Miner Sherwood that the people's desire for lies amazed her; it amazed her more how newspapers filled that desire.[10] It is this early, perhaps, that Cather came to distrust journalists—in Pittsburgh, when she was an insider. Cather's distrust might have reflected a growing public discontent. In the autobiography of Cather's much-admired Clara Morris, Morris wrote:

> And trembling at the idea of being attacked or sneered at in print, without one thought of asking what *Herald* the unknown represents, . . . she [the innocent young actress] hastens to grant this probably ignorant young lout [an interviewer] the unchaperoned interview.[11]

Much later in her life, Cather would become renowned for her reticence concerning her private life. Those who became so obsessed by Cather's reserve that they branded her a recluse forgot to note that Cather knew journalism from the inside, knew that only a stiff guard could repel an industry which sought to invade private spaces which turn-of-the-century ideology had placed safely away from the office.

It was Cather's reconstituted voice, the Willa Sibert Cather voice that she had developed for journalism, which so often wrote fiction during her Pittsburgh years. Willa Sibert Cather could combine the personae of Helen and Henry to create "bilingual" or "crossdressing" stories. As in the Moned article, once Cather learned how to place Helen and

Henry's fundamentally different points of view in juxtaposition, she could manipulate audience reaction and audience expectation. Helen and Henry's feud could become the essence of story itself, and Cather's writing could adopt modernist irony as one of its hallmarks. Indeed, I wonder if a study broader than the present one—that is, examining more authors—might show that journalism's clash with the sentimental, plus a hefty dose of contact with pre-and post-war Europe, created modernist irony in America.

Although Cather's early, uncollected short stories have been examined at length before, it is worth analyzing them in terms of Helen and Henry's contributions. In these early Pittsburgh stories, Cather begins to drop the mask, blend the voices, appropriate Helen's feelings and Henry's realistic eye. It is here that Cather first really begins to use her journalism to feed her fiction.

Nine Stories from the *Home Monthly*

Working at the *Home Monthly* compelled Cather to fill empty pages with her own poems and short stories, and it is no wonder that her year there was one of great inventiveness and productivity. She signed most of her *Home Monthly* short stories with her own name. Thus, while all of Helen Delay's reviews maintained Helen's even, didactic tone and chaste subject matter, Cather's short stories show some realistic—or even fantastical—characters caught in deterministic circumstances, subject, and plot that sometimes run counter to Helen's advice.[12]

"Princess Baladina—Her Adventure," "The Strategy of the Were-Wolf Dog," and "The Way of the World" are, or seem to be, directed toward children. "Princess Baladina," which Cather published under a pseudonym, is a fractured fairy tale. The princess leaves her father's castle in order to find her prince, but she comes up with the miller's son instead. "Princess" sets up a Helen tale of matrimony and confounds the reader with an ironic ending by Henry. "Were-Wolf Dog" is a Christmas tale whose characters are all animals, in imitation of Kipling (whom Cather admired as a realist). The evil were-wolf dog leads the reindeer to their death. An old seal with one fin (he's also drunk) is the only animal brave enough to say that he will help pull Santa's sleigh. The other animals are shamed by the seal's bravery, and together they save the day. The story has an ideal hero, like Helen's favorite idealistic novels. "The Way of the World" has greater depth, and it is not so much a story for children as it is a story about children directed at adults. In "The Way," Speckle Burnham has set up a cardboard-box city named Sand Town in his back yard, complete with businesses and politicians, but lacking in houses. Everything goes well until a girl asks to join. Finally, because the girl's presence causes competition among the boys to attract her, Sand Town becomes a ghost town (and that is "the way of the world"). The story presents a conflict of ideologies, Men's Sphere meets the New Woman. The moral of the tale, if read literally, is one that Helen's readers would have enjoyed; a more ironic reader could have read the story as a protest.

In "Burglar's Christmas," a starving man breaks into a house to steal jewelry and silver that he can pawn for food. When he finds his own baby cup in the house, he realizes that he is in his parents' home and becomes filled with remorse. His mother finds him and forgives him, taking him into her arms. In "Burglar's Christmas," the Swedenborgian mother-child bond persists, turning the burglar into a penitent man who can be redeemed into society.[13]

Most of the other stories published in the *Home Monthly* allude, in one way or another, to the theater, the world that Cather had come to know so well as a reviewer. "The Count of Crow's Nest" is a Jamesian tale, complete with a nosey journalist, a European nobleman, and a purloined letter. The story is notable for a few effects. In addition to describing boarding house life with a few deft, bitter strokes, the story profiles scrupulous and unscrupulous money makers in the art world. The count lives in reduced circumstances in a boarding house on the pittance left him after he fled Europe. Nevertheless, he remains a gentleman who does not need to work for his upkeep. His daughter is a singer with a higher opinion of her talents than circumstances warrant. Her greed leads her to steal her father's family letters (which are full of embarrassing revelations) and sell them to a journalist looking for a "scoop." A dramatic confrontation at the end of the story stymies the daughter's plans and the journalist's invasion of private space. "Count" shows Cather's first evil journalist, who is willing to use another person's embarrassment for gain. In "Count," Cather begins to portray the politics and the economics of yellow journalism.

"Tommy, the Unsentimental" is one of Cather's strangest stories. Tommy, a girl, loves Jay Ellington Harper. Tommy's best friend is Jessica, and Tommy loves her, too. Tommy operates her father's bank when he's not in town; her ideal is to pursue Henry's life, a life of business. Tommy's girlfriend, Miss Jessica, wears fine clothes and falls in love with Jay. Jay, an ineffectual clerk in the bank in the next town, has let his bank's ready cash run low the same day that there is a run on his bank. Tommy and Miss Jessica join in a crazy bicycle ride over rough roads to deliver money to Jay in time to save his bank. Miss Jessica tires and cannot finish the ride; Tommy saves the day but renounces her claims on both her girlfriend and her boyfriend so that he can feel free to love Miss Jessica. "Tommy" presents parallel stories, a Henry story—with Tommy playing Henry's role—about dedication to work and renunciation, and a Helen story—of which the ultra-feminine Jessica is the heroine—about falling in love. The lovers are ineffectual workers; the worker is an ineffectual lover.

"Tommy," the earliest story that Cather had written for *The Home Monthly,* ironically comments on the type of writing her new job demanded: Cather gave the magazine a story in which the hero was a mannish woman and in which the happily-ever-after love story looked somewhat tarnished. James Barrie, from whose *Tommy, the Sentimental* Cather had playfully derived her title, was the author of *Peter Pan.* Peter's hallmark is that he is determined to be a boy forever, avoiding such obligations as work and school. Wendy and her brothers toy with staying in Peter's world, but return from Never-Never Land to take up their proper positions in society. In Cather's story, Tommy, a girl with a boy's name, is dedicated to work. The marginalized characters are those who choose love instead.

Cather's story "A Resurrection" comes directly from her realist reporting, and perhaps from a yellow squib in the *Nebraska State Journal.* "Resurrection" is set in Brownville, Nebraska, and its atmosphere is that of decay which Cather had reported in her yellow article, "An Old River Metropolis," during her college days. Perhaps Cather took the germ for her idea from the gossip columns: on 1 September 1890, the *Journal* had printed a story of a man who ran away with Estelle Lebon, a French Canadian woman, leaving his wife and two children. Cather's story is about Martin Dempster (the name is from a Hall Caine novel), who jilts his fiancée to elope with Aimée, one of Henry's too-passionate Frenchwomen. Aimée dies, and Martin asks Miss Margie, his former fiancée, to raise his motherless child, Bobby. Martin works hard until he earns enough money to ask Miss Margie to be his wife once more. He sees her on Easter Sunday in a shaft of Swedenborgian light, holding Easter lilies. She says "yes." Helen's contributions in "Resurrection" are multiple rhetorical partings, the Swedenborgian symbol (light), and the love story that redeems all. Henry's contributions hover more quietly in the background: the setting of the decaying town of Brownville, the illicit pairing of Martin and Aimée, and Henry's sociological notes on the tendencies of the French.

"Nanette, an Aside" is a character sketch from the theater. To some readers of the *Home Monthly,* theater people would have still been outsiders to polite society, and therefore, becoming voyeur on their private scenes would have been titillating. In the story a singer, Madame Tradutorri, is aging; her husband, a n'er-do-well, gambles away her earnings. They are estranged. On top of these small tragedies, the singer's lady's maid ("Nanette") has fallen in love and asks to leave. "Nanette" appeals more to Henry's aesthetic than to Helen's; the short story shows the tattered underside of theater life, a side that Cather would have observed during her interviews.

"The Protegies" is a story that Cather took directly from her Lincoln journalism. Previously Cather had written about the lives of twin child protegies.[14] In the short story, Cather exaggerates the real protegies' more ordinary lives and fictionalizes them as lives under the tyranny of ambitious parents. Cather uses her Henry voice to pry beneath the surface of the charming child entertainers and note how their ideally free childhoods are constrained by their parents' greed for fame.

Seven *Library* Stories

The *Library* was solvent for only six months or so. Cather managed to publish seven stories in the magazine, of which three are discussed here. Of those not discussed, "A Night at Greenway Court" and "Peter" were recycled from her college years, and "Dance at Chevalier's" has been handled earlier. "A Singer's Romance" is "Nanette" slightly rewritten from the original *Home Monthly* publication.

Henry-type stories about racial and national types present characters who are true to "type" and who do not develop. Cather's Henry stories are the most breathtakingly racist of her works: in "Grover Station," a murder mystery, the murderer's evil tendencies can be explained by his parentage—he's half Chinese, and Chinese blood is so cold that Chinese people have no feelings.[15] In "The Conversion of Sum Loo," it is no wonder that the Chinese family who converts to Christianity converts right back to their native religion when their baby dies. In a time when "The Heathen Chinee" was popular, one of the features of the "Chinese racial type" was a seeming indifference to religion.[16]

In "The Sentimentality of William Tavener," the title character is one of Henry's middle-aged, small-town farmers. His farm is hard work, and his mind has narrowed until it considers only farm equipment and wheat prices. When his sons want to go to the circus, he cannot understand their desire for such frivolity. William's wife, Hester Tavener, reminds William of their younger days, when they went to the circus, too. Cather sustains the moment of remembering, draws it out, until it becomes the opposite of the rhetorization of suffering—the rhetorization of joy. Tavener relents, and, for a moment, he even experiences something like passion. In "William Tavener," the realistic scene and William's single-minded concentration on work is entered and destroyed by a moment of sentiment, a plot that Helen and Helen's readers would have approved, long after Cather had left the *Home Monthly*.

Independent Publication before *The Troll Garden:* Four Stories

When the *Library* folded, Cather lost her easy avenue of publication and had to seek space in magazines such as *Scribner's, Everybody's, Lippencott's, Youth's Companion,* and the *Saturday Evening Post.* In the three and a half years before her first short story collection was published in 1906, she independently published six stories. Of these, two are part of the *Troll Garden* proper and will be handled there. Of the remaining four—all original—I have handled "The Namesake" elsewhere, leaving "Jack-a-Boy," "El Dorado—A Kansas Recessional," and "The Treasure of Far Island" for discussion here.

Readers see the title character of "Jack-a-Boy" as Cather's little brother, Jack, but Jack himself did not die young as the short-story character does. Cather published "Jack-a-Boy" immediately after the death of Ethelbert Nevin, the composer, who, Cather had noticed, had "an exquisite sensitiveness, that fine susceptibility to the moods of others"—that is, his ability to sympathize, to move others, was especially strong.[17] Nevin had faced his death "naturally," like the Greeks, without feeling the terror of dying that Cather attributes to the Judeo-Christian inheritance.[18] "Jack-a-Boy" as a short story makes more sense as being about Nevin reimagined as a child. The story is about two things: the ability of a child to school the denizens of an apartment building to learn wonder and love; and how Jack's untimely death teaches those around him how to become better people. Although Jack is a boy, his message to the apartment dwellers is the "feminine" one about love and sympathy. Cather's fascination with Ethelbert Nevin had been that he was a "girl-boy," a man who had deep feelings.[19] Jack's existence as a child who had not yet come to sexual maturity and who did not exist solely to make money allowed him to be an especially "real" portrait of Nevin for Cather, since she always thought of Nevin, although near forty, as childlike.[20] Jack's kindnesses are so manifold that they have the capacity to heal an old wound: Jack causes an old scholar to leave his books and enter meaningfully (for Cather) the social world of the apartment building. Jack's freedom from commercial ties and sexual desire rendered his actions "purely" benevolent, and for these uses, Helen's voice was the only appropriate vehicle.

"El Dorado" is another of Cather's stories about money and ethics, and it comments on real estate speculation in the West. Josiah Bywaters, a man from the east, has heard about the town of El Dorado, Kansas, which is attracting so many people that it will soon be a small metropolis. He goes to Kansas to make his fortune in the dry goods business. However, the advertisements for the boomtown turn out to be puffery concocted by the members of one family to bilk speculators of their investments. After Bywaters invests his money in land and a store, the Gump family leaves with his money, which had been deposited in their bank. The streets become dusty, buildings decay, but Bywaters must remain because he has no money with which to leave. El Dorado has an ending that Helen would have approved of: Apollo Gump, a dandy, riding near the decaying town, is bitten by a rattler and dies. Bywaters takes all the money from the dead man's pockets and leaves El Dorado.

In "The Treasure of Far Island," Cather sets the scene in a place familiar to her as she grew up—a sandbar in the Republican River, which ran at the southern edge of Red Cloud. Douglass Burnham and Margie van Dyck, boyfriend and girlfriend as children, return as adults to Far Island to dig up the treasure they had buried years ago. The story ends according to Helen's dictum, with the two protagonists plighting their troth. As in "William Tavener," sharing a moment out of the past brings two people together in the present.

Seven Stories from *The Troll Garden*

Cather published her first book of collected short stories after she had become a schoolteacher. Their publication by McClure, Philips in 1906 was the result of a meeting with S. S. McClure, the publisher of the New York muckraker *McClure's*. As Bernice Slote has shown in her essay in *The Kingdom of Art,* Cather intended the short stories to illustrate common themes, which readers can understand only by becoming familiar with Cather's epigraphs.[21] The first epigraph is from Christina Rossetti's poem "The Goblin Market." In the poem, two sisters meet the strange goblin men and one buys their seductive fruits with gold coins. This sister begins to pine and waste away for want of more fruit. The other sister, for love of her sibling, seeks out the goblin men and asks to buy their fruits to keep her sister from starving. Instead of selling their fruit, they smear their fruit all over her in a scene whose violence and symbolic content (smeared "fruit") indicate a rape. When she staggers home, her sister discovers the violence inherent in her desire, and she becomes cured of her addiction. The two sisters substitute love for each other for the goblin men's strange fruits.

In Rossetti's fable, a woman is seduced by the men's beautiful goods; she spends her coin for the fruits, which, in the poem's language becomes associated with the woman's love as well as her sexual act. Rossetti reveals the exchange between male producers and female consumers to be full of danger for the consumer—it is best that she step out of that dualism and enter instead a bond with her sister that is not based upon the exchange of coins, but the exchange of caring and loving acts.

The other epigraph is from Charles Kingsley's *The Roman and the Teuton,* and it gives the book its title. In the book, the Anglo-Saxon, barbarian "forest people" come upon the garden of the classic Romans, with its fantastic fruits and elaborate decoration. The Roman civilization, for all its cleverness with garden-making, has become decadent, so involved with its own luxuries that it has forgotten to defend itself. The forest people invade and sack Rome, but the fabulous garden falls into decay because the forest people care only about waging war and gaining spoils; they know nothing of art. In the second epigraph, Cather alludes to an idea which Slote says particularly attracted her. In turn-of-the-century America, Cather saw elements of both the Roman and the forest people. As she told in an article that she wrote for the *Courier,* American culture had come to be directed by luxury-loving decadents; however soon they would be conquered by a small group of "forest people" whose "natural" devotion to competition had made them invincible. The fable can be read as a struggle between the new consumer capitalism and what Cather saw as the nineteenth century's excess. Cather writes in her article that the victory of the forest people was necessary to renew the artistic but decadent civilization. Afterward would arise the new *pax romana,* in which a new breed of people would have enough competitiveness to survive, but enough knowledge of art to make living gracious.[22]

Like Cather, Henry James had read *The Roman and the Teuton,* and he retells its story briefly in his *Partial Portraits* (1887), which Cather had read.[23] James, praising Robert Louis Stevenson's works, notes the novelist's aversion to writing about marriage. To Stevenson, reports James, men and women are the Roman and the Teuton, artist and barbarian, who can never dwell together in peace. Cather's *Troll Gar-*

den, like so much of her work, traces unhappy marriages and incompatible partners. Cather does not repeat James's (Stevenson's) misogyny: not all the "Teutons" are women, and not all the "Romans" are men. Instead, Cather's seven fables reveal her ideas about honest and dishonest "art-work." Her characters tend to be either Romans or Teutons; often these are married to each other. Cather used marriage and other family relations to draw opposites into conflict and show the result of the battle. Embattled families showed on a small and personal scale her feeling that serious art in America was threatened by the equivalent of the "forest people." Most troubling to Cather was that the forest people came, not from some distant place, but from within, from America itself.

Cather's book begins with "The Garden Lodge." In the short story, a woman has grown up in a houseful of artists who believed in *l'art pour l'art* and who therefore were a financial drain on the family. The woman, having seen her own mother live in infatuation of her father—and therefore in constant want—determines to support herself by giving piano lessons and playing at recitals. Only she forgets to balance her need for money with any "higher" goals (any ideals), so when a famous French singer—d'Esquerré—visits at her house and his singing stirs her to longing, she does not know what she longs for or how to satisfy what she feels. Cather's scene-painting of an opera star and how his groupies use his passion to augment their own attenuated lives is pointed here; it came directly from her views and interviews of so many of the famous. "The Garden Lodge" shows just how sophisticated Cather had become by the time she had collected the short stories of *The Troll Garden.* The protagonist's deep fear of the *art pour l'art* attitude is believable and poignant. Still, her rigorous subordination of her own desire to create has left her unfulfilled, and she must seek fulfillment in the success of others.

Cather uses her Henry-the-watcher character in her short stories. Henry's point of view, which Cather had exploited in her Mulberry Street and Lizzie Hudson Collier articles, allows an often gruesome or troubling scene to unfold without editorial comment. Henry's point of view was Cather's realist narrative voice: it proved that she could report a scene without her text's showing her emotional involvement. "The Sculptor's Funeral" is such a realist story. Steavens, the young Bostonian and the sculptor's student, comes to Sand City, Kansas, a tiny western town, to attend his mentor's funeral. Steavens is aghast to find that living in a small town "closer to nature" has not made the sculptor's parents and the townspeople kinder. In fact, all are deeply flawed, and the sculptor's death does not teach by its dignity, but rather brings out the townspeople's worst vices. Steavens is helpless to do anything but see as the drama of the watch over the coffin plays itself out. Cather's story about Steavens-the-watcher is a direct offspring of Cather's journalism: "The Sculptor's Funeral" was born in the death of Pittsburgh painter Charles Stanley Reinhart; Cather had watched and reported his funeral.[24]

In "A Wagner Matinée," Clark, the male protagonist, observes the actions and appearance of his Aunt Georgiana. The scene reprises Cather's *Home Monthly* article about how she learned Byron at her Aunt Franc's knee. But in the short story, Aunt Georgiana is grown old, and Clark observes her flaws with Henry's realist eyes instead of with Helen's sentimental ones. As "Matinée" unfolds, Clark tries to sympathize with his aunt, but cannot. He is repelled by her age and by her country clothes, by the contrast she makes with Boston society when he welcomes her to Boston, his home. Clark cannot read in his aunt's appearance anything positive in her dedication to her farm and family: he cannot "read" the sentimental stories written on her body. Clark takes the Hamlin Garland position, in which country living wears life down to a nub. "Matinée" is about the aunt's untold story and the story that Clark does tell; the contrast is ironic.[25]

In "Flavia and Her Artists," the plot hinges on a newspaper article. Flavia, a society woman who invites "collections" of artists to her home just to be able to say she had hob-nobbed with the great, becomes the butt of a joke, played by one of her guests. The guest, a French novelist, publishes his negative views of American women in a newspaper that Flavia takes. To save Flavia's feelings, her husband burns the newspaper, then gives a rude speech before the rest of the guests (who were in cahoots with the French author) to drive them away. Flavia, unaware of the sacrifices her husband has made for her, is appalled. Cather reveals Flavia to be a short-sighted woman desperate enough for greatness that she must invite it over in the persons of famed artists. Cather would have been in sympathy with the artists—whom she had interviewed, and whose lives she had come to know—enough to write a thoroughly unsympathetic picture of an artist's intellectually and emotionally impoverished hanger-on.

The short story "Flavia" is loaded with details from the world of journalists. Will Maidenwood, one of the guests, writes for the magazine *Woman,* which specializes in reading for "the young person" (a dig at the *Home Monthly,* the *Ladies' Home Journal,* and William Dean Howells, who said that magazine literature ought to be safe for "young girls"). "Jimmy" Broadwood, a comic actress, has, like Cather, traits considered to be both male and female (her coworkers in the Pittsburgh press called Cather "Bill"). Two points of view—artist and artist's groupie—lead to the ironic ending. Cather, as a journalist, would have been familiar with both groups, both points of view. Her point-of-view character is in the position in which Cather found herself as a journalist: an informed watcher, neither artist nor groupie.

In " 'A Death in the Desert' "—the title quotes Robert Browning—a plot that could have been taken from *Camille* unfolds: a beautiful woman dies of tuberculosis. However, in the rest of the story, Cather's Henry point-of-view undercuts the sentimental superstructure which an emotional actress would have erected upon the play *Camille*. In the short story, it is as if Cather had reached back and snatched a moment of Eleanora Duse performing Dumas's play. Duse always hinted at the French emotional school, but understated the most heated emotions and melted them to irony. In Cather's story, the woman, Katherine Gaylord, loves Adriance Hildegard, a famous composer, but he lives only for his art. Adriance's brother, Everett, loves Katherine, but he cannot have her, as her heart belongs to his brother. Everett witnesses Katherine's last days when she asks him to come to her and speak of his brother. In this case, Everett-the-witness could be compounded of the girl Helen, who watched and waited at the knee of her elderly aunt, and of Henry the realist reporter, who watched without blinking. Katherine's illness fails to spiritualize her; instead, Cather describes her wasted body, a realistic touch. Love given or withheld, that currency of sentimental fiction, is absent from Cather's short story. The story seems to exist to cut sentimental tropes with its fine irony and realistic descriptions of no marriage, no love affair, no love triangle, no happy ending.

"Paul's Case" comments on art, beauty, work, and ethics. Cather herself had conflicting desires: her desire to be an artist and therefore to remain untainted by commercialism and her concomitant need to support herself. Her dual needs had forced her to think about art, work, and money; and what work should be like, be for.

In "Paul's Case" Cather writes, "Perhaps it was because in Paul's world the natural nearly always wore the guise of ugliness, that a certain element of artificiality seemed to him necessary in beauty." Because he did not have the money, power, or talent to remedy the ugliness of his lower-class family home, the boy Paul stole money from his employers and fled to New York. There, living in a hotel, Paul surrounds himself with beautiful things, trying to create "unnatural beauty" from his unethical gains.[26] "Real" beauty, which is created by hard-working actresses, is beyond Paul's grasp, and he knows it. When Paul runs out of money, he throws himself under the wheels of a train and dies. "Paul's Case" is subtitled "A Study in Temperament" to remind readers that a persona like Henry's had taken notes on Paul's troubling or "disturbed" character.

April Twilights: Business and Poetry

Cather's fiction had been strongly shaped by the realist bent to include narratives about labor and class, and, as a result, Cather had always written about work, poverty, greed, and success in her prose. Realism had come to shape not only fiction, but also painting and the theater; however by 1903, when Cather published *April Twilights,* the greatest number of poems still remained the sanctuary of the idealist. Cather had begun writing poetry in Lincoln, perhaps in response to assignments by her college teachers.[27] Both her early works in Lincoln and later the poems that she collected in her first volume, take as subjects the swains and goddesses who, in that time, seemed to stand for all who sighed in love and all who had power, but found that not enough.

Cather's poems did change as the twentieth century progressed: her later poems "Spanish Johnny" and "The Swedish Mother" are perhaps more marked by realism than the early attempts of her first volume. However, by the 'teens, when Cather published "Spanish Johnny," Eliot and Pound were beginning to publish their more radical experiments. After Eliot and Pound, Cather's poetic voice could no longer be said to enter the twentieth century's dialogue with modernity. It was through her fiction that she was most new and most a leader. The volume of poems is a side road, then, but an interesting one.

When she was still living in Lincoln, Cather had discovered Bliss Carman and had praised that poet, whom she had originally believed to have been a woman.[28] Carman attracted Cather; "she" was modern because "she" did not write poems about men and women falling in love. Instead, Bliss Carman created a poetic persona who wandered the countryside. Shunning traditional work, the vagabond poet worked for herself, making verses out of the free raw materials of the fresh air without waiting for factories to manufacture or trains to deliver what she needed. Carman typified a turn-of-the-century "type," the vagabond poet. Modeled on the troubadours of fourteenth-century France, such a poet wandered the land, uttering verses. "Buyers," attracted to the poet's utterances, gave money and lodging. At the moment of heightened industrialization, the vagabond circumvented capitalism's encumbrances. The poet remained free from the confines of an office, the entanglements of unions, the whims of bosses. The vagabond poet was magically part, and not yet part, of American labor.

At least two actual poets of Cather's day tried on the mythic vagabond's disguise: in America, Chicago Renaissance poet Vachel Lindsay chanted his verses on street corners. In France, Paul Verlaine's outlaw life had become the stuff of legend. His example was so magnetic that while condemning the *Yellow Book* and the *Chapbook,* the literary organs of the Aesthetics movement (*la décadence*) in Europe and America, Cather wrote a supportive review of Verlaine and of his life.[29] According to Cather's review/obituary of Verlaine, while Bliss Carman had been freed from many of society's fetters by "her" vagabond life, the same fetters trapped Verlaine.

Verlaine, according to Cather, had been born only to write poems. His desire to write had driven him mercilessly until he made his home in the jail, the street, or the hospital. Verlaine, according to Cather, longed to be ordinary ("a Philistine"), but like an oyster, only the ineradicable "disease" or artistic temperament led to "pearls." In 1903, when Cather came to publish her first book, the collection of poetry *April Twilights,* one poetic persona (which was a mask or a speaker of each poem) available to Cather was the vagabond poet. Her own vagabond persona, which she created from her comfortable study in the McClung home, was more like Verlaine's diseased oyster instead of Bliss Carman's free wanderer.

As she wrote her poems, perhaps Cather was troubled, not only by a clash between tradition and an artistic temperament, but by a personal tragedy as well: her good friend, the composer Ethelbert Nevin, had died in March 1901. Many of Cather's poems address an absent "troubadour." He had embodied an oxymoron to Cather: a "girl-boy," a sentimental man, and a male artist who had avoided the country's masculine cult of virility. Through Nevin, Cather had understood how an artist could be both sentimental or feeling, and serious at the same time. To Cather, the sentimental, once identified with those "scribbling women," had sometimes seemed a bogey in the night, and as an artist, she had sometimes felt such a need to avoid being labeled "sentimental" that her prose had become almost a cliché of realist writing. Nevin showed Cather how a "serious" artist could use sentiment: like Cather herself, he had appropriated some of the cultural attributes of the opposite sex. Now this important model was dead, and many of the vagabonds who wander through Cather's poems, who had once lived the good life, are in Cather's book dead or dying, done to death by the world's harsh censure. For instance, in Cather's poem "Sleep, Minstrel, Sleep," it is winter, and walking the roads has become cold comfort. The minstrel is dead; his traveling companion, the speaker and vagabond poet, mourns the minstrel's passing, but he is thankful that he has not lived to see that their audience "does not grow more kind."[30]

The vagabond in Cather's "Encore" is old and forgotten. He is not pitiful, but rather angry and powerful. He chastises his audience: "Ye never cry 'long live the King' / until the king is dead," he tells his audience.[31] Cather's vagabond-king derives his authority and strength from the earth: his cockleburr-coat and his mullein scepter make his vagabondage "natural"; his audience, however, is out of step with nature and cannot hear his message. Another vagabond, the persona of "The Poor Minstrel," mourns her burdensome life. The "crowd" "jeers" at her efforts. The freedom of vagabondage has become a kind of beggarhood. Winter, the traditional figure for death, has taken the vagabond's "troubadour."[32] The vagabond, in fact, mourns the conditions under which people labor. Living a "natural" existence close to the land, producing her product, poetry, as a result of naturally inspired feeling, had once been a good way to live, assert Cather's vagabonds. In the world which *April Twilights* creates, that way of living has been subsumed by different modes of living and of making a living. Poetry, a product once much in demand, has lost its market, and poets who once made their music from easily gotten raw materials find the modern world bleak and wintery, offering neither food nor shelter.

At the fin de siècle, several poetic personae were available for Cather to use as speakers of her poems in *April Twilights*. The vagabond was one who implicitly protested the conditions of modern labor. Another far less safe persona was that of the Aesthete. After Oscar Wilde's imprisonment, Cather had damned the Aesthetics movement as unhealthy. Wilde's posture of Aesthete had become linked in the public mind with his homosexuality, which had gotten him imprisoned. However, as Richard Gilman and Linda Pratt have shown, the Aesthetics movement, like vagabondage, protested philosophical positivism, whose adherents held that rational thought, science, and industry could solve all problems. Championed by Walter Pater in Oxford, England, the movement ignored the rational and elevated the irrational and "useless" products of the imagination. In addition, the aesthete renounced Darwinism and everything deemed to be natural, since natural would remain a part of the construct "nature red in tooth and claw" and its attendant competitiveness. According to Pratt, the Aesthetics movement elevated two new personae whom Cather could have emulated: the male dandy (Wilde) and the female New Woman. Both new personae renounced conventional gender stereotypes and donned clothing more appropriate for the opposite sex—an act that today we call "crossdressing." The Aesthete and New Woman were artificial constructs who avoided "natural" roles of childbearing (for women) or vicious competitiveness and incessant sexual desire (for men). The Aesthetics movement accepted homosexuality, since non-heterosexual love was deemed "unnatural" and "artificial" and therefore fit in with the Aesthete's public posture of renouncing the natural.

In a time when homosexuality was deemed at least a sin and at worst a felony punishable by imprisonment, homosexuals adopted code words to refer to themselves. The word "Greek" referred to gay love; poems of the era (like the famous "Atalanta in Calydon" by Swinburne, which Cather had praised) adopted Greek titles, if not explicitly to signify a gay subtext, then at least to refer to a heightened "eastern" and irrational sexuality. Fin de siècle poets who embraced the Aesthetics movement designed poems which looked safe—after all, a poem's Latin and Greek references were a hallmark of the age's neoclassicism. However, such designs covered the more radical subtext of the Aesthetic poem, whose subject was irrational passion or desire that was publicly *inutile*.

Today's readers may have difficulty pinpointing the *décadence* in Cather's collection *April Twilights*. However, many of her poems have Greek titles like "Eurydice" and "Anacreon." In her poems (as well as in her short stories), Cather "crossdresses," trying on male ("unnatural") personae. In her poem "The Namesake," for instance, the male persona figuratively asks his uncle, dead in the Civil War:

> Tell me, Uncle, by the pine,
> Had you such a girl as mine,
> When you put her arms away
> Riding to the wars that day.[33]

After admiring the uncle's valorous acts, the poet renounces "his girl" so that "he" can join in battle and gain glory. In a similar crossdressing poem, "The Night Express," the speaker is not expressly male, but "he" is awaiting the night express with the boys in a western town to meet the coffin of one of their number.[34] The dead boy's return, after a brief, successful life, inspires the persona to seek "his" fortune. In both "The Namesake" and "The Night Express," Cather chooses a male "crossdressing" persona who could aspire to those acts not deemed "natural" for a woman—fighting a battle or going off to seek her fortune.

One theme in Cather's poems is as old as poetry: lovers renouncing love. Renunciation may not seem to have to do with work, but for the New Woman, another persona created by the Aesthetics movement, it did. In the days before legalized birth control, renouncing love and marriage was one way a woman could gain enough freedom to pursue an ambition such as work or education. Ida Tarbell, another New Woman who would become, with Cather, a New York journalist, recounts the minor subterfuges that she pursued in college to maintain her single state.[35] Tarbell does not seem to have agonized over her choice, but Cather dramatized the tragedy of her need to stay single, again and again, in her verse. Cather's "renunciation" poems tell about female protagonists' renunciations, and their concomitant need to suppress sexual desire.

Cather's favorite poem from her first book was "Grandmither, Think Not that I Forget."[36] In the Scots dialect poem, the "lass's" grandmother has died; the "lass" has grown sad because her lover has left her, and she wishes to change places with the dead grandmother:

> Grandmither, gie me your clay-cold heart that has forgot to ache,
> For mine be fire within my breast and yet it cannot break.
> It beats and throbs forever for the things that must not be,—

In the poem, "things that must not be" are lovers' meetings. Whether the love is directed toward a woman or man, the poet does not say; instead, the poem, verse by verse, tries to put away all feelings of longing or regret so that the persona, like the grandmother, will be immune to desire. It is a twist of irony that to be so immune can be achieved only by dying.

In "Eurydice," the speaker, the mythic Eurydice, is following Orpheus from the underworld back to the surface of Earth, where they can be lovers once more.[37] Cather writes only about the moment when Eurydice, walking behind Orpheus, cannot see his face. She desires to touch him, but all she can have of him is his music. Once more, the poem is a meditation on how not to give in to desire. Two more poems of longing, "Aftermath" and "Sonnet," mourn lovers who have left.

Two poems late in *April Twilights* imagine a life without conventional love. "Since thou come'st not at morn, not at even," the poet begins in "I Have no House for Love to Shelter Him," "Let Night close peaceful where it hath begun," the persona commands. She warns a "kingly stranger" away, repeating the poem's title, and then resolves to remain alone.[38] Cather closes the collection with "L'En-voi": "No matter on what heart I find delight / I come again unto the breast of night," she says. In the last poem, the speaker decides that "loneliness" will be her most constant companion: "loneliness . . . loves me best of all, / And in the end she claims me, and I know / That she will stay, although the rest may go."[39]

Cather's poetry avoids the enclosing space of the office, in fact seeking, more often than not, some timeless and placeless moment, like Arcady or Winter. As Dana Gioia has shown, many of the male modernist poets who began writing early in the twentieth century (Wallace Stevens, T. S. Eliot) were employed in offices—but their poetry rigorously avoided referring to the telephone calls, the desk drawers full of paper clips and pencil stubs, the 10:30 meetings.[40] The problem was not just that the working day has given its name—workaday—to our most forgettable moments, but rather, near the turn of the century, several forces had come to separate work and poetry, so that each avoided the other. A ghost of the old coterie ideal still placed authors among "gentlemen" whose title and standing precluded them from working. The Aesthetics movement still sought to place art somehow "above" or "beyond" the utilitarian and rational forces of management, labor, machines, and factories. To male aes-thetes, the office had come to be the theater where men circled each other like animals, ready to pounce and assert their fitness to survive. Indeed, to social Darwinists of the time, losers, the down-and-out, and those killed during mining strikes, were the inevitable detritus of human life on a survival-of-the-fittest stage. Aesthetes avoided the pattern posited by the social Darwinists by defining their laboriously crafted works as "art-ificial," not natural, products.

One more ingredient: women's sphere had come to be defined as anti-Darwinist space. The home, properly run, could sooth the savage beast inside the working man and tame him to the household. Women's work kept her from exploitative relationships, and her soothing influence was absolutely essential to the man freshly come from the snarling jungle of the office. Because of the women's sphere/men's sphere split, authorship had come to be an employment which women could pursue without entering men's intensely competitive existence. At the same time, however, women's work, which avoided one of the age's most intense debates (those fostered by Darwin's theories), was seen as less important. Cather would have felt the need to keep work out of poetry, yet at the same time, a desire to make her poetry "serious" and involved in its moment's most important cultural discussions. Her poetry may not be set in offices, but work is a theme that is strongly present in her poetic *oeuvre*.

Cather's life in Pittsburgh ended in triumph. First, she met Isabel McClung, forming a close friendship that shook when Isabel married in 1916, but broke only when McClung died many years later. Cather moved from her boardinghouse into the McClung mansion March 1901; the story of her love for the house and for Isabel can be found, in part, in *The Professor's House*. McClung became Cather's audience and her family; her residence in the mansion meant that she no longer had to spend money on her room and board—and so Isabel, and Isabel's house, allowed Cather to labor over writing literature that was not paid for by the column-inch like journalism. With her spare time, she began to write the stories that she collected in *The Troll Garden*, and she began to put together her book of poetry.

Pittsburgh marked a time when Cather temporarily left journalism to become a schoolteacher. During her teaching years, 1901–1906, her journalistic pen was relatively quiet (only 37 articles and reviews appear in Curtin's bibliography). She spent the time preparing her two books for publication. However, as she published *The Troll Garden*, a new era in her life, and in her life as a journalist, was about to open. Soon she would go to New York to edit for *McClure's*.

5

Helen Loves Henry: New York City

Well we, most of us, start out to write epics and end by writing advertisements.[1]

—Willa Cather

I took a salaried position . . . because I didn't want to write directly to sell. I didn't want to compromise.[2]

—Willa Cather

The beginner should do things his employer's way.[3]

—Willa Cather

Mary Baker G. Eddy, from Cather's biography of Eddy

Events in New York City were conspiring to remove Cather from her life in Pittsburgh. Cather seems to have settled down to a peaceful existence there (the evidence: two books in three years). Leaving journalism in the spring of 1901, she took a position, first, teaching high school Latin, then English. As a freelance journalist, Cather had had to scramble for the next paycheck; her teaching brought in a regular salary of $650 a year, and there were summers off for writing. Meanwhile, she had moved in with Isabel McClung, in whose friendship she found the support that she needed to be a writer.

But S. S. McClure, who had published Cather's collection of short stories, *The Troll Garden*, in 1905, lost his business partners in 1906. With no senior personnel left to help him publish his *McClure's* magazine, his thoughts turned to the impressive young journalist from Nebraska, and he travelled to Pittsburgh to convince her to come to New York. As a result, Cather began packing to leave her pleasant Pittsburgh life and to arrange another home.

S. S. McClure: The Man with the Muckrake

S. S. McClure, who had founded *McClure's* magazine in 1893, had come to America a poor Irish immigrant. By working as a peddler and hired hand he had put himself through Knox College in Galesburg, Illinois. Travelling to Boston, he got work in a bicycle shop. When the shop began a cycling magazine in 1882 (the *Wheelman*, which Cather, an avid wheelwoman, might have even read), McClure became the editor. After his first editorial venture, he had married, and, needing a business, decided to start a syndicate, buying manuscripts and placing them in periodicals. When he came to found his magazine, he had two thousand unplaced stories in his safe from such writers as Stevenson, Kipling, James, Whitman, Zola, Crane, O. Henry, and London. It is this list of authors that he brought to *McClure's*.[4]

He modeled his magazine after the new Sunday supplements in the newspapers: *McClure's* had literature, exposés, and stories of the lives of the wealthy and famous, all richly illustrated by photographs and artist's renderings. McClure's childhood, a rags-to-riches ascent, had given him sympathy for immigrants and the poor in America. As the owner of *McClure's* he gave his reporters time and money, two commodities he had most lacked as a young man. The results were reports of graft that were so well-researched and well-written that articles in *McClure's,* during the years of hectic yellow journalism, seemed to breathe the very truth.

McClure gathered a top-notch staff, and soon Ida Tarbell, Ray Stannard Baker, and Lincoln Steffens were turning out a new kind of socially conscious reportage. Ida Tarbell, trained as a biologist, put together a fact-filled and iron-clad case against Rockefeller's Standard Oil trust in her *History of Standard Oil*.[5] Ray Stannard Baker uncovered an alliance between unions and industrialists which left nonunion workers open to violence from both groups in articles such as "Right to Work."[6] He conceived of his journalism as a "mission" akin to searching for the "grail."[7] Lincoln Steffens's "Shame of the Cities" series (the articles were later collected into a book of that title) chronicled how the government of the people had come to take power from the people in Minneapolis, St. Louis, and Chicago. Steffens's articles were exciting because he interviewed crime and political bosses and wormed from them the story of their rise to enormous power.

But by 1906 S. S. McClure's immersion in the business of publishing a magazine had begun to conflict with his star reporters' findings. In *Shame of the Cities,* Steffens indicted big business, which made McClure uncomfortable. McClure himself was aging, reports Ida Tarbell in her biography.[8] He fought age's inevitable depredations by frantically seeking to recoup the losses: in between dashing from one health spa to another, he began a rather public love affair. In addition, without his partners' consent, he made plans to enter some big businesses of his own: set up a bank, open a school, and found an insurance company—to form, in effect, a trust. It was this desperate bid to reclaim his health and his youth that caused the partners to walk out. With his employees gone, McClure thought of Cather in Pittsburgh.

Cather had been reading *McClure's* at least since November 1895; in February 1906 she found herself one of the makers of the *McClure's* image. Joining the magazine, she gained the editorial power to shape the public's taste in letters and writing; however, she entered in the shadow of her predecessors, Ida Tarbell, Lincoln Steffens, and Ray Stannard Baker. As a longtime reader of the magazine, she would have felt pressure to imitate, to repeat the magazine's past successes. Since she was immersed in the culture of the muckraking magazine and drawn to its subject, it is worth looking at this new type of journalism, which mixed realism and sentimentalism to urge readers to take action against injustices.

Muckraking, a new method of factual reporting, came of age during the ascendence of realism in fiction and employed realism's cast of characters—the Common Man and the Downtrodden—and realism's story—the workings of intractable forces upon character. Unlike realistic writers, though, muckrakers reported actual social injustice.

America was industrializing quickly, and there was no safety net to protect workers from unethical industrialists, mine owners, an rail-road trusts.

A muckraker, telling the story of a worker's exploitation, expected to arouse the audience's pity, exactly like a sentimental play. The audience's anger at those injustices rehearsed in muckraking articles served to inspire them to activity, such as righting wrongs and lifting the downtrodden. Like the literary sentimental, muckraking showed the helpless victims of circumstance. Muckraking "worked" because its spectacle of the destruction of innocents by the enormous forces wielded by politicians or industrialists mimicked the spectacle of an emotional actress playing *Camille:* both the real and fictional dramas engendered sympathy in an audience. Muckraking was thus a marriage between those observably bitter enemies of the 1890s: realism and the sentimental. It is as if Cather's two pseudonymous reporters during her Pittsburgh days, Henry Nicklemann and Helen Delay, had merged into one androgenous being and lifted the pen. Muckraking evoked the same feelings as the frontispiece from Jacob Riis's *Out of Mulberry Street.*[9] The illustration shows an impoverished family (realism). They are grouped symbolically around a miserable Christmas tree; the children's want is particularly apparent (sentimentalism).

Symbols of real cultural moment can be discerned by the excitement that ensues over defining them. *Muckraking,* as a term, was invented by Theodore Rooseveldt, in a speech delivered in 1907 to curb the movement's power. He took the term from John Bunyan's "man with a muckrake" in *Pilgrim's Progress.* Rooseveldt's speech, like many muckraking articles, used emotion to make a point. Who would want, said Rooseveldt, to always be raking filthy muck, when there were more noble things to be doing? "Raking the filthy muck" means digging up unsavory doings—true and untrue—of politicians and bosses to be presented to the public for entertainment. Rooseveldt was in fact describing yellow journalism. What the muckrakers actually did was more complex. For instance, the muckraker Ida Tarbell eschewed emotion, such as that engendered by the yellow press, in her articles. She believed that "the facts" would speak for themselves, and that knowledgeable Americans would act upon "the facts" as soon as they had read them. Facts exercised the mind and led to more knowledge, Tarbell believed, but emotion was dangerous.[10] When Cather finally wrote a muckraking article of her own, it could be said of her that she took Tarbell and her camp as her model.

Muckraking assumed that a kind of political Eden once existed, an Eden whose description may be found in the Declaration of Independence and the Bill of Rights. In the perfect world delineated by these two documents, which muckraking assumes once existed and attempts to recreate, there was "equality,"[11] happiness was everybody's right,[12] business was a peaceful pursuit,[13] and "old-time ethics" was once the law of the land,[14] a law administered by a "pure and efficient" government.[15]

The muckraking reporter was a hero figure who sought the help of "the People" in returning America to its Edenic state. Reporters had "notions of justice" and "regard for the rights of others."[16] The muckraking reporter blamed poverty, not on the poor, but on modern society, a revolutionary idea in America at the turn of the century.[17] The reporter was, of course, one of "the people": "We, the people of the United States . . . must cure whatever is wrong," declared Ida Tarbell;[18] and "[newspapers] are on the side of the people," assured muckraker Irwin.[19] The reporter assumed that as soon as the people read the muckraking article they would hasten to correct America's wrongs.[20]

"The interests," which were the powerful industrialists and corrupt politicians, were "predatory";[21] they were on the side of Britain, that ancient enemy of America, because they represented "the feudalism of privileged wealth."[22] The interests, shouted the articles of the period, were thieves, frauds, pimps, misers, paranoids, enemies of Christianity, warmongers, and corrupters of youth. The interests were the villains of the sentimental drama, thoroughly evil, because they were depicted as ideas, not as people.

Since the muckraking reporter was one of the people, the common souls who often were the victims of the interests, the people received the reporter's sympathy. The reporter dramatized victims' wrongs, rhetoricizing their suffering as if muckraking were a nineteenth-century sentimental novel. In "The Newark Factory Fire," for instance, author Mary Alden Hopkins described the dead: three sisters died in each other's arms; a shoemaker recognized his daughter by the special shoe he had made for her crippled foot.[23] At its highest pitch, the sentimental reportage asked the reader to become a spectator of a tragic scene, to participate by feeling with the sufferer, and by experiencing catharsis at the end of the tragedy. This was the muckraking side of working for *McClure's*.

McClure's nose for the drama of good muckraking reportage also led him to seek out good literature, and he was responsible for the American publication of such authors as Kipling and Stevenson, writers Cather admired. During her editorship, which lasted nearly six years, Cather's own writing imitated that of the writers appearing in *McClure's* pages. It seems as if the pages of the magazine, and particularly three authors—Henry James, Robert Louis Stevenson, and Rudyard Kipling—came to form Cather's literary tastes in the 1890s, tastes which she brought with her to New York.

The record shows that, in Pittsburgh, Cather and the Seibels were enjoying James's *Partial Portraits,* which Scribner's had brought out in 1887. *Portraits* reads like a roll-call of Cather favorites of the '90s: George du Maurier (who had written *Trilby*), George Eliot (the only other woman besides George Sand, Sappho, and Christina Rossetti whom Cather had admired as a cub reviewer), Daudet (whose *Sapho* had caused such a scandal when it was dramatized in 1900), and Robert Louis Stevenson.[24] Perhaps it was James himself through whose eyes Cather first consumed Stevenson's work, or at least, perhaps James shaped her ability to fit Stevenson into her ideal of writerly behavior. According to James, Stevenson was "as different as possible from the sort of writer who regards words as numbers" (i.e., he would not have liked Professor Lucius Sherman).[25] Stevenson wrote "books without women" which had no moral message; that is, he modeled how to avoid the realist accusation of sentimentality.[26] Stevenson avoided the marriage plot in his books because he believed that marriage conflicted with and diluted an artist's work.[27] Stevenson was the true chronicler of youth, that unmarried and untrammelled moment that Cather, too, came to celebrate.[28] Stevenson, reported James, was ill most of his adult life, and for Cather, that fact probably placed Stevenson into the décadent scheme of the artist dying young.

Kipling, for Cather, narrated her experiences as a journalist—work—and made it romantic and exciting. Period critic John Palmer notes the illusion presented by Kipling's narrators—that they are soldiers, adventurers, or engineers—powerful workers and producers who make things happen, and yet, miraculously, at the same time, passive writers or speakers.[29] They made Cather's chosen art an honest job that her grandmother would have approved of. Kipling started the way Cather did—as a journalist—and became famous by age 22—an admirable career path. The territory he narrated—India—paralleled Cather's imaginary West, where [white] people could act their will on a wild land.

James himself was known as the literary craftsman who lived a life of contemplation.[30] He was an American who had somehow gained the respect of European authors Turgenev, Daudet, Kipling, and Stevenson. James avoided the heavily plotted sentimental style and instead presented studies in character development.[31] The Alvin Langdon Coburn photographs for James's New York edition of his works (which began coming out in 1907–8) did not illustrate. Instead, they did a new thing entirely, symbolizing or evoking a mood implicit in each volume, but never stating it.[32] To Cather, James, Kipling, and Stevenson in their persons and in their works embodied choices that she, too, could make as she became an author. It is no wonder that, joining *McClure's,* she should come to feel their presence there, and copy their successful strategies.[33]

In 1906, Cather was hired as associate editor of the magazine; one of her jobs seems to have been to buy muckraking reportage.[34] However, she also bought poetry and fiction. One can imagine Cather at work, keeping in touch with a network of writers by memoranda. Business correspondence from one disgruntled author is still extant. In 1906, Cather paid writer Percival Gibbons twenty dollars for a poem—triple the fee paid to George Seibel for an article in years gone by.[35] In 1909 she was still trying to satisfy Gibbons: he thought that the magazine had lost one of his manuscripts. Besides, he wrote, *McClure's* never paid him what he was worth. In replying, Cather used a ploy that must have been several years old by that time. Unfortunately, she replied, her boss set all the prices, and she couldn't quarrel with him.[36] In the office, Cather used her ingenuity to quell differences between personalities, meet deadlines, entice authors, and establish the right mixture of fiction, nonfiction, and poetry.[37] This was her job for the year 1906.

In 1907, however, Cather had the experience of actually becoming a muckraking reporter herself, when an important but poorly written manuscript fell into McClure's hands. For Cather, working with the Eddy manuscript added another possible character about which Cather could write, and shaped her prose style as well.

Mary Baker G. Eddy: Helen Delay on the Verge of a Nervous Breakdown

The life story of Mary Baker Eddy and the Church of Christ, Scientist, written by Georgine Milmine, must have come to McClure near the time that Cather was hired. McClure wanted to publish the work, since Eddy's recent trial had aroused public interest in her church, and a long series of articles about Christian Science in a magazine would insure good circulation.[38] What Milmine gave McClure was a pile of facts, so McClure hired writer Burton J. Hendricks to convert Milmine's facts into a readable biography.[39] After the first installment, however, McClure stopped Hendricks—his work was too biased, Mc-

Clure thought.[40] McClure then moved Cather to the Eddy project. After months of research in the vicinity of Boston, Cather completed all the rest of the project's installments and laced her writing with facts to avoid Hendricks's mistake.[41] Although Cather essentially rewrote the manuscript, Georgine Milmine's name appeared as the author.

Cather's book-length work is loaded with dates, names, and places; these were necessary to prove that Eddy's story was the Truth with a capital *T*. Such proof was a hallmark of S. S. McClure's style of muckraking, and it raised his work beyond reproach, or at least beyond the reach of the libel suit.[42] It was a very different style of writing for Cather, and she found it uncongenial.[43] However, researching the real-life passions that drove Eddy altered Cather's fiction writing style for good.

To begin to imagine Cather the muckraker at work, one need only glimpse the pages of the Eddy biography. Even if Milmine had supplied all the facts, McClure still had Cather double check them. Dates on depositions seem to indicate that Milmine's research was incomplete, and Cather had to fill in.[44] Thus the biography, while the product of several hands, was molded and shaped into its story by Cather.

Cather used several kinds of sources. For example, for the four installments that ran in *McClure's* volume 28, Cather had to read the back files of at least eight rural newspapers for ads and articles penned by Eddy and her detractors (opposing camps frequently went public with their accusations). To give her installments the correct ring of truth, Cather published the depositions of people who had known Eddy and who would swear before notaries to the truth of their statements. Cather took six such depositions for volume 28.

Cather read at least five books by Mary Baker Eddy and by Dr. P. P. Quimby, from whom Eddy had initially drawn her ideas.[45] Cather traced how Eddy honed her ideas through six different versions of her own work, growing her assertions from a manuscript originally authored by Quimby. Cather's comparisons clearly show that Eddy derived her text from previously existing sources—a fact which Eddy had tried to suppress.[46]

The articles are richly illustrated, as was typical of *McClure's*. The illustrations, often photographs, provide "proof" to back up Cather's text. For instance, the installments just for volume 28 of *McClure's* are illustrated with forty-eight photostats and photographs, material that Cather probably had to find herself.[47] She must have raised a lot of dust on the back roads north of Boston, travelling between little towns, following leads, and knocking on doors.

All the while her search carried her, not in Milmine's paths, but in her own. Although she hated her research and complained about it to friends, she brought to it intelligence, plus a real knowledge, gained from years as a short-story writer and theater reviewer, of how to make dead facts come to life. As Stouck points out, making good fiction out of fact was exactly Cather's challenge when she later wrote such historical novels such as *One of Ours* in 1922 and *Death Comes to the Archbishop* in 1927.[48]

"Christian Science," says Cather, "is a kind of autobiography in cryptogram; its form was determined by a temperament."[49] Cather had been thinking about inborn "temperament" and how exterior forces acted on a person at least since she had written the realistic story called "Paul's Case" and subtitled it "A Study in Temperament." For her study of Eddy's temperament, Cather set up the Eddy biography as a kind of mystery to be solved: in 1907 Eddy was the richest and most powerful woman in America.[50] How could a poor, intellectually impoverished farm girl grow to this stature? Cather used psychological realism to portray young Eddy. "Her girlhood," writes Cather, "had been a fruitless, hysterical revolt against the sordid monotony of her environment. The dullness and meagerness of her life had driven her to strange extravagances in her conduct . . . she had been a helpless dependent. Up to this time her masterful will and great force of personality had served no happy end . . . like disordered machinery her mind was beating itself to pieces."[51] According to Cather, Eddy's temperament was both the devil and the angel that drove her to enormous successes; Eddy's mind drove her as senselessly as the big steam generators drove a printing press.

Cather reasoned that Eddy's need to be the center of attention was inborn, and that it drove her even as a child to try various ways to gain notice. When she learned to have fainting spells to attract her family's notice, she secured her first audience.[52] Cather herself, remembering the attention-getting realistic journalism that she had written to provoke others, had recalled how desperate she had been for approval.[53]

From there, Cather portrays Eddy as a master actor, a type of person about whom Cather had written frequently in her newspaper work. She draws Eddy's portrait with sure strokes: "The stage did not exist that was so poor and mean nor the audience so brutal and unsympathetic, that Mrs. Glover [Mrs. Eddy] could not, unabashed, play out her part."[54] Eddy's poverty as a girl allowed her to tolerate low pay and a sparse audience in the beginning,[55] and her ambition to escape her past forever drove her to ask more and more money from her followers. According to Cather's portrait, followers were only too ready to pay: Eddy's eyes had an almost magical hold on those who beheld them. She was Svengali to thousands of Trilbys.

Patiently Cather explains Eddy's slow progress to her high position and its accompanying wealth. Her first followers brought others, who, in turn, were drawn by something in Eddy's appearance. What about those who never met her? Cather deduced an answer from her own past. There existed, says Cather, "lonely places in Nebraska and Colorado, where people had much time for reflection, little excitement, and a great need to believe in miracles."[56] In the case of Eddy, Cather's upbringing in the West helped her understand how Eddy motivated people isolated in small towns. Cather's special gift was to portray a woman who moved from real rags to real riches, a woman who once hired murderers to further her ambitions. Cather knew how to make clear the connection between the powerful woman and her converts. Cather's Eddy is as believable as Eddy's Nebraska converts, desperate people on the prairie in search of some panacea for their ills.

The Eddy biography ran most of two years in *McClure's,* and then in 1909 was published by Doubleday (which had bought out S. S. McClure's book publishing interests). As Cather's first book-length work, it schooled the young novelist in many ways. Here, a full-blown characterization drives the plot. Cather could not just portray a Paul, as in the short story, "Paul's Case," at the moment when his hatred of his middle-class home drove him to steal and commit suicide. Cather had also to bring to life those inconsequential days leading to and trailing from the climax of her story.

Of course, Eddy was not a Paul at all, but a Helen, a Helen rising abruptly from her hearthside, leaving the kids and the husband, her novel-reading and her darning. This Helen was real; she was not the paper-doll construction of the *Home Monthly:* she was astonishingly prickly. There was nothing for Cather to do with this prickly Helen but to write her story; McClure's strictures would not allow her to avoid unpleasant facts. Cather's commitment to realism, particularly to psychological realism, impelled her to seek reasons for Eddy's actions, and then make of the reasons the story itself.

The storying forth of days and years, the character-driven plot, psychological realism, the female protagonist: these became the ingredients for Cather's first novels. Another puzzle piece gained during her writing of the Eddy biography—the story of an ambitious woman—had not long to wait for fruition. *Alexander's Bridge* (1912), Cather's first novel, sketches two ambitious characters, Bartley Alexander and Hilda Burgoyne. Bartley's ambition is destructive, while Hilda's is constructive. Alexandra, the hero of Cather's second novel, *O Pioneers!,* rises quietly, inexorably, from poverty to wealth, setting

all obstacles firmly aside. Cather's 1915 novel, *The Song of the Lark,*
is about an ambitious woman who is driven by her inborn artistic
temperament to seek fame as an opera singer. Thea Kronborg, the
hero in Cather's naturalistic work, is an admirable character, but readers often remember Thea Kronborg and forget Marian Forrester, the
protagonist of *A Lost Lady* (1923) whose inmost need to lead an
active social life while stuck in the role of traditional wife in a small
town drives her to drink and to have an affair. Readers also forget
Myra Henshawe, the protagonist of *My Mortal Enemy* (1926), whose
need for wealth leads her to hate her impecunious husband. Sapphira,
the protagonist of Cather's last novel, *Sapphira and the Slave Girl*
(1940), is perhaps the character most like Eddy. Determined, ambitious, manipulative Sapphira works behind the scenes to bring about
the rape and downfall of her slave, Nancy, whom she envies. Ann
Romines has said of the shape of Sapphira's revenge that it was a
cultural construct handed down to Southern women: to acquiesce to
their husbands' desires to their husbands' faces, then to act upon their
own plans behind their husbands' backs. Romines: "At the novel's
center, then, is the conjunction of Sapphira's enormous power and
her humiliating helplessness as woman."[57] These same conjunctions
of interior and exterior deterministic forces, according to Cather, had
driven Eddy.

Just how "modern" Cather's life of Eddy was is hard to appreciate
in 1995. Attributes such as Eddy's—pride, vengefulness—are Byronic and were reserved, in traditional women's fictions, for the villainess.[58] In Cather's Eddy series, the villainess becomes the
protagonist. In an earlier piece of journalism written under her pseudonym Helen Delay, Cather had told about her aunt Frances Cather
reading Byron to her. Frances Cather had used the act of reading
Byron—an unconventional, slightly scandalous act—to represent her
intellectual freedom and to communicate this freedom to the girl,
Willa Cather. In her Helen Delay column, Cather had "read" Byron
to her magazine audience. Later, writing Eddy's life, Cather—still
masking, this time as Georgine Milmine—presented an unconventional, scandalous Byronic woman, a "real" woman (realistic reporting: just the facts). In her later fictions, female protagonists often
retain those attributes of the Byronic hero or villain: pride, vengefulness, tempestuousness, alienation. Before she could write her fictions, Cather would learn to create characters in Byron's mold
without the convenience, however, of hiding behind a pseudonymous mask.

As Cather finished work on the Eddy biography, works such as
Sapphira were thirty-two years in the future. McClure was so pleased

with Cather's Eddy series that in 1908 he promoted her to the managing editorship of the magazine. In that post, she read manuscripts submitted by hopeful writers, voyaged to London and to Boston to sign new talent, red-penciled poorly written muckraking pieces, got on the telephone to patch up her boss's indiscretions, and searched for illustrators for stories that were going to press.[59]

Cather's New York years were a time of achievement as a journalist, but increasingly her editorial responsibilities interfered with her fiction writing: there were no summers off.[60] Sharon O'Brien chronicles, through Cather's letters, her feeling that she had lost direction as a writer at the same time that she became important at *McClure's*. Her letters reveal, not only spiritual and emotional exhaustion, but also illnesses. Her difficulties were real: her employment at *McClure's* brought in enough money to support her and to send some home to her family. Suddenly, Cather was a success, managing editor of one of America's high-profile periodicals, living in a Greenwich Village apartment, catching the fast boat to Europe to find talent. As in the days of the flamboyant journalist Nellie Bly, the position of journalist became a significant topic. Journalism seemed to shape the face of America. As an index of its popularity, the magazines and newspapers of Cather's day were filled with advertisements for correspondence courses in journalism and in ad writing.[61] It was a seller's market.

But there was no time to write. Cather had voice and vehicle but no hours to spare. The scholar Barbara Rippey, working on Nebraska author Mari Sandoz, notes that a basic theme of women's writing is not being able to quit their day jobs to write. A similar fate haunted Tillie Olsen, also of Nebraska, who has said in her book *Silences* that an economic system which does not count creative writing as work silences that writing.[62]

Cather apparently felt real affection for S. S. McClure. O'Brien documents Cather's and McClure's office and personal dynamics. Cather was solid and dependable, McClure's anchor and lighthouse in his self-created, one-man storm.[63] McClure paid Cather well and praised her constantly. With him, she wrote, she felt as if someone else believed in her; his belief drove her on.[64] On the other hand, McClure did not like Cather's most experimental stories—those dealing with immigration and the West for which she would become famous.[65] He kept her believing that her writing talent was less than her talent as a reporter and a manager,[66] and that her most intriguing experiments were too *outré* to sell. It came to pass that, only a few months later, *outré* is exactly what sold.

Earlier in her life, Cather had written letters to Will Owens Jones trying to prove her worth to him by telling about her fame and her higher and higher salaries. Cather's feeling for this boss, McClure, was pitched differently. In a letter dated 12 June 1912, she wrote that she would be glad to help McClure write his autobiography— but at this point in the letter, instead of bragging, Cather became very modest. She recalled chapters that she had written three and four years before in the Eddy biography. McClure had apparently edited her work, heavily enough that she remembered. Would her chapters for McClure's autobiography be acceptable to him?[67] No longer desperate to prove herself as a journalist, as she was during her Nebraska years, Cather worried about whether she was a good writer.

In the end, she ghosted the autobiography for nothing. McClure had just been relieved of his business and his support, and he was without a steady income. McClure would come to Cather's apart- ments and tell his story to her. After he left, Cather would write from memory what she had heard. She disguised her own voice and tried to write using McClure's tricks of phrasing.[68] McClure's story is that of a poor immigrant who, arriving nearly penniless in America, first helps work his mother's farm, then works as an itinerant peddlar and a country schoolteacher to finance his own education at Knox College, in Indiana. Cather wrote McClure's rags-to-riches story in a disguised narrative voice—as she saw it, the choppy, excited voice that typified her boss's boyish energy. The McClures, grateful for what Cather had done, shared with Cather the reviews from all over the country. If Cather had been indeed doubting her narrative force (and if her doubt had not been yet another mask—of "becoming" "feminine" modesty), her doubts must have been laid to rest. It is her S.S. McClure voice, she wrote to Will Owens Jones, that gave her the courage to try *My Ántonia*.[69]

At its close, the *McClure's* chapter of Cather's life was more positive than negative. Indeed, if McClure had never called her from Pitts- burgh, she might have remained the schoolteacher who wrote slightly decadent short stories during summers off. *McClure's* took up too much of Cather's time, but, as with all of her journalism before, the *McClure's* years provided raw material for her art. It is easy to see how Cather the artist changed during her early New York years by examining the short stories she wrote during her stay at *McClure's*.

Cather's New York Fiction

In New York, Cather's journalism had both multiplied and reduced her literary strategies. By working at *McClure's* as associate, then managing editor, Cather had once again placed herself in a context where literature was debated seriously. Being in charge of day-to-day details of a national magazine forced Cather to weigh whether an article, short story, novel, or memoir was "good" and what "good" meant. One definition of "good" was that it sold well, and its imitations also sold. It was here, she said, reading "some thousand short stories," that she decided that the only writing that counted was not imitation of someone who was famous, like Henry James, but a kind of loving remembering of what mattered most to the self.[70] The jump, from imitation to trust in the self's vision and memory, was a big one for Cather.

As a magazine editor, she had to be aware of the two currencies by which a writer could be measured: popularity and notoriety were measured by fan letters and copies of the magazine sold; and critical esteem was measured by reviews by "respectable" or powerful makers of literary prestige such as the *New York Times Book Review*. Henry James had had such a strong showing in the "respectable" reviews that in her early fiction Cather had copied James, to her disadvantage. Unfortunately, her strength was not dissecting drawing-room discussions. Disappointed reviewers noted Cather's imitation and pronounced her work less than original:

Hilda: I can't stand seeing you miserable.
Bartley: I can't live with myself any longer.[71]

The *McClure's* years enriched her as well, however. McClure's rigorous editing of the Eddy manuscript changed Cather's prose.[72] She called her early, pre-*McClure's* prose her "purple flurry" of adjectives,[73] but in fact, her early prose does not seem to be more adjective-laden. Instead, the early prose juxtaposed "situations" or plot elements, many of which were "yellow" or sensational, designed to play on the emotions. After Eddy, plot elements become separated by slower paced background or scene painting. McClure had insisted that the Eddy articles be free of bias (emotion): Cather was to report the facts. After Eddy, Cather invented "facts" which were background or scene-painting in her fiction, against which a few emotion-laden events stand like grain silos in Nebraska. Cather's New York fiction displays this change. The Eddy biography also gave her a model for a protagonist—the ambitious man or woman. After her work on Eddy, she knew, by "getting inside a person's skin," how a person could be driven to do anything to reach her goals. Writing Eddy's life did not break her of the Henry James habit, but it showed her how to escape his influence. Soon she did.

The physical attributes of Cather's job shaped her prose as well. Cather had once more gained control of an outlet for publishing her own work. She soon took advantage of her position: "The Namesake," "The Profile," and "Eleanor's House" appeared in the March, June, and October issues for 1907. Perhaps professional ethics kept her from using her power to its uttermost, for her short story "The Willing Muse" appeared in August 1907 in *The Century* and not in her own publication. By 1908, Cather was busy fulfilling obligations for the Eddy biography—the problem with a serial was that it forced her to write a certain number of words per month. Consequently, during the years 1907–1908, she published only one short story, "On the Gull's Road," in the *McClure's* December 1908 issue. Afterwards, Cather published three stories in other venues: "The Enchanted Bluff" appeared in *Harper's* in April 1909, "The Joy of Nellie Deane" appeared in the *Century* in October 1911, and "Behind the Singer Tower" was printed in *Collier's* in May 1912. "The Bohemian Girl" appeared in *McClure's* only after she had already begun to cut ties to the magazine in August of 1912. Only two more Cather stories would ever run in "her" magazine: "Consequences" in November 1915, and "The Diamond Mine" in October 1916. After that, the magazine truly foundered and soon ceased publication altogether.[74]

The reasons behind Cather's publishing outside of *McClure's* throughout her early New York years are not clear, but the record furnishes hints. As she sought publication for "The Bohemian Girl," she showed it to Cameron MacKenzie, who had become the managing editor of *McClure's* after she left. She was sure, she told MacKenzie, that her short story was too highbrow for the magazine.[75] He bought it anyway. "Highbrow" here probably means that the setting is western and the characters are immigrants. Cather's intention with her stories—to place her work beyond the reach of *McClure's* "popular" or "mass" audience and to seek the esteem of the reviewers—was perhaps one she adopted at least beginning with "The Enchanted Bluff."

Helen and Henry had been Cather's pseudonymous narrators of her Pittsburgh journalism. In Pittsburgh, Cather had begun writing stories that mixed the two voices, two points of view, realist and sentimental. The muckraking in *McClure's* would have reinforced Cather's strategy of joining attributes from Helen and Henry's voices to create works that were blends. Cather's later New York short stories and her first four novels had used the "married" voices of Helen and Henry to add depth and texture.

When McClure asked Cather to ghostwrite his autobiography, he unconsciously helped Cather the fiction writer. Cather had used a male narrator before, when she had Henry narrate her Pittsburgh newspaper reporting. Later, she had other male voices tell the stories of "The Namesake" and "On the Gull's Road." However, McClure had been an exacting editor, a man who would stop Hendricks from continuing on the Eddy biography and give it to Cather instead, and the request for a ghostwriter, coming from such a man, boosted Cather's confidence and gave her practice in yet another book-length work.

Cather's work on the magazine had given her a richer range of narrators, plots, and characters, as well as more practice using her Helen and Henry narrators. In addition, the character of S. S. McClure was an immigrant boy, and to write about him in the first person was to enter his world sympathetically, not to brand him as *other* or *outsider* as Henry had often done. In writing McClure's autobiography, Cather had worked in Henry's voice, yet modified that voice so that it understood (not just watched) the immigrant man as he sought an education and founded his magazine. Sympathizing with the immigrant was the last step that Cather had to take before she could write *O Pioneers!, Song of the Lark,* and *My Ántonia,* the works that would make her reputation. Cather's short fiction written while she was still employed by the magazine shows her working through these concerns.

Four Early New York Short Stories

The Namesake

In Pittsburgh, Cather had invented the pseudonym Henry Nicklemann and described Henry's coming-of-age years for her Pittsburgh readers. Cather continued to write Henry's coming-of-age story several times during her early New York years. "The Namesake" (published in *McClure's* [March 1907]) tells the story of a young man's artistic growth—and it also tells Cather's story as a young Pittsburgh journalist. Lyon Hartwell, the protagonist of "The Namesake," is a young sculptor searching for direction. He is called to America from France, where he makes his home, to stay with a dying relative. Rummaging in the attic, he finds an old trunk with his name on it. It belonged to an uncle who had died at age seventeen in the Civil War. Fingering the dead boy's copy of the *Aeneid,* Hartwell is overcome by his namesake's determination to give up his home and his books, his bravery in joining the war. Returning to France, the sculptor finds new inspiration and direction, fashioning figures of American male conquerors, pioneers, and soldiers.

Hartwell's story recapitulates Cather's rediscovery, during her Pittsburgh years, of her "namesake," William Seibert Boak, who died in the Civil War. When in Pittsburgh Cather took the name "Sibert" as her middle name, thereby grafting William's "important," self-sacrificing career of soldier onto her own. (It is interesting that William was on the side of the Confederacy. When Willa Cather wrote her story about Lyon Hartwell, however, Lyon's namesake became a Union hero.) Lyon's "frivolous" career of artist became affirmed by the blood in his veins, just as Cather's "frivolous" aspirations as artist—and perhaps as journalist—were likewise strengthened. Boak's relatedness to Cather would have been especially appropriate given the realist belief that "blood" determined "temperament," which in Cather's psychology was the force one brought to bear against that other force, "environment."

The Profile

In "The Profile" (published in *McClure's* [June 1907]), Cather explores a conflict in the realism versus idealism war: whether art should be about truth or beauty. Aaron Dunlap, an artist, paints idealized portraits of the famous women of Europe. When he is commissioned to make a portrait of a young woman, he is horrified to find that one side of her face is disfigured. He loathes the disfigurement, yet is drawn to it. When she seats herself to him in profile, she turns her scar away from him, presenting her ideal, beautiful side for him to paint. Later he marries her, his idealizing vision leading him to view her with both fascination and pity. Their marriage is tormented by Aaron's tendency to idealize women, and by Virginia's true makeup, which, after all, has both realistic (scarred) and ideal elements.

Cather's story capitalizes on the difference between her two pseudonyms, Helen Delay and Henry Nicklemann. Virginia lives by Henry Nicklemann's realistic strategy, accepting her scar as a realist writer accepted poverty as a fit subject for literature. Aaron lives by Helen Delay's dicta, carefully excluding from his life that which could be thought offensive. The story ends, realistically, in divorce. In "The Profile," Cather explores the difficulties of having Helen and Henry forge their separate stories into one story.

The work, in imitation of Hawthorne, James, and Wharton, explored the psyches of well-heeled American tourists in Europe; since Willa had visited that world only briefly, she does not evoke the European background (which would have been her strength). Instead, the short story remains rather bloodless: Cather's omniscient narrator lingers on neither Aaron nor Virginia. Virginia's scar offers no real pain, and Aaron's disappointment in his aesthetic object does not seem to be deep enough to end their marriage. On another plane, Virginia, the "real" object, which a realistic writer would have cherished, remains an object, not a person. Cather traces Aaron's aesthetic vision, which was dependent upon ideality, ironically, almost satirically, and so his attempts to stretch his aesthetic, and his subsequent failure, is no tragedy.

The Willing Muse

"The Willing Muse" (*Century* [August 1907]) presents two caricatures. One, Bertha Torrence, is a Scribbling Woman, a type that Cather often reviled in her Lincoln days. Bertha turns out one best seller after another; her public loves her. Bertha, however, complicates her life by marrying Kenneth Gray, the Serious Artist. Kenneth is so serious about his art that he cannot bear to finish a book. He polishes sentences and words and never quite completes a paragraph, all for the finest of reasons.

If Cather reviled the Scribbling Woman, the artist who did it for the money and the fame instead of for art's sake, then she held up John Ruskin, Robert Louis Stevenson, and Stephen Crane as artists who slowly turned out masterpieces. However, by the time she produced her portraits of Kenneth and Bertha, she had modulated her views of coterie-type publishing: the work had to be good, yes, but it also had to support and advertise its creator. By the time she wrote "The Willing Muse," Cather, the author of two published books, had begun to come to terms with her ideas about money and about art as a product. Bertha is not entirely bad—she is brisk and efficient, turning out back-to-back best-sellers. At the end of the story, Kenneth simply runs away to China. Because both characters represent ideals, they never come to life. The story is a satire of artistic manners.

Eleanor's House

"Eleanor's House" (published in *McClure's* [August 1907]) is about a man who cannot relinquish the memory of his dead wife. In the short story, Robert and Harriet travel in France with Harold and Ethel. Harold has lost his first wife, Eleanor, and, although he has remarried, he does not allow his new wife, Ethel, to enter meaningfully into his affections. He remains among his memories, and she remains on the outside. Cather uses Robert and Harriet to comfort

Ethel and reveal Ethel's story to readers. At the dénouement, Harold sneaks off to the house which he and Eleanor had inhabited. Ethel confronts him there, revealing her pregnancy, and he resolves to leave Eleanor behind and make a go of his marriage with Ethel.

The bare bones of the plot do not address Cather's real subject—the young man's story, or *Bildungsroman*. Cather had written the *Bildung* many times before, often in Henry Nicklemann's newspaper contributions. However, in other venues she had remarked that the young man's story was too self-centered.[76] In "Eleanor's House," Harriet is not merely a *ficelle* character, but an alternative point of view who corrects the story of the *Bildung*. "Youth was a disease with him," she says of Harold.[77] "He was so absorbed in his own waking up, and he so overestimated its importance." Harriet interrupts the *Bildung*, and the ending of this short story interrupts Harold's self-centered love for Eleanor, and later, his self-centered grief. He disappears into another story with a nineteenth-century plot: that of being married and becoming a father.

Three Breeches Parts: "On the Gull's Road," "The Enchanted Bluff," and "Behind the Singer Tower"

On 20 May 1919, after having written *My Ántonia*, Cather wrote in a letter to Will Owens Jones that ghostwriting S. S. McClure's autobiography had been a refreshing experiment in speaking through a male narrator.[78] However refreshing it was, it was no experiment for Cather, but a tried-and-true method of conveying ideas, for with her Henry Nicklemann articles twenty years before, she had already put on the male narratorial voice and found it useful. Cather's self-fashioning, her experiments in self-advertisement during the 1890s, forced her to develop a past for Henry, a boyhood. In the first years of the twentieth century, Cather made this journalistic boyhood into the fiction of *Bildungsroman*. Likewise, Helen Delay's girlhood, scarcely sketched in the 1890s, became a full *Bildungsroman* during Cather's New York years.

When Cather disguises her voice as Henry's, she enacts one of the most entertaining roles of the late-nineteenth and early-twentieth century: the breeches part, in which a female plays a male role. The most famous breeches part of recent years had been Sarah Bernhardt's 1905 re-creation of Hamlet. Cather was familiar with Bernhardt's Hamlet, recalling it in her short novel, *My Mortal Enemy* in 1926. Of course, crossdressing to play theatrical roles was as old as Shakespeare. But near the turn of the century in America, the breeches part became so popular that certain of Shakespeare's plays, for instance, *The Merchant of Venice,* achieved a new vogue. The breeches part asked a woman to take on the character and clothing of a man, an artificial, staged role that in turn-of-the-century America imitated a movement in real life: the New Woman taking on the "male" role of worker in the American scene.

In three later New York short stories, Cather created male narrators and played the breeches part in fiction, continuing to tell "Henry's" story. In "On the Gull's Road," Cather the writer remembers a beautiful woman through a male character's conventional love for her. In "The Enchanted Bluff," Cather lets Henry give voice to her memories of playing on a sandbar in the Republican River in Nebraska, of lying beneath the stars and envisioning the places she would discover. In this story, an apparent masculinity disguises female ambition to explore. "The Enchanted Bluff" prefigures Cather's 1915 novel, *The Song of the Lark,* in which the protagonist Thea Kronborg puts on the robe of ambitious woman, conqueror, discoverer. "Behind the Singer Tower," a fiction, attempts to imitate nonfiction muckraking. The three "breeches parts" avoid the most typical Jamesian setting— the interiors of houses—although they do explore a part of the psyche: memory instead of the moral sense. All three plots could have happened, or in the case of "Singer Tower," were modeled on newspaper reports of actual accidents that would have made the papers.[79]

On the Gull's Road

In "On the Gull's Road," the nameless narrator (an "ambassador," readers learn from the subtitle) falls in love with Alexandra Ebbling, a beautiful, dying woman. To make her male narrator believable, Cather has him bristle with jealousy at Alexandra's callous husband, even thinking that he would like to hit him with his fists.

Yet in his quieter moments, the narrator suffers sentimentally for his hopeless love. In the modern, psychological fashion, Cather made the words that speak the character's suffering become thoughts, and therefore suffering became, not a conversation, but a state of mind: "But even in those first days I had my hours of misery," the ambassador remembers.[80] The ambassador is a sentimental sufferer whose primary act in Cather's short story is to feel and to relate feeling to his audience.

Alexandra Ebbling, the female protagonist, argues the virtues of the real and the ideal with the ambassador. Italy was her fairy tale, her ideal:

> The coast of Sardinia had lain to our port for some hours and would lie there for hours to come, now advancing in rocky promontories, now

retreating behind blue bays. It was the naked south coast of the island, and though our course held very near the shore, not a village or habitation was visible; there was not even a goatherd's hut hidden away among the low pinkish sand hills. Pinkish sandhills and yellow headlands, with dull-colored scrubby bushes massed about their bases and flowing through the dried watercourses. A narrow strip of beach glistened like white paint between the purple sea and the umber rocks, and the whole island lay gleaming in the yellow sunshine and translucent air.[81]

Later Alexandra says, "I shall never go to Sardinia, . . it could not possibly be as beautiful as this."[82] Then, as they pass the strait of Gibraltar, the waters become cold and rough. These waters, she insists, are the real, just like her birthplace in Finmark, "where the doings of the world go on." "These are the waters that carry men to their work," she insists.[83] The climate of her birthplace is cold and harsh, wild and lovely. It is not to be trusted, but eventually, it is where she returns to die.

The narrator interrupts Ebbling's thoughts about the real, begging to stay within the confines of the ideal. "[This cold sea] is not our reality, at any rate," he says.[84] Ebbling, however, insists that they are surrounded by their reality, and however much their dreams give them joy, all must come to reality. In the end, Alexandra Ebbling disappears into a reality created by death and the arctic sea. The narrator is left with only his memories and his ideal.

Cather had fashioned her narrator years before. This is a Henry Nicklemann figure, who had watched Lizzie Hudson Collier step off the train, Henry through whose voice Cather had articulated realistic stories and discussed the job market in Pittsburgh. Henry, as usual, is only *watching*. He watches the object that his male pseudonym allowed him to watch in Pittsburgh—a pretty woman—but the act of watching and of being unable to act despite his desire to do so, makes him a sentimental sufferer whose sentimental suffering has been internalized into modern angst. Henry's characteristics are joined with those of Helen, as if Cather's pseudonymous narrators had joined their voices together.

The Enchanted Bluff

"The Enchanted Bluff" (*Harper's* April 1909) again takes up the story of a young man's coming of age. Cather would have thought of her short story as starting with a "situation" instead of a "plot." To Cather, the plot would have been an artificial bringing together and separation of lovers, while a situation would have set up the temperaments of characters, a time, a place; and then she would have let the story unfold "organically." "Enchanted Bluff" unfolds organically.

The situation is one that Cather had used in a Henry Nicklemann article in the late eighteen nineties in Pittsburgh: an older man remembers what it had been like to be a boy, to share a boy's strong young body, a boy's allowed ambitions, and a boy's dreams that were free from two "stories" that shaped grown men's lives: love and money. In the Henry Nicklemann original, Henry pauses before a painting of boys in a swimming hole and discusses the painting with another man. In the New York City short story, several men remember when they were children and lay on a sandbar in a Nebraska river and dreamed of climbing a mesa that had been inhabited by the Anasazi. Because the story of the enchanted bluff takes place in characters' memories, Cather's "Henry" narrator—telling the "male" story of the swimming hole—is passive like Helen, remembering but not doing.

"Behind the Singer Tower" as Muckraking

Cather published one short story which took its outward form from the muckraking movement: "Behind the Singer Tower." Here she consciously adopted the hallmarks of journalistic forms. Writing to the *Century* magazine when she submitted the story, Cather pointed out that it was "yellow."[85]

In "Behind the Singer Tower" (which she finally published in *Collier's* [May 1912]), Cather divides the dialogue among Helen- and Henry-like characters. The characters, however, are all male, spokesmen for opposing schools of the sentimental and the real, here brought together to tell the Common Man's wrongs. "Behind the Singer Tower" tells many "modern" stories. As in "The Enchanted Bluff," there is no plot, just talk. The talk, it turns out, is about the two temperaments, Helen's and Henry's, and the acts that such temperaments feel compelled to perform.

The multiple stories of "Singer Tower" take their situations and characters from Cather's early journalism. Caesarino, an Italian laborer, is crushed and killed because his boss did not keep equipment in good repair. The conflict, one between labor and capital, was muckraking's most persistent theme. Cather draws Caesarino as a "type": an uneducated Italian laborer, he is simple and happy. His death is the snuffing out of a bright creature, but he is a creature who is neither complex nor entirely human. Cather's portrait of Caesarino is straight from Henry's yellow journalism. Henry the reporter is responsible for the other ethnic "types" in the short story: the boss whose negligence caused the death of Caesarino is part Jewish, and, according to Hallett, another character in the short story, it is his Jewishness that caused him to seek wealth at the expense of others' safety. Cather portrays another Jewish character, Zablowski, as having no backbone; ethnic insults sent his way slide right by him. His refusal to become offended by an insult is part of his "type."

In another story-within-the-story, Fred Hallett is paradoxically both an engineer of America's skyscrapers and a sentimental audience, one of "the people" who is moved by the muckraking plot—Caesarino's death at the hands of "the interests." Hallett forces Caesarino's boss to mail the laborer's last paycheck to his mother in Italy. In addition, Hallett gives Caesarino a decent burial, not just a pauper's funeral (in muckraking articles, the storyteller was empowered to set things straight, to fix what was wrong with America, and often, what was wrong between the dominant culture and immigrants).

The narrator of "Singer Tower" tells still another story. The narrator is a Henry-like journalist. Like Henry, and like a young Willa Cather who reported Brownville's decay in 1894, the narrator likes to report disaster and destruction. Behind the Singer Tower in New York, the Mont Blanc hotel has burned, killing many. This narrator with no feelings mentions that he or she saw the hand of the wealthy opera singer Graziani clinging to the window ledge of the Mont Blanc. The rest of Graziani, presumably, fell to the pavement. In the same way that Henry reported Mulberry Street, the narrator records shocking details to titillate the audience.

Through "Behind the Singer Tower," Cather invoked muckraking as well as several other journalistic styles that she had used during her almost twenty years reporting and editing. One could almost say that the subject of "Singer Tower" is journalism itself, and that the conversations between the characters in the short story argue the virtues of various journalistic plots, characters, and narratorial stances toward character and audience. Caesarino's decent burial and the portrait of the chief engineer as a scurrilous businessman argue for muckraking's concern with the way the powerful did business in America. However, despite Cather's complex, artistic construction of the narrative, the story does not work. Readers cannot identify with Caesarino, whom Cather's "Henry" style of narration portrays as scarcely human. In addition, the great skyscrapers, which in a muckraker's hands would be wholly symbolic of power gone awry, become in Cather things which are terribly wrong, yes, but also things whose very size commands respect. Muckraking as a type of writing ultimately failed Cather, but some of its conventions helped her later on.[86]

Two Western Stories: "The Joy of Nellie Deane" and "The Bohemian Girl"

"Helen's" story is scarcely pieced together in Cather's Pittsburgh journalism. In the nineteenth century, Helen's allowed activity was to sit by the hearth, waiting for her husband or children to call upon her talents as helpmeet. Cather's Helen, reflecting her time, was still. She seemed to have no history, because Cather herself had not lived Helen's history: Cather had gone to college instead, driven by her ambition to write. Helen has no ambitions, because to have them or aspire to work was not ladylike and was opposed to the ideals of motherhood, as they were then understood. However, Cather's "Helen Delay" pieces, combined with a few comments from Cather's Nebraska journalism, can serve to fill in Helen's history and ideals. As a little girl, Helen was read to. Her work was to sit still and listen. As an older girl, her only business was to fall in love. As a woman she married, had children, and kept house. What ambitions she was allowed to have were circumscribed by her sex. By the 1890s, Cather sanctioned one kind of professional ambition for women—the stage. The home and the stage allowed the woman to display the affectations of sentimentalism to the fullest: at home, she became the adult-taught-by-the-child. On stage, she became the objective correlative for the audience's emotions. Helen's life is so confined by her sex that Cather could not really expand her story into fiction. Instead, Cather transports Helen's story wholesale into her fiction and has other characters comment on the smallness of Helen's world.

The Joy of Nellie Deane

Before Cather wrote a full-fledged Nebraska novel, she wrote a Nebraska short story. In "The Joy of Nellie Deane," Cather uses her first woman narrator, who was Nellie Deane's high-school friend. She tells Nellie's story as a memory, using the "natural" narrative technique espoused by the realists. "Nellie Deane" is the story of Nellie's marriage and early death. Readers learn of Nellie's death through a letter, written to the narrator by another woman. The letter is psychologically realistic: the writer is so overcome that she sketches Nellie's death in the barest of prose. In "Nellie Deane," Cather began to let Helen tell her story.

Readers immersed in a woman's story were prepared by the narrator's sex for Nellie's last words to her husband, to her little baby. Nellie's suffering would surely uplift. It would be noble. Instead, they read Nellie's story as told by an older woman to the narrator. Nellie's husband is an unimaginative, avaricious man whose dour personality dampens Nellie's high spirits. During Nellie's labor her husband hires an inexperienced (and cheap) young doctor who does not know what to do, and so she dies. Cather's trick of telling of suffering that occurred in the past (instead of as it happens) silences the rhetoric of suffering, leaving only the bones of the story: a well-off but avaricious man bends his wife's outgoing personality to his, finally skimping when he shouldn't have. Nellie, a victim, remains silent.

In this realism that reports a woman's psyche, Cather used a story opening typical of Helen Delay to set reader expectations. However, Cather fashioned the speakers of the story along realistic guidelines: their small-town rhetorical simplicity reveals volumes about Nellie's passing. For instance, Mrs. Daws, a friend, relates Nellie's last days in a few words: "We won't talk about that . . . We did get Nellie fixed up nicely before she died."[87]

A realistic narrator, trappings of the sentimental overturned and thwarted by determinism—the organic shape of "Helen's" life—these form Nellie Deane's tragic story, which Cather published in the *Century* in October 1911.

The Bohemian Girl

"The Bohemian Girl" at first seems to be free of journalistic influence. However, its main conflict is one that Cather had explored at length while in Lincoln: there, she had insisted that beauty exists for its own sake, and not because it could make one wealthy. The story's paradox was replayed every time Cather sought publication: her short stories had to be "beautiful," that is, they had to fulfill the function of literary art. However, she likewise expected to be paid for their "beauty."

In "The Bohemian Girl," Nils Ericson returns home to the Divide after years away from his family. In his absence, his father has died, leaving his land to Nils's brothers. Olaf, one of the brothers, has married Nils's best girl, who is not Norwegian like the Ericsons, but Bohemian. Clara the Bohemian is one of "Henry's" racial types, but she is a positive one. Beautiful, daring, and unconventional, she is a New Woman not by choice but because of her "blood."

Nils's brothers have all become stodgy, concerned only with money. Cather had explored at length in her *Journal* columns what happens to an artist who becomes concerned with the bottom line instead of beauty: the story inevitably suffers. True art, by contrast, affirms the position of the gentleman in the coterie, who does not seek a profit on his words. In "The Bohemian Girl," Clara's beauty exists for itself.

Cather emphasizes Clara's "uselessness"—she does not cook or clean; she has no children. She roams the plains on horseback, turning her ankles and skinning her knees in the process. Like the actresses that Cather revered, Clara was worth her style and her verve. She is what she dramatizes herself to be, nothing more.

Olaf, her husband, bestirs himself only to make money and gain power. He has appropriated beauty, in the person of the woman Clara, and tried to use her for his utilitarian ends. Since Olaf is running for political office, he hopes that Clara's presence in his home will gain for him the Bohemian vote—yet he must be careful. Clara's father is a tavern keeper, and if his wife is seen too much with her own father, she may ruin his chances with the prohibitionist Protestants. Olaf is even bilking two orphan children of their inheritance: he is a caricature of the money-grubber.

In the end, Nils, at first affecting pennilessness, steals Clara away. We learn that he is in fact a "gentleman" in standing, that is, he is wealthy. Clara can be herself with him; he will love her for what she is and where she comes from.

The story gains its fairy-tale quality from Nils, who has money but who got it all offstage, like a "gentleman." Readers do not see him as "the interests" even though he has gained a fortune in shipping. In running away from the farm, he escaped his brothers' on-stage squabbling and maneuvering, their sordid stories the very plot of the yellow journalist. However, in her short story, Cather sympathizes with the immigrant character, bringing Clara and her kin to life and making them fully human. "The Bohemian Girl" was a necessary stair-step to Cather's second novel, *O Pioneers!* Cather's novel would take on many of the short story's attributes: stodgy characters, portrayed as Scandinavian "racial types," stand in the way of the new. Aligned against them are farmers whose experiments in farming enrich them and allow them to stay on a harsh land—they are the very type of pioneer. In the novel, however, there is no fairy-tale escape; it would have heros, but feel like realism.

The End of Cather the Muckraker, the Beginning of Cather the Novelist

By 1909, muckraking was in trouble. The journalist William Irwin remarked in a late muckraking article that big business owned the transportation that carried magazines, the banks that financed them, and the advertising dollars that kept them solvent.[89] When big business became tired of the journalists' attacks, it withdrew media loans and advertising and made transportation difficult. By the fall of 1911 *McClure's* had become insolvent. Soon afterward, its founder was forced to retire. In this atmosphere, Cather had composed "Behind the Singer Tower," her editorial on the journalistic trade. Ultimately in 1912, Cather began to cut her ties to *McClure's*, taking longer and longer leaves of absence, until she became a novelist and free. In New York, Cather finished the process of transforming her long journalistic foreground into her years as a novelist.

Reading "some thousand short stories"[90] at the magazine led her to realize that she should use for inspiration, not the works of other writers like Henry James and Rudyard Kipling, but the events reported as fact by the magazine: "I can remember when Kipling's *Jungle Tales* [sic] meant more to me than a tragic wreck or a big fire in the city," Cather said in an interview in 1915.[91] Cather went on to cement her solidarity with realist newspaper reporters and to take one last jab, both at her youthful admiration of successful writers, and at academics: "If I hadn't again grasped the thrills of life, I would have been too literary and academic to even write anything worth while."[92] Ultimately she transformed a style of reportage—muckraking, which was meant to be consumed and then discarded—into a literary art intended to be handed down to the next generations.

After her stint at *McClure's* Cather did something radical: for her next four novels, she used the *outré* setting, Nebraska.[93] However, traces of the long foreground remained. Helen the homemaker became a familiar subject; so did Mary Baker Eddy, the ambitious woman. Occasionally Henry's deadpan reporting chimed in to tell a brief, horrible, deterministic story—about immigrants. She had changed, however. Cather discarded much that she had learned as a seller of images, of fiction. Immigrants became point-of-view characters, named, important. Henry receded so that he did not always control the story. She sometimes chose the "wrong" setting and the "wrong" subject, such as "Nebraska" or "Immigrants." However, Helen and Henry, S. S. McClure, and Mary Baker Eddy remained to help her, providing voices, points of view, temperamental types, and plots as Cather turned to Nebraska subjects.

Notes

Preface

1. L. Brent Bohlke, *Willa Cather in Person: Interviews, Speeches, and Letters* (Lincoln: University of Nebraska Press, 1986), 14.

2. Willa Cather, *The World and the Parish: Willa Cather's Articles and Reviews* (Lincoln: University of Nebraska Press, 1970), 146 (hereafter cited as WP).

3. Ibid.

4. James Woodress, *Willa Cather: A Literary Life* (Lincoln: University of Nebraska Press, 1987), 88.

5. More specific studies are as follows: John P. Hinz discusses Cather's use of pseudonyms in a *New Colophon* article. Peter Benson discusses Cather's years at the *Home Monthly* in his article in *Biography*. Mildred Bennett and Helen Cather Southwick each offer articles on Cather's years in Pittsburgh. Bennett's *The World of Willa Cather* and James Shiveley's *Writings from Willa Cather's Campus Years* bring Cather's times in Nebraska and Pittsburgh alive. However, none of these works studies journalism's influence on Cather's later writing.

6. Peter Benson, "Willa Cather at *Home Monthly*," *Biography* 4., no. 3 (Summer 1981), 244.

7. Sharon O'Brien, *Willa Cather: The Emerging Voice* (New York: Oxford University Press, 1987), 346.

8. The theater-goer watching the deeply moving performance seems to have been a kind of Ur-text of early modernism—perhaps a way for a late Victorian to express the passionate, the sexual, without arousing the censor's ire. In "A Wagner Matinée," Aunt Georgiana is deeply moved by a performance of Richard Wagner's music. The passionate music awakens Aunt Georgiana's memories of being a music student in Boston; she wants to give up her life on the Nebraska Divide (the short story appears in *Willa Cather's Collected Short Fiction, 1892–1912* [Lincoln: University of Nebraska Press, 1965], hereafter cited as *WCSF*). In Edith Wharton's *The Age of Innocence*, all the *dramatis personae* gather, at the beginning and the end of the novel, to view a performance of the opera *Faust*. Between is sandwiched a tale of extramarital passion. The heroine of Ellen Glasgow's *Barren Ground* tropes the expected plot by renouncing passion at the moment she is most carried away by a performance of Beethoven's music.

9. She was so much an oddity that the copyboy had to walk her home after a late night at work. *Lincoln Journal* (today's version of the *Nebraska State Journal*) editor Kathy Rutledge reports that, up until the 1970s, the management of the *Journal* still called a cab for its women reporters who had put in late hours. Fanny Butcher, who was of the third wave of female journalists, reports that her friends disapproved of her working on the *Chicago Tribune* because it was "no place for fair womanhood" (*Many Lives—One Love* [New York: Harper, 1972], 40). Butcher be-

came Cather's friend in 1913 when her first book to review as book page editor for the *Tribune* was *Alexander's Bridge*.

Sarah Josepha Hale (1788–1879) was the "Lady of Godey's" from 1837 to 1877. Sara Payson Willis (1811–72), whose pseudonym was Fanny Fern, worked for the *New York Ledger*. Her articles were collected in *Fern Leaves from Fanny's Portfolio* in 1853. Margaret Fuller (1810–50) wrote a front-page column for the *New York Tribune*.

10. Linda Wagner-Martin, *The Modern American Novel, 1914–1945: A Critical History* (Boston: Twayne, 1990), 9.

11. Cather, *WP*, 261–62; *Lincoln Courier* (21 September 1895).

12. Blanche Gelfant, "'What Was It . . . ?' The Secret of Family Accord in *One of Ours*," *Modern Fiction Studies* 36, no. 1 (Spring 1990): 61–78.

13. Cather to Grace [surname not known], 29 August 1894, Willa Cather Papers, Willa Cather Pioneer Memorial, Red Cloud, Nebraska (hereafter cited as *WCPM*). Cather calls her work at the *Home Monthly* "liberty" and refers to choosing how to spend her money in a letter to Mariel Gere dated 10 January 1898 *(WCPM)*.

By the terms of Cather's will, no one may quote her letters. I follow the tradition of biographers who have mentioned their contents only in paraphrase.

14. Jean Schwind's article on Cather and the Benda illustrations, which appears in *Approaches to Teaching Cather's* My Ántonia (New York: MLA, 1989), was the first to discuss Cather's concerns with the mechanics of book-making. My discussion here draws heavily on her work.

Chapter 1. Introduction

1. Adrian Forty, *Objects of Desire* (New York: Pantheon Books, 1986), 9.

2. Willa Cather, *The World and the Parish: Willa Cather's Articles and Reviews* (Lincoln: University of Nebraska Press, 1970), 271–72 (hereafter cited as *WP*).

3. H. W. Boynton, Review of *A Lost Lady, Independent* 111 (27 October 1923): 198–99.

4. J. B. Edwards, Review of *A Lost Lady, Sewanee Review* 31 (October/November 1923): 510–11.

5. Cather to Mrs. John Fisher, 2 September 1916, Willa Cather Papers, Willa Cather Pioneer Memorial, Red Cloud, Nebraska (hereafter cited as WCPM).

6. Frank Luther Mott, *American Journalism* (New York: MacMillan, 1950), 422 (hereafter cited as *J*).

7. Sidney Kobrey, *The Yellow Press and Gilded-Age Journalism* (Tallahassee: Florida State University Press, 1964), iii, 6.

8. Mott, *J*, 526.

9. Kobrey, *Yellow Press* (Tallahassee: Florida State University Press, 1964), iii.

10. Mott, *J*, 503.

11. Edith Lewis, Cather's companion after 1907, worked for an ad agency after *McClure's* magazine folded.

12. Willa Cather, *Nebraska State Journal* (1 May 1895).

13. Forty, *Objects of Desire*, 11–12.

14. Nellie Bly is the pseudonym of Elizabeth Cochrane (1867–1922). Cochrane took her name from a song by Stephen Foster.

15. Mott, *J*, 489.

16. Rpt. in Nan Robertson, *The Girls on the Balcony: Women, Men, and the* New York Times (New York: Random House, 1992), 24.

17. Fanny Butcher, *Many Lives—One Love* (New York: Harper, 1972), 40–41.

18. Robertson, *Girls,* 19.

19. Arthur J. Riedesel, *The Story of the Nebraska Press Association, 1873–1973* (Lincoln: Nebraska Press Association, 1973), 37.

20. Joan Stevenson Falcone, "The Bonds of Womanhood: Sisterhood in Chicago Women Writers—The Voice of Elia Wilkinson Peattie." Diss., Illinois State University, 1992, 51.

21. Ibid., 34.

22. Frank Luther Mott, *A History of American Magazines, 1885–1905* (Cambridge, MA: Belknap, 1938–1957), 36 (hereafter cited as *M*).

23. For example, Cather damned *The Heavenly Twins,* a novel by Sarah Grand (pseudonym of Sarah Elizabeth McFall), because it dealt with syphilis, a "popular" subject, not a literary one.

24. Mott, *J,* 411–12.

25. Ibid.

26. I searched for the transcript of this speech when I was in Lincoln and Red Cloud, and Woodress before me looked for it as he was preparing his biography, but it seems to be lost. The best place to understand its flavor is Bernice Slote's opening essays in *The Kingdom of Art.*

27. Robert E. Wenger, "The Anti-Saloon League in Nebraska Politics, 1898–1910," *Nebraska History* 52, no. 3 (Fall 1971): 269.

28. Ibid., 267.

29. Cather, *Journal* (1 September 1890).

30. Anne L. Wiegman Wilhite, "Sixty-Five Years Till Victory: A History of Woman Suffrage in Nebraska," *Nebraska History* 49, no. 2 (Summer 1968): 150–55. Wyoming had entered statehood with full woman suffrage; Colorado granted woman suffrage in 1893; thus Nebraska would have been a logical place to stump for it. Historian Frederick Leubke, in a 7 April 1995 private conversation, noted the political designs that engineered the suffrage vote in western states. Wyoming's powerful railroad interests supported the suffrage issue because, they felt it would attract women and their families to the state, a development that would be good for railroad business. Utah's Mormon men supported suffrage because, in their highly patriarchal society structure, they felt that women would simply vote as their husbands did.

31. Ibid., 154.

32. To Cather, to seek the vote meant to align herself with the most reactionary elements of her state. The record shows that Cather, for whatever reason, did not stump for suffrage, even though she had a column in which she could have done so. New York journalist Ida Tarbell also avoided seeking the vote. The reason that she gives in her autobiography is that she sought employment and education to assert her style of being modern and female (*All in a Day's Work: An Autobiography* [New York: MacMillan, 1939], 34).

33. See, for example, Ford, *The Wooing of Folly* (New York: Appleton, 1906).

34. Letter, 2 January 1894, WCPM.

35. Frances Gere to Mariel Gere, 11 April 1900, Bernice Slote Collection, Love Library, the University of Nebraska, Lincoln, (hereafter cited as LOVE).

36. Mott, *M,* 11.

37. Ibid., 5.

38. Christine Bold, *Selling the West: Popular Western Fiction, 1860–1960* (Bloomington: Indiana University Press, 1987), 3.

39. "The medium is the message" is, of course, the theme of Marshall McLuhan's groundbreaking *Understanding Media: The Extensions of Man* (New York: McGraw-Hill, 1965).

40. Sharon O'Brien, *Willa Cather: The Emerging Voice* (New York: Oxford University Press, 1987), 18–22.

41. Ibid., 22–24.

42. Ibid., 79.

43. Cather, *WP*, 350–53; *Home Monthly* (June 1897).

44. "A Wagner Matinée," "The Bohemian Girl," and other pre-1913 short fiction by Willa Cather appears in Cather, *Willa Cather's Collected Short Fiction, 1892–1912* (Lincoln: University of Nebraska Press, 1965) and is cited herein as *WCSF*.

45. James Woodress, *Willa Cather: A Literary Life* (Lincoln: University of Nebraska Press, 1987), 59.

46. L. Brent Bohlke, *Willa Cather in Person: Interviews, Speeches, and Letters* (Lincoln: University of Nebraska Press, 1986), 26.

47. Woodress, *A Literary Life*, 17, 25.

48. Ibid., 15.

49. Ibid., 45.

50. Willa Cather, *A Lost Lady* (New York: Random House, 1972), 29–30.

51. Woodress, *A Literary Life*, 56.

52. Cather, *WP*, 642; *Lincoln Courier* (16 December 1899). Lillian Nordica is the stage name of Lillian Norton. Cather later modeled her short story, "The Diamond Mine" on the singer's life. In the story, the singer, who is a success, is a diamond mine for her toadies and hangers-on.

53. O'Brien, *The Emerging Voice*, 7.

54. Hermione Lee, *Double Lives* (New York: Pantheon Books, 1989), 37.

55. Willa Cather, *The Kingdom of Art: Willa Cather's First Principles and Critical Statements, 1893–1896* (Lincoln: University of Nebraska Press, 1966), 276; *Journal* (23 April 1895).

56. George C. D. O'Dell, *Annals of the New York Stage* (New York: Columbia University Press, 1945) lists each year's most important or popular plays and those who played in them. Volume 14 is pertinent to the discussion here.

57. Bohlke, *Willa Cather in Person*, 26.

Chapter 2. The Waltz and the Real

1. Willa Cather, *The World and the Parish: Willa Cather's Articles and Reviews* (Lincoln: University of Nebraska Press, 1970), 233 (hereafter cited as *WP*).

2. Ibid., 740.

3. Loretta Wasserman. *Willa Cather: A Study of the Short Fiction* (Boston: Twayne, 1991), 9.

4. Lincoln's newspapers were the *Nebraska State Journal,* an independent daily newspaper with a Sunday edition, owned by Charles Gere and edited by Will Owens Jones; the *Evening News,* which put out a daily evening edition, owned by the Westermanns (on whom were modeled the Erlichmanns in *One of Ours*), for which Lucius Sherman wrote a book column; the *Daily Call,* once the *Daily Democrat,* which folded not long after it tried to change its politics and compete with the other dailies; the *Lincoln Herald,* a weekly; and the *Lincoln Courier,* an arts and entertainment weekly owned by W. Morton Smith, edited by Sarah B. Harris, and for which Herbert Bates did a music column.

5. Sharon O'Brien. *Willa Cather: The Emerging Voice* (New York: Oxford University Press, 1987), 120.

6. Cather changed the title of her *State Journal* column many times. "One Way of Putting It" lasted until 21 January 1894; after that, Cather modified her style and purpose and called her column "With Plays and Players" for one month, 11 February–11 March 1894. She tried another title for the next month, calling it "Between the Acts" from 25 March to 29 April 1894. Perhaps she found these last two titles too confining. Her column usually consisted of many short (2–3 paragraphs) pieces strung together—and they were not always on the theater. "Utterly Irrelevant" became her next title, 16 September–28 October 1894. On 11 November Cather's writings appeared under "As You Like It." She did not change the title again until after her graduation in June 1895, but after that month, her work could be found under "The Passing Show" (see Curtin's bibliography).

As Curtin has pointed out, "The Passing Show" was Cather's intellectual property, and, when she quit the *Journal* to help edit the *Lincoln Courier,* a position which she filled 24 August until late November 1895, "The Passing Show" went with her (186). As she returned to the *Journal,* and later, sent columns from Pittsburgh, it remained "The Passing Show." Simultaneously, Cather published frequent daily reviews under the titles "Amusements" and "Music and Drama." Her last *Journal* column appeared 19 October 1902, after she had become a teacher. Her *Courier* contributions continued under the titles "Observations" and "The Theaters" until 24 August 1901.

7. In 1862, the Morrill Act allowed for the setting aside of land for agricultural and mechanical colleges, the so-called land-grant schools.

8. A very unsympathetic portrait of men who have no business sense appears in Cather's short story, "The Garden Lodge" (1905). The short story "A Sculptor's Funeral" (1905) contrasts the successful artist, who lived for his work, with small-town shysters who preyed on each other in a kind of sterile anticreation.

9. It is not too strange to imagine that Cather's more sensational plots came from the papers. Barbara Rippey notes that Nebraska author Marie Sandoz's (1896–1966) authorial voice and story plots were much influenced by frontier newspapers. Indeed, in Cather's article for the *Home Monthly* magazine, "Nursing as a Profession for Women" (May 1897), Cather (under her pseudonym of Elizabeth L. Seymour) mentions a woman drinking carbolic acid to escape her childbearing-related illness.

10. James Woodress, *Willa Cather: A Literary Life* (Lincoln: University of Nebraska Press, 1987), 72–73.

11. Cather's other short stories finished during her Lincoln years: "Lou, the Prophet" (1892) and "The Fear that Walks by Noonday" (1894) exploit the age's fascination with ghosts and the supernatural. "A Tale of the White Pyramid" (1892) attempts the genre of Oriental tale but fails because Cather did not then know how to evoke the otherness of Egypt. "A Son of the Celestial" (1893) succeeds in creating that otherness in the jingoistic portrayal of a man of Chinese descent. "A Night at Greenway Court" (1896) is straight out of Thackeray's *Henry Esmond,* set in Virginia in the seventeenth century. I have cited Cather's short stories from *Willa Cather's Collected Short Fiction, 1892–1912* (Lincoln: University of Nebraska Press, 1965); hereafter *WCSF.*

12. Cather, *WP,* 256.

13. Gerald Graff and Michael Warner, eds., *The Origins of Literary Study in America: A Documentary Anthology* (New York: Routledge, 1989), 104.

14. By the mid-nineteenth century, writing was still an avocation for upper-class gentlemen, and those men who needed to work had better ways of making money.

As a result, women writers made the profession of authorship their own. Susan Geary in her article "The Domestic Novel as Commercial Commodity" documents who held the largest share of the writer's market and why, from mid-century until near the turn of the century ("The Domestic Novel as a Commercial Commodity: Making a Best Seller in the 1850s," *Papers of the Bibliographical Society of America* 70 [1976]).

15. Daniel Borus, *Writing Realism: Howells, James, and Norris in the Mass Market* (Chapel Hill: University of North Carolina Press, 1989), 114.

16. Judith Fetterley, "*My Ántonia:* Jim Burden and the Dilemma of the Lesbian Writer," *Lesbian Texts and Contexts: Radical Revision* (New York: New York University Press, 1990), 159.

17. Cather, *WP*, 131.

18. Says an anonymous columnist in volume 192 of *Littel's Living Age,* "The staple English commodity which circulates in 3 volumes is a conventional product . . . a refuge for distressed needlewomen . . ." ("English Realism and Romance," 192: 131). According to Cather, the author of "Peter," she uncommodified "Peter" by making it shocking (by making it end in suicide, by making it about an inebriate and about a poor man)—only the few, the best thinkers, the most vociferous male critics, would "buy." "Peter" was a kind of luxury product not read by just everybody. Just everybody read "commodities." Paradoxically, however, "Peter" and other realistic novels sought to become a kind of ultimate commodity, luxury goods.

This year's luxury product is next year's commodity. In the 1850s, in America, Sarah Orne Jewett was using new advertising techniques to sell Harriet Beecher Stowe's new novel, *Uncle Tom's Cabin* (Geary, "Domestic Novel," 375–76). Jewett's modern tactics helped change the book trade forever, but the product, Stowe's book, was one that Cather looked down her nose at.

19. Borus, *Writing Realism,* 20–22.

20. Ibid., 91.

21. Cather, *WCSF.*

22. *Hesperian* (27 September 1893), Slote Collection, Love Library, Lincoln, Nebraska (hereafter cited as LOVE).

23. Woodress, *A Literary Life,* 76.

24. "Old Peter" became Mr. Shimerda in her 1918 novel. Ántonia Shimerda was modeled on the Bohemian woman Annie Sadilek Pavelka, whose father had committed suicide. Even if Cather had not known Mr. Sadilek and Annie, even if all she knew was what she read in the papers, she would have had ample stories in her head about violent deaths brought on by insanity, the weather, crop failure, childbirth, jealousy, and greed. "Samuel Deeters," begins a 1 September 1893 *Journal* article, "a prominent farmer living near here [Butler, Indiana], suddenly developed insanity today. He shot his mother twice. He also shot Amos Beechel in the stomach . . . He then attacked Beechel's daughter, Mrs. Lowe, and shot her twice . . ." (1).

25. Frederick Leubke, *Immigrants and Politics: The Germans of Nebraska, 1880–1900* (Lincoln: University of Nebraska Press, 1969).

26. Bismarck's purges, remarks Frederick Leubke, were especially hard on Catholics, who fled Germany in the 1870s (230). Others left because of a vigorous advertising campaign by frontier land companies.

27. Leubke, *Immigrants,* 66, 69, 128, 130, 137.

28. In a letter to Mariel Gere, Cather apologizes to her friend for having inflicted her various personae—Cather-the-Scholar and later, Cather-the-Bohemian—on her (2 May 1896, Willa Cather Papers, Willa Cather Pioneer Memorial, Red Cloud, Nebraska [hereafter cited as WCPM]).

29. Helen Horowitz, *Campus Life: Undergraduate Cultures from the End of the Eighteenth Century to the Present* (New York: Knopf, 1987), 15.

30. Ibid., 201.

31. Horowitz reports a novel written by Olive Anderson, *An American Girl and Her Four Years in a Boy's College* (1878), which follows the fortunes of Wilhelmine, who shortens her name to Will (Cather's nickname was Billy or Bill). Will, like Bill Cather, wished to become a doctor of medicine (reported in Horowitz 194).

32. Ibid., 28–29.

33. Willa Cather, *The Kingdom of Art: Willa Cather's First Principles and Critical Statements, 1893–1896* (Lincoln: University of Nebraska Press, 1966), 165 (hereafter cited as KA); *Nebraska State Journal*, 21 January 1894. Cather is quibbling over a spelling error: "Vitalis" is the correct spelling for the Latin word.

34. Cather, *WP*, 115; *Journal*, 28 October 1894.

35. Karen Blair, "Club Movement," *Oxford Companion to Women's Writing in the United States* (New York: Oxford University Press, 1994).

36. Cathy Davidson, *Revolution and the Word: The Rise of the Novel in America* (New York: Oxford University Press, 1986).

37. Elizabeth Ammons, *Conflicting Stories: American Women Writers and the Turn into the Twentieth Century* (New York: Oxford University Press, 1991), 6.

38. Of course, by the time her stay in Nebraska had reached its end, Cather had joined the Ladies' Auxiliary of the Nebraska Press Association. Her good friend Elia Peattie was very active in the women's club movement, which was in its heyday—perhaps it was Peattie who helped Cather correct her narrow prejudices on this account. In addition, Cather became the editor of the *Lincoln Courier*, an arts and entertainment weekly, whose sister publication was a club organ. (See Karen J. Blair for a discussion of the club movement.)

39. Herbert Bates, *The Odyssey of Homer* (New York: Harper, 1929), xvi.

40. Ibid., xxiii.

41. Ibid., xxxviii.

42. He appears as the sympathetic character Gaston Cleric in *My Ántonia*.

43. Borus, *Writing Realism*, 27–28.

44. It should be clear that the seeds of the New Criticism were planted long before I. A. Richards and John Crowe Ransom published their ground-breaking studies. Innovations such as Sherman's were needed. Land-grant schools and compulsory education laws began to place a college education within reach of the sons and daughters of the middle class, young men and women who had not been steeped in literature, for whom reading practice might be necessary.

45. Woodress, *A Literary Life*, 81.

46. *Hesperian*, December 1893, rpt. in Woodress, 80–81.

47. Cather, *WP*, 681; *Courier*, 2 December 1899.

48. Cather, *WP*, 703; *Leader*, 11 November 1899.

49. Cather, *WP*, 534; *Courier*, 5 February 1898.

50. Bernice Slote's speculations about when Cather first began writing for the *Nebraska State Journal* appear on pages 13–14 of *The Kingdom of Art*. She concludes that Cather may have begun earlier than the first datable piece of 5 November—but if she did, the subjects she addressed are not those that she customarily handled, and thus do not provide a positive identification.

51. Woodress, *A Literary Life*, 68.

52. Ibid., 90. By comparison the compositors in the back made three dollars per day, which was enough to support them.

53. Nebraska scholar Betty Stevens, in a telephone interview with the author (31 July 1994), notes that Nellie Bly came to Valentine, Nebraska, to cover the drought in 1894.

54. John Jakes, *Great Woman Reporters* (New York: Putnam's, 1969), 45.

55. A few pieces were signed "W.C." and "Deus Gallery."

56. Edith Lewis, *Willa Cather Living: A Personal Record* (New York: Knopf, 1953), 37.

57. Woodress to the author (20 August 1994), letter in possession of the author.

58. WPA, *Printing Comes to Lincoln* (1940), 49. Later, Cather's books would be set by Knopf in "handmade" fonts designed by the art book school—but cast on monotype and linotype machines.

59. The human interest story was invented when newspapers became businesses instead of purely political organs whose space was devoted to a politician's point of view. Newspapers of the late nineteenth century began to manufacture "news" with which to fill their pages. The practices of independent papers were called the New Journalism (Frank Luther Mott, *American Journalism* (New York: MacMillan, 1950), 436–37).

60. Willa Cather Papers, Willa Cather Pioneer Memorial, Red Cloud, Nebraska (cited hereafter as WCPM).

61. *Journal,* 12 August 1894: 13.

62. Letter to Grace [surname unknown], 29 August 1894, WCPM.

63. Cather used her Brownville material again in her 1897 short story, "A Resurrection" and recycled it as another article in *The Library,* calling it "The Hottest Day I Ever Spent" (Cather, *WP,* 778–82; 7 July 1900).

64. Cather wrote her enmity in a letter to Helen Seibel, dated 20 August 1898 (WCPM).

65. Cather to Jones, (8 September 1897), Slote Collection, Love Library, Lincoln, Nebraska.

66. Ibid.

67. Ibid.

68. Larzer Ziff, *The American 1890s: The Life and Times of a Lost Generation* (New York: Viking, 1966), 164.

69. Cather, in addition to being steeped in the "classics," was a pop culture junkie. When the bicycle became popular, she had one. As soon as the Victorian era floor-length dress became passé, Cather was in shirtwaists and "sensible" skirts, which in those days were not "sensible" at all, some thought, but rather disturbingly short. When *Trilby* was in, she read Trilby. When the nation experienced Kipling and Stevenson crazes, Cather was likewise bowled over. She didn't necessarily *like* everything that swam into view—Oscar Wilde and Chicago's *Yellow-Book* lookalike, the *Chapbook,* particularly disgusted her (Cather, *WP,* 155; *Journal* 26 May 1895)—but she seems to have sampled it all.

70. When Cather wrote a magazine article on Mary Baird (Mrs. William Jennings) Bryan, she portrays Mr. and Mrs. Bryan's teamwork. When William made political speeches, Mary signaled her husband from the balcony to change the pitch and volume of his voice (Cather, *WP,* 313; *Home Monthly,* September 1896).

71. In Harold Frederic's *The Damnation of Theron Ware* (1896), one of the marks of Theron's fall (he is a Methodist minister) is his buying a biography of the Frenchwoman George Sand, which he keeps wrapped in brown paper (214, 218). Frederic was foreign correspondent for the *New York Times.*

72. Cather, *KA,* 138; *Courier,* 28 September 1895.

73. Josephine Donovan's article on Sarah Orne Jewett and Emmanuel Swedenborg provides the information for my discussion of Swedenborg. Theophilus

Parsons's long life (1797–1882) allowed him to spread Swedenborgianism to more than one generation of New Englanders (*American Literature* 65, no. 4 [December 1993]). Parsons and Sampson Reed (1800–80) attended Harvard with Emerson, whose transcendentalism is Swedenborgian. Parsons published books that popularized Swedenborg, such as *Outlines of the Religion and Philosophy of Swedenborg*, late in his life (1876); these books brought his ideas to a new generation of readers and writers.

74. Cather mouthed Swedenborg's ideas about children being their elders' teachers. In Cather's 12 November 1893 *Journal* vignette, a man in jail sobs when his wife brings their new son to him (Cather, *WP*, 19). This vignette falls easily into the Swedenborgian pattern of the child teaching wisdom (or here, contrition) to an adult. In another vignette, (*Journal*, 17 December 1893), Cather uses the figure of the child to attack the equation, Time is Money. Since the exchange of gifts at Christmas between parents and children was not a monetary transaction, the business equation temporarily did not hold (Cather, *WP*, 8–9). The narrator tarries before the picture windows, trying to find just the right gift for a child whom we later learn is dead, the narrator's dearest love (Cather, *WP*, 9).

Many years after the *Trilby* episode, Cather was still using Jim Burden's (a child's) point of view to tell the story of *My Ántonia* and opening *O Pioneers!* with children, a lost kitty cat, a dying father who was a poor farmer from the old country.

75. This is the didacticism that Nina Baym notes in *Woman's Fiction*, with resignation, that crept into woman's writing after the Civil War.

76. Donovan, "Jewett and Swedenborg."

77. Cather reacted with impatience when she read authors who felt that they had to impart a message (see, e.g., her Sarah Grand review, Cather, *WP*, 132–34; *Journal* 23 December 1894). Her newspaper reviews sneered when authors portrayed a heavy Swedenborgian symbol: "Why should Mr. Belasco arrange with the regulator of the universe," Cather asked in a 27 January 1895 play review, "to have the sun rise at just the right moment to light up the figure of the Christ over the hero's repentance?" (Cather, *WP*, 221).

"[Belasco] claimed to have spent $5000 experimenting until he got just the right lighting for the last scene of the sunrise in the mountains [in *Girl of the Golden West*]," says Newman in her introduction to *Girl*. Belasco's dramas were about technology, pageant, and show, as when he had real horses and sheep on the stage—another kind of stage realism (viii).

78. Cather, *WP*, 70–71; *Journal*, 21 October 1894.

79. Cather, *WP*, 79; *Journal*, 5 April 1894.

80. Cather, *WP*, 275–77; *Courier*, 23 November 1895. Ouida is the pseudonym of novelist Marie Louise de la Ramée.

81. American actress Matilda Heron brought French actress Madame Doche's staging of *La Dame aux Camélias* to America in 1855, and because of this event, critics called Heron's acting and that of her imitators the "French emotional school." An "emotional" actress strove to feel the staged emotion. Her business was to dramatize passion and to disregard discipline and control (Garff B. Wilson, *Three Hundred Years of American Drama and Theatre: From* Ye Bare and Ye Cub *to* Hair [Englewood Cliffs, NJ: Prentice-Hall, 1973], 171–72). Wilson reports that Clara Morris could weep real tears on stage (266).

82. "The theater," hypothesizes Arthur J. Pulos, "shares with advertising the distinction of having been the early source of industrial design in America" (*American Design Ethic: A History of American Design to 1940* [Boston: Massachusetts Institute of Technology, 1983], 288). Pulos cites as evidence the necessity of the stage to

show, by shape, color, position, as well as to *tell,* via a script or libretto. My study posits that Cather, too, is a kind of designer, and that her special need as a journalist to involve herself in the dramatic arts rubbed off on her.

83. K. Cowper in Littell's *Living Age* magazine wrote how she deplored the acting of Sarah Bernhardt, premier actress of the French emotional school. She asked, "what is to be said about some of the horrible death-scenes adopted in modern plays? In this it was Madame Bernhardt who first sets the example" (201: 293). At the turn of the century, it seems as if anything that was new or imported from France was called "realism," and anything that had become comfortable was labeled "sentiment." "Realism" became the signifier for the new (and in America, the new was a moneymaker); sentiment was always old.

84. The suppression style of Duse left the signified undefined, and it was inevitable that some of those who saw her filled in the blanks with illicit sexuality. According to K. Cowper in *Littel's* volume 201, Duse as Camille dying in her nightgown was just too revealing a sight. There should have at least been a curtain around Duse's bed to preserve her modesty (293).

85. Cather, *WP,* 119–20; *Journal,* 11 November 1894.

86. Cather to Mariel Gere, 2 May 1896, WCPM.

87. Cather to Charles Gere, 14 March 1896, WCPM.

88. Woodress, *A Literary Life,* 105.

89. Cather, *WP,* 187.

90. The *Courier's* sister publication was a club organ. Whether Cather's views of women's clubs changed is unrecorded, but after she joined the *Courier,* she certainly tempered her writing on the subject.

91. Cather, *KA,* 68.

92. Cather, *WP,* 202; *Journal,* 3 May 1896.

93. Cather, *WP,* 277; *Courier,* 23 November 1895.

94. Cather, *WP,* 194; *Journal,* 7 April 1895. Male artists shouldn't marry either. She rhetorically shakes her head at the French actor Mounet-Sully when she learns that he and his wife do not get along (Cather, *WP,* 95; *Journal,* 16 June 1895). She castigates Rudyard Kipling with his own words, saying, "He rides the fastest who rides alone" (Cather, *WP,* 138–39; *Journal,* 30 December 1894).

95. Cather, *WP,* 222; *Journal,* 27 July 1895.

96. Borus, *Writing Realism,* 61.

97. Cather, *WP,* 299; *Journal,* 17 May 1896.

98. Cather, *WP,* 103; *Journal,* 12 August 1894.

99. *Journal,* 19 January 1896; 22 March 1896.

100. Cather, *WP,* 696; *Courier,* 23 November 1895.

101. Cather, *KA,* 27.

102. Cassandra Laity, "H. D. and A. C. Swinburne: Decadence and Sapphic Modernism," *Lesbian Texts and Contexts: Radical Revisions* (New York: New York University Press, 1990), 220.

103. Cather, *WP,* 146; *Journal,* 13 January 1895.

104. Letter, 2 January 1896, WCPM.

105. Cather, *KA,* 192; *Journal,* 19 January 1896.

106. Cather was still attracted to the risqué; Mott reports that Swinburne's name was synonymous with "sin" during the period under consideration (*A History of American Magazines* [Cambridge, MA.: Belknap, 1938–1957], 123).

Chapter 3. Selves and Others

1. Reported in Frank Luther Mott, *A History of American Magazines, 1885–1905* (Cambridge, MA.: Belknap, 1938–1957), 32 (hereafter cited as *M*).

2. Mildred Bennett to George and Helen Seibel, 10 April 1958, Willa Cather Papers, Willa Cather Pioneer Memorial, Red Cloud, Nebraska (hereafter cited as WCPM).

3. Reported in Mott, *M*, 39–40.

4. In his 1981 *Biography* article Peter Benson reviews the scholarship on how Cather met James Axtell. While E. K. Brown maintains that Cather met the Axtells at Charles Gere's home (Benson, "Home Monthly," 228), Slote believes that George Gerwig, who preceded Cather as the *Nebraska State Journal* critic, was the intermediary (Benson, "Home Monthly," 229). Axtell's wife's family was from Lincoln, and the two families may well have known each other socially (Benson, "Home Monthly," 231). At any rate, by June 1896, the deal was closed, and Cather had informed the *Journal* that she was leaving. Her salary was to be one hundred dollars a month (James Woodress, *Willa Cather: A Literary Life* [Lincoln: University of Nebraska Press, 1989], 125), and her duties—anything that was needed.

5. Willa Cather, *The World and the Parish: Willa Cather's Articles and Reviews* (Lincoln: University of Nebraska Press, 1970), 305 (hereafter cited as *WP*).

6. Helen Woodward, *The Lady Persuaders* (New York: Oblensky, 1960), 63.

7. George Seibel, "Miss Willa Cather from Nebraska," *New Colophon* 2, no. 7 (September 1949): 201.

8. Kathleen Byrne and Richard C. Snyder, *Chrysalis: Willa Cather in Pittsburgh, 1896–1906* (Pittsburgh: Historical Society of Western Pennsylvania, 1980).

9. Cather to George Seibel, 29 January 189[7], WCPM. During the same period that Cather edited the *Home Monthly*, the editor of the *Atlantic* could expect four thousand dollars annually; a young man of thirty on the make in New York City could expect two thousand dollars (Mott, *M*, 35). An unknown writer could expect anywhere from one cent per word to ten dollars per page from *Harper's* (Mott, *M*, 39); however, Mrs. Humphrey Ward, whose *Robert Elsmere* was a best seller, published a novel in *Harper's* and received fifteen thousand dollars for it (Mott, *M*, 39). Fanny Butcher reports her 1913 salary—almost fifteen years later—as book reviewer for the *Chicago Tribune* as seventy-five dollars a month, or nine hundred dollars a year (*Many Lives—One Love*, 39).

In the magazine business, so often did words became equivalent to pennies or fractions of them that Borus was led to say, "the language of equitable financial exchange easily replaced that of art" (*Writing Realism: Howells, James, and Norris in the Mass Market* [Chapel Hill: University of North Carolina Press, 1989], 43). Not only was time money, but words were, too.

10. Cather to Will Owens Jones, 15 January 189[6], Jones Papers, Nebraska State Historical Society, Lincoln, Nebraska (hereafter cited as NSHS).

11. Edith Lewis, *Willa Cather Living: A Personal Record* (New York: Knopf, 1953), 41.

12. See, for example, L. Brent Bohlke *Willa Cather in Person: Interviews, Speeches, and Letters* (Lincoln: University of Nebraska Press, 1986), 13.

13. John P. Hinz recognizes the following names and pseudonyms under which Cather wrote in Pittsburgh: Willa Cather, her "real" name, she seems to have reserved for her short stories and poems published in the *Home Monthly* from August 1896 to December 1899. Willa Sibert Cather, her "real" name plus her self-created nickname, appears in most venues for Cather's writing after 1900: the *Library*, the *Pittsburgh Leader*, the *Pittsburgh Gazette*, and the *Index*. It is also the byline for most of Cather's stories and poems, as well as some reported articles, 17 March 1900 to 29 November 1903. W. S. C., John Esten, Mildred Beardslee, Emily Vantall, Charles Douglass, Elizabeth Seymour, Mary K. Hawley, W. Bert Foster, George Overing, and John

Charles Esten each appear only once or twice over poetry, short stories, and newspaper stories (1896–1900). Mary Temple Bayard, CWS, and Mary Temple Jameson wrote for the *Library* and the *Home Monthly*, 1897–1900. Clara Wood Shipman (possible) submitted poems to the *Library*, May–June 1900 (John P. Hinz, "Willa Cather in Pittsburgh," *New Colophon* 3 [1950]: 198–207).

Helen Delay appeared most often as Cather's book reviewer persona for the *Home Monthly*, January 1897–February 1898, but she also wrote a few articles, the latest appearing 14 April 1900. Henry Nicklemann (or Nickelmann) wrote only one short story, "Dance at Chevalier's" (*Library*, 28 April 1900); the rest of the time he remained true to his persona of reporter for the *Library* and for the *Pittsburgh Gazette*. "Sibert" reviewed books, magazines, and theater for the *Pittsburgh Leader* (September 1897–March 1900). Gilberta S. Whittle wrote for the *Leader* and the *Gazette* 1898–1902. Byrne and Snyder add Mary D. Manning, Marie Catheron, Ira Brevoort (possible), and Lawrence Brinton to the list. All of these Byrne and Snyder additions were pseudonyms used only once (*Chrysalis*, 7).

Cather was not terribly clever with titles for her works and pseudonyms. Most she got from a book, short story, poem, song, or from a relative or acquaintance. Charles Douglass, a pseudonym, for instance, came from Charles, her father, and Douglas, her brother (Bennett, "Names," 37).

Cather came into journalism at a period of transition. *Godey's Ladies' Book* (1830–98), the upper-class journal for "ladies," not "women," had female authors contributing under male pseudonyms or anonymously (Woodward, *Lady Persuaders*, 22). Edward Bok, who took over the *Ladies' Home Journal*, a middle-class magazine, in 1889, had female contributors sign their names (Woodward, *Lady Persuaders*, 41). Male authors as well used pseudonyms frequently in the era under study (e.g., Hall Caine, Anthony Hope, and Anatole France). The pseudonym could keep the "authorial self" separated from the authors' other public personae, personae such as politician, landholder, or lawyer.

14. The Cather behind all the Pittsburgh pseudonyms was a progressive woman of her time. Jeanette Barbour in the *Pittsburgh Press* (28 March 1897) included a profile of Cather in "Pittsburgh's Pioneers in Women's Progress," calling Cather "a thoroughly up-to-date woman" (reported in Bohlke, *Willa Cather in Person*, 1–2).

15. Mott asserts that the practice of assigning pseudonyms to disguise the fact that one author was supplying multiple contributions was common practice (*M*, 38). Cather told Mrs. Gere in a letter that she was using half a dozen pseudonyms (13 July 1896, WCPM).

16. Willa Cather, *The Kingdom of Art: Willa Cather's First Principles and Critical Statements, 1893–1896* (Lincoln: University of Nebraska Press, 1966), 188; 12 January 1986 (hereafter cited as *KA*).

17. Cather, *WP*, 115; *Nebraska State Journal*, 28 October 1894.

18. Helen Woodward describes the voice that was the foremother of all women's journals: the voice of Sarah Josepha Hale. It "combined flattery, advice, command, all soft and feathery. That has been the pattern of women's magazines ever since, never quite hitting on the dirty spot, but flipping at it" (*Lady Persuaders*, 32). My comparison of Cather with Hale is not meant to be facile. Cather recognized her belonging to a community of women editors. In the *Home Monthly* for November 1896, Cather wrote an appreciation of Hale, the editor of *Godey's*. Cather's July 1897 *Home Monthly* article celebrates "The Great Woman Editor of Paris: Madame Juliette Adam."

19. Cather to Mrs. Gere, 13 July 1896, WCPM.

20. *Lincoln Daily Star,* 24 October 1915; reported in Bohlke, *Willa Cather in Person,* 13.

21. Letter, 4 August 1896, WCPM.

22. Reported in Byrne and Snyder, *Chrysalis,* 4.

23. Elizabeth Ammons, *Conflicting Stories: American Women Writers and the Turn into the Twentieth Century* (New York: Oxford University Press, 1991), 7.

24. Cather's employing a secretary was a symbol of having arrived. See the letter that Cather wrote Mariel Gere bragging about the fact (13 July 1896, WCPM).

25. Cather to Mrs. Gere, 13 July 1896, WCPM.

26. Cather, *WP,* 589; *Pittsburgh Leader,* 8 April 1898.

27. Byrne and Snyder, *Chrysalis,* 15. Ida Tarbell, New York journalist, like Cather, used clothing as a symbol (see *All in a Day's Work: An Autobiography* [New York: MacMillan, 1939]). Tarbell wore the shorter skirts to indicate that she was a modern businesswoman who had work to do. Later generations, choosing even shorter dresses and skirts, would call Cather and Tarbell's skirts and shoes "sensible" and consider them unfashionable.

28. Byrne and Snyder, *Chrysalis,* 7.

29. Anne Romines, *The Home Plot: Women, Writing, and Domestic Ritual* (Amherst: Univesity of Massachusetts Press, 1992), 135.

30. According to Ruth Miller Elson, the city streets were responsible for all sorts of ills: they were vicious and dirty, they were artificial, not real (*Myths and Mores in American Best Sellers, 1865–1965* [New York: Garland, 1985], 27–31). Men who went to the city were seduced by gambling and drink; women were seduced by rakes (Nina Baym, *Women's Fiction: A Guide to Fiction by and about Women in America, 1820–1870* [Urbana: University of Illinois Press, 1993], 184). American landscapes, as they were storied in Cather's day, were immediate products of the industrial revolution (Lewis Baltz, *Landscape: Theory* [New York: Lustrum, 1980], i): industrial noise and pollution drove the home to the suburbs and created the ideal of a "natural" landscape as one with no sign of technology. Writing of suburban homes was Cather's way of writing to her audience, but it can also be seen as Cather's comment on industry and technology. One of her attitudes toward technology in Pittsburgh is of a piece with her *State Journal* comments of years gone by, in which technology was somehow allied with Lucius Sherman and against "the people." For instance, Cather had said of actor Joseph Jefferson: "You have touched the large world of men who feel more closely than the small world of men who formulate" (Cather, *WP,* 681; *Courier,* 2 December 1899).

31. Cather, *WP,* 335.

32. Edna Lyall is a pseudonym of Ada Ellen Bayly.

33. Cather, *WP,* 336.

34. Ibid., 345.

35. Ibid., 506; *Journal,* 17 January 1897.

36. Cather, *WP,* 335.

37. Cather was apparently defending Mark Twain here. His work was not considered proper for a ladies' magazine (Woodward, *Lady Persuaders,* 10).

38. Cather, *WP,* 363.

39. See Ibid., 258, n. 4.

40. Ibid., 343–44.

41. Ibid., 346.

42. Ibid., 357.

43. Marcia Jacobson, *Being A Boy Again: Autobiography and the American Boy Book* (Tuscaloosa: University of Alabama Press, 1994), 3.

44. Ibid., 14.

45. Jacobson's term, 7–8.

46. Cather, *WP*, 337.

47. Woodward notes very astutely that while men had their architecture and farming magazines, the woman's magazine was a trade journal, too. It was didactic and utilitarian (*Lady Persuaders*, 5, 7); here Cather informs her readers about how to be, and how to teach their daughters and sons to be.

48. Sharon O'Brien, *Willa Cather: The Emerging Voice* (New York: Oxford University Press, 1987), 152.

49. Anthony Hope was the pseudonym of Sir Anthony Hope Hawkins.

50. Cather, *WP*, 354.

51. Anatole France was the pseudonym of Jacques Anatole Thibault.

52. Cather, *WP*, 238.

53. Ibid., 574.

54. Ibid., 575.

55. Ibid., 341.

56. Ibid., 342.

57. Some of Helen Delay was Cather's real and closely felt sentimental view of art. However, Helen was also a mask that Cather put on for work—her favorable review of Hall Caine, for instance, belies her true feelings about that writer. Another opinion is available through George Seibel, who, writing of Cather and of his wife Helen, stated that they would all rather go hungry than write like Caine and become millionaires ("Miss Willa Cather," 196–97). But concerning a childhood among books, Cather seemed to write at times clear *through* her medium, the woman's magazine. Helen Woodward says of her days on the *Woman's Home Companion* beginning in 1908: "To the uninitiated, a woman's magazine may be a powdery bit of fluff. No notion could be more unreal or deceptive. That is just the style in which the magazines express themselves" (*Lady Persuaders*, 1–2).

Later, Cather used the "fluff," exploring children's coming-of-age or using a child's point of view in her novels: *O Pioneers!*, *My Ántonia*, *Song of the Lark*, *One of Ours*, and much later *Shadows on the Rock* are all examples.

58. Cather, *WP*, 344.

59. The Alger myth was a very comfortable one, reports Ruth Miller Elson, the author of a study on American best sellers. It remained one of popular literature's most important themes until war and depression of the 1930s and 1940s weakened its hold (*Myths and Mores in American Best Sellers*, 25).

60. Kirk Jeffrey, "The Family as Utopian Retreat from the City: The Nineteenth-Century Contribution," *The Family, Communes, and Utopian Societies* (New York: Harper & Row, 1972), 23.

61. Cather, *WP*, 349; *Home Monthly*, May 1897.

62. Cather, *WP*, 349.

63. Cather said of Aunt Franc that she distributed "manna" (in this case, learning) in the wilderness (Cather, *WP*, 349); she seems to have been a model of a learned woman for young Cather. Fanny Butcher, another western journalist (born in Fredonia, Kansas, in 1893), remarks how another older woman showed the way for her. The woman, a friend, had also graduated from Mt. Holyoke and was concerned with writerly style. As a reviewer for the *Chicago Tribune*, Butcher's first book to review in 1913 was Cather's *Alexander's Bridge*. Her intelligent comments made Cather her friend (*Many Lives—One Love*, 358)

64. Lewis, *Willa Cather Living*, 43.

65. In the 1890s and after, newspaper work was a common way for authors to support themselves. Eugene Field wrote a column in the *Chicago Morning News* (later the Chicago *Record*); he sometimes published his own poems there. William Dean Howells sat in the editor's easy chair at *Harper's;* Cather's own friend Elia Peattie worked for the Chicago *Tribune;* Theodore Dreiser worked as a newspaperman in St. Louis, Chicago, Pittsburgh, and New York; Stephen Crane worked for the Bachellor-Johnson syndicate, and Bret Hart edited the *Overland Monthly.* Later, Ernest Hemingway would take a job at the *Kansas City Star.* All began in the press; some used their press connections to publish. By 1900, however, Cather was reaching the end of her newspaper career—the rest of her journalism would be for magazines. To Helen Seibel she wrote that she avoided reading newspapers; in fact, she wouldn't even look at one (20 August 1898, WCPM).

66. The spelling of the name varies, appearing as either Nickelmann or Nicklemann.

67. Cather, *KA,* 39.

68. *Journal,* 11 February 1894.

69. Cather, *WP,* 865; *Pittsburgh Gazette,* 17 November 1901.

70. Cather, *WP,* 506; *Journal,* 10 January 1897.

71. George Seibel, "Miss Willa Cather from Nebraska," 206.

72. Cather, *KA,* 43.

73. Cather, *WP,* 555–57; *Courier,* 4 March 1899.

74. Cather worked briefly for a weekly called the *Index of Pittsburgh Life.* In it she published "Winter Sketches at the Capital," a column, as well as articles. Her latest contribution appeared in March 1901.

75. Edith Lewis, *Willa Cather Living,* 37; the Crane "interview" appears in Cather, *WP,* 772–73.

76. Cather's meeting with Crane is highly fictionalized. I am indebted to James Woodress for the idea that Cather's words about Stephen Crane are also about herself. Bernice Slote's article "Willa Cather and Stephen Crane," which appeared in 1969 in *The Serif,* notes the incongruities between Cather's article and actual events (for instance, Stephen Crane was fair, and Cather depicts him as dark-haired).

77. Sanford C. Marovitz, "Bridging the Continent with Romantic Western Realism," *The American Literary West* (Manhattan, KS.: Sunflower University Press, 1980), 17.

78. The book from whose title Cather took the name of her poem, James Lane Allen's *Summer in Arcady* (1896), is about young lovers whose affairs were troubled by their parents' hatred of their chosen partners and by their poverty. Arcady was, for Cather, a loaded word which celebrated sentimental untroubled love, condemned change and death, and condemned poverty.

79. See, for example, Cather, *WP,* 702–3; and see the short story "Jack-a-Boy," *Willa Cather's Collected Short Fiction, 1892–1912* (Lincoln: University of Nebraska Press, 1965; hereafter cited as WCSF).

80. It was not long before Cather began to forgive teachers and use them as positive, or at least interesting, characters. When she became a schoolteacher in March 1901, she wrote a story about a professor who forgets his prepared speech at the party celebrating his retirement. Lucius Wilson, a philosophy professor, is the affable *ficelle* in *Alexander's Bridge.* By the 1920s, Cather could write a novel like *The Professor's House,* in which she was in whole-hearted sympathy with a history professor's quandary.

81. Cather, *WP,* 536; *Courier,* 5 February 1898.

82. Cather, *WP,* 696; *Pittsburgh Leader,* 17 June 1899.

83. Borus, *Writing Realism*, 66.

84. Ibid., 36.

85. See Susan Geary's article on how advertising helped women writers gain a wide market in the mid-nineteenth century ("The Domestic Novel as a Commercial Commodity: Making a Best Seller in the 1850s," *Papers of the Bibliographic Society of America* 70 [1976]:365–93).

86. Borus, *Writing Realism*, 114.

87. Frank Norris, reported in Borus, *Writing Realism*, 20–22.

88. Takaki and Borus discuss the same economic and social forces as driving the literary types now known as "realism" and "naturalism"; thus, although it is not traditional to do so, I have collapsed those two categories in my discussion. Both take immigrant life or economic inequality as subject matter, and it was these subjects that Cather has Henry write about. Realism and its child, naturalism, were responses by the art world to Charles Darwin's *Origin of Species* (1859). Ronald Takaki's work is titled *Iron Cages: Race and Culture in Nineteenth-Century America* (New York: Knopf, 1979).

Cather herself knew the terms "realism" and "veritism"; the latter term she used only once, to my knowledge, and in parentheses, in a derogatory review of Hamlin Garlin. She used "realism" as the broad term to describe the revolution that changed western art near the end of the nineteenth century, and that is what I use here. Much later, Elizabeth Sergeant, Cather's friend and biographer, would use the term "naturalistic" to describe Cather's novel *The Song of the Lark,* but her use of the term is much later than the time under discussion here (Sergeant's work is *Willa Cather: A Memoir* [Philadelphia: Lippencott, 1953]).

89. Elizabeth Blackwell, *Pioneering Work in Opening the Medical Profession to Women* (New York: Source Books, 1970), 97.

90. Edith Wharton says in her autobiography, *A Backward Glance,* that she wrote *Ethan Frome* to correct the "rose coloured spectacles" of an earlier generation of women writers. Wharton's book is a love story, but it is one about poor people living proscribed existences ([New York: Appleton, 1934], 293–94). An intimate of Henry James, who, with William Dean Howells, was one of the creators of American Realism, Wharton wished to prove just how different she was from those "scribbling women."

91. The *Pittsburgh Leader,* for which Cather wrote and worked the telegraph desk, was yellow, according to John P. Hinz ("Willa Cather in Pittsburgh," 199).

92. "Dance at Chevalier's" appears in WCSF.

93. According to Takaki, white men, caught up in the rapid industrialization of America, created a fortiori "reasons" for their successes and failures (*Iron Cages,* 143). An easy reason was that race, religion, sex, or nationality could hamper or help a person's attempts at success. To many white nineteenth-century thinkers, America's major industrialists, all white protestant men, had the right moral and physical equipment for success, while everyone else lacked something—of course, what the "other" Americans really lacked was a voice, a language, money, acceptance, freedom from race prejudice. People of color, Catholics and Jews, non-English speakers, and women as well were "othered." The term is Edward Said's.

94. Ronald Takaki, *Iron Cages,* 143. Ignorance about the role of genetics hindered turn-of-the-century understanding of race. "National traits" in the 1890s and 1910s were fixed, not mutable or learned, scientists believed. Racial and national traits were in the blood (Elson, *Myths and Mores in American Best Sellers,* 96–99).

Even customs associated with class were inherited somehow, although Alger preached that one could "rise."

95. See, for example, Woodress, *A Literary Life*, 160–62.

96. According to Elson, the French were "light, effervescent, intellectual, harmless, decorative." However, Paris was the city of sin; it especially encouraged sexual deviation (*Myths and Mores in American Best Sellers*, 154 ff.).

97. Cather, *WP*, 643; *Courier*, 16 December 1899.

98. Cather, *WP*, 49; *Journal*, 25 March 1894.

99. Elson, *Myths and Mores in American Best Sellers*, 162. Cather would have known about Mexican stereotypes from the newspaper. The *Nebraska State Journal* published the story of a Mexican, Don Pedro, who stabbed a woman through the heart out of jealousy (1 September 1893).

100. Takaki, *Iron Cages*, 156–8.

101. "A Chinese View of the Chinese Situation," *Gazette* 28 July 1900; "Pittsburgh's Richest Chinaman," *Gazette*, 15 June 1902; and "A Factory for Making Americans," *Gazette*, 8 June 1902.

102. See Cather, *WP*, 712–13.

103. Blanche Gelfant's introduction to *O Pioneers!* describes Cather's literary contributions as "pioneering" (New York: Penguin, 1989). Gelfant describes the end result of "Henry Nicklemann's" experiments in Pittsburgh. By 1913 Cather would come to identify with those immigrants whom Henry "othered"; she began to see her career, which she followed to the top, her risk-taking, when she quit to write fiction, and her new techniques for novel-writing as "pioneering." Her books told of a period in American history, and also of her life.

Chapter 4. Pittsburgh Short Fiction

1. Dana Gioia, "Business and Poetry," *Hudson Review* 36, no. 1 (Spring 1983): 148.

2. Willa Cather, "The Novel Démeublé," *On Writing: Critical Studies of Writing as an Art* (Lincoln: University of Nebraska Press, 1988).

3. Besides *The Troll Garden* and *April Twilights,* the books she actually published, Cather planned two other books during the Pittsburgh years. One, to be called *The Player Letters,* would collect a series of open letters to American dramatists. The letters, some of which appeared in periodicals, did not interest the publishers to whom she sent them (James Woodress, *Willa Cather: A Literary Life* [Lincoln: University of Nebraska Press, 1987], 138).

In addition, in 1905 Cather began a novel, whose setting was to have been Pittsburgh. However, when she sent the manuscript to S. S. McClure, he did not publish it, and she ceased sending it out (Woodress, 181).

4. Woodress, *A Literary Life*, 165.

5. Ibid., 170–71.

6. Ibid.

7. For a discussion of Cather's self-created middle name, see Sharon O'Brien, *Willa Cather: The Emerging Voice* (New York: Oxford University Press, 1987), 7.

8. Letter, 11 April 1900, Slote Collection, Love Library, Lincoln, Nebraska (hereafter cited as LOVE).

9. " 'One of Our Conquerors'," *The World and the Parish: Willa Cather's Articles and Reviews* (Lincoln: University of Nebraska Press, 1970), 765 (hereafter cited as *WP*).

10. Cather to Carrie Miner Sherwood, 22 December 1906, Willa Cather Pioneer Memorial, Red Cloud, Nebraska (hereafter cited as WCPM).

11. Clara Morris, *Stage Confidences: Talks about Players and Play Acting* (Boston: Lathrop, 1902), 24.

12. Stories which are discussed elsewhere, or which show no influence from journalism, are not mentioned.

13. Willa Cather, *Willa Cather's Collected Short Fiction: 1892–1912* (Lincoln: University of Nebraska Press, 1965), 51 ff (all of Cather's short fiction not published in *The Troll Garden* was read in this edition, which is cited as *WCSF* hereafter). "Burglar's Christmas" is one of the few short stories that Cather published under a pseudonym. In this case, she signed her story, which appeared in the December 1896 issue of the *Home Monthly,* "Elizabeth Seymour." A complete discussion of "Burglar's Christmas" may be found in O'Brien, *The Emerging Voice,* 51–54.

14. Willa Cather, *Lincoln Courier,* 14 September 1895.

15. Cather, *WCSF,* 342–43; 351.

16. "The Heathen Chinee" appeared in Bret Harte's *Plain Language from Truthful James,* and it appeared as well in the *Overland* in September 1870. The Chinese man who won the epic poker game in Truthful James's tale was named "Ah Sin."

17. Cather, *WP,* 538; *Courier,* 5 February 1898.

18. Cather, *WP,* 639.

19. Ibid., 535.

20. Ibid., 534.

21. Willa Cather, *The Kingdom of Art: Willa Cather's First Principles and Critical Statements, 1893–1896* (Lincoln: University of Nebraska Press, 1966), 93 (hereafter cited as *KA*).

22. See Cather, *WP,* 268–70; *Courier,* 2 November 1895; Cather, *KA,* 93.

23. George Seibel, "Miss Willa Cather from Nebraska," *New Colophon* 2, no. 7 (September 1949), 203.

24. Cather, *WP,* 510; *Courier,* October 1897. See Mildred Bennett's "Willa Cather in Pittsburgh" *Prairie Schooner* 33 (Spring 1959), 70–71 for details of Cather's acquaintance with Reinhart.

25. The home folks could not, in turn, read Cather's irony. Will Owens Jones offered a scathing attack of the story in the *Nebraska State Journal.*

26. Cather, WCSF, 251.

27. One poem was called "Shakespeare, A Freshman Theme." Another was a translation of one of Horace's odes.

28. Carman's book of poems, which he published with Richard Hovey, was called *Songs from Vagabondia* (1894).

29. Cather, *WP,* 282–86; *Nebraska State Journal,* 2 February 1896.

30. Willa Cather, *April Twilights* (Lincoln: University of Nebraska Press, 1962), 14.

31. Ibid., 34.

32. Ibid., 47–48.

33. Ibid., 25–26.

34. Ibid., 36–37.

35. She teasingly calls chapter 6 "I Fall in Love"; however, the love object is the city of Paris.

36. Cather, *April Twilights,* 5–6.

37. Ibid., 23.
38. Ibid., 46.
39. Ibid., 51.
40. Gioia, "Business and Poetry," 148.

Chapter 5. Helen Loves Henry

1. Willa Cather, *The World and the Parish: Willa Cather's Articles and Reviews* (Lincoln: University of Nebraska Press, 1970), 722 (hereafter cited as *WP*).

2. Reported in L. Brent Bohlke, *Willa Cather in Person: Interviews, Speeches, and Letters* (Lincoln: University of Nebraska Press, 1986), 21.

3. Reported in Bohlke, *Willa Cather in Person*, 15.

4. James Glenn Stovall, "S. S. McClure," *Dictionary of Literary Biography*, 91 (Detroit: Gale Research Company, 1990), 216–225.

5. The woman journalist still was unwelcome in some circles. When Tarbell wrote a life of Lincoln for the magazine, Richard Watson Gilder, editor of the conservative *Century*, sneered, "they got a girl to write a life of Lincoln" (Stovall, 223).

6. *McClure's Magazine* (January 1903).

7. Robert C. Bannister, *Ray Stannard Baker: The Mind and Thought of a Progressive* (New Haven, CT: Yale University Press, 1966), 105.

8. See Ida Tarbell, *All in a Day's Work: An Autobiography* (New York: MacMillan, 1939), chap. 13.

9. Henry Nicklemann took the title of one of his realistic human interest pieces from Riis's book.

10. Tarbell, *All in a Day's Work*, 241–42.

11. Ida Tarbell, "History of Standard Oil," *McClure's Magazine* 20: 259.

12. Hutchins Hapgood, "The Spirit of Labor," in *Years of Conscience: An Anthology of Reform Journalism* (New York: World, 1962), 193–94.

13. Tarbell, "History," *McClure's* 23: 671.

14. Will Irwin, "The American Newspaper," in *Years of Conscience: An Anthology of Reform Journalism* (New York: World Publishing, 1962), 385.

15. Benjamin O. Flowers, "The Monthly Magazines in the Grip of Priveleged Wealth," *Arena* 41 (January 1909): 106.

16. Tarbell, "History," *McClure's* 23: 672.

17. For a discussion of this point, see Cornelius Regier, *The Era of the Muckrakers* (Gloucester, MA: Peter Smith, 1957), 195; see also Michael Lewis, *The Culture of Inequality* (Amherst: University of Massachusetts Press, 1978), 7.

18. Tarbell, "History," *McClure's* 23: 671.

19. Irwin, "The American Newspaper," 386.

20. Garff B. Wilson, *Three Hundred Years of American Drama and Theatre: From Ye Bare and Ye Cubb to Hair*. Englewood Cliffs, NJ: Prentice-Hall, 1973. 200–201.

21. William Kittle, "The Making of Public Opinion," *Arena* 41 (July 1909): 440.

22. Flowers, "Grip of Priveleged Wealth," 106.

23. Mary Alden Hopkins, "The Newark Factory Fire," *McClure's Magazine* 36 (April 1911): 668.

24. Concerning Daudet's play, see Cather, *WP* 687–88. Olga Nethersole played the part of the artist's model, whose name was Sapho. Cather reviewed the play,

praising it highly in the *Pittsburgh Leader* (9 January 1900). After the run in Pittsburgh, the play moved to New York, where the censors shut it down.

25. Henry James, *Partial Portraits* (New York: Scribner's, 1887), 40.

26. Ibid., 41.

27. Ibid., 44.

28. Ibid.

29. John Palmer *Rudyard Kipling* (London, Nisbet, 1918), 8–9.

30. Ibid., 11–12.

31. Leon Edel, *Henry James*. 5 vols. (Philadelphia: Lippincott, 1953–1972), 331–32.

32. This dance, between meaning emerging in a reader's mind and the scarcely hinted at author's intention, is what Cather refers to in her essay "The Novel Démeublé," in *On Writing: Critical Studies of Writing as an Art* (Lincoln: University of Nebraska Press, 1988), 33–43.

33. Cather would have been reminded of Stevenson often. S. S. McClure's son was named Robert Louis Stevenson McClure.

34. She met her friend and biographer Elizabeth Sergeant when Sergeant sold a piece of muckraking to her in 1911 (Sergeant, *Willa Cather: A Memoir* [Philadelphia: Lippencott, 1953], 31).

35. Gibbons and Cather's letters are preserved in the Lilly Library, Bloomington, Indiana. I read them as photocopies at the Love Library, University of Nebraska, Lincoln (cited hereafter as LOVE).

36. Cather to Gibbons, LOVE, photocopy.

37. Bohlke, *Willa Cather in Person*, 12–16.

38. On 1 March 1907, Eddy's son filed a Bill in Equity against the managers of the church's assets, claiming that the managers were mishandling the funds, and alleging that his mother was not able to properly handle her finances. See Sibyl Wilbur, *The Life of Mary Baker G. Eddy* (Boston: Christian Science Publishing Society, 1913).

39. See David Stouck's excellent preface to *The Life of Mary Baker Eddy and the History of Christian Science* (Lincoln: University of Nebraska, 1993), xvi.

40. Stouck, *Life of Mary Baker Eddy*, xvii.

41. Stouck's article on Cather and the Eddy article is entitled "Willa Cather and *The Life of Mary Baker G. Eddy*," published in *American Literature* (May 1982): 288–94. Stouck discovered that Cather had written the article, a fact that she had kept secret until she wrote a friend, Edwin Anderson (24 November 1922) of her connection with the work (reported in Stouck, "Life of Mary Baker G. Eddy.").

42. James Woodress reports that church members visited McClure in his office and threatened him and his magazine (*Willa Cather: A Literary Life* [Lincoln: University of Nebraska Press, 1987], 193). However, nothing came of it.

43. Ibid., 193.

44. Ibid., 195.

45. The upshot of the Christian Science controversy at the time Cather's articles were published was that Eddy had not originated her doctrines, but had learned them from Quimby, even down to the word *Christian Science,* then called these doctrines her own.

46. See, for example, *McClure's Magazine* 29, no. 1.

47. Woodress asserts that one of Cather's jobs was to find illustrators for stories in *McClure's* (*A Literary Life*, 189).

48. Bohlke, *Willa Cather in Person*, xxii.

49. *McClure's Magazine* 29, no. 3: 336.

50. Ibid., 28, no. 2: 211.

51. Ibid., 28, no. 4: 347.

52. Ibid., 28, no. 2: 236.

53. Woodress, *A Literary Life*, 239.

54. *McClure's Magazine* 28, no. 6: 620.

55. Ibid., 28, no. 2: 211.

56. Ibid., 29, no. 6: 688.

57. Anne Romines, *The Home Plot: Women, Writing, and Domestic Ritual* (Amherst: University of Massachusetts Press, 1992), 75.

58. Nina Baym, *Women's Fiction: A Guide to Fiction by and about Women in America, 1820–1870* (Urbana: University of Illinois Press, 1993), 279.

59. Woodress, *A Literary Life*, 188–89.

60. Sharon O'Brien (*Willa Cather: The Emerging Voice* [New York: Oxford University Press, 1989], 292) and Woodress (*A Literary Life*, 190) both document this process in their biographies. Especially telling is Cather's output of fiction during her New York years. In 1907 she published four stories, stories which Woodress suspects she wrote in Pittsburgh. In 1908, Cather published one story; in 1909, one story; and in 1910, nothing at all.

61. See, for example, *Munsie's* (1902 vol.).

62. See "When the Claims of Creation Cannot Be Primary," *Silences* (New York: Delacorte Press, 1978).

63. O'Brien, *The Emerging Voice*, 290.

64. Cather also had found a stage upon which to exercise her ingenuity and power. O'Brien reports that she frequently published her own work in *McClure's* without asking others (*The Emerging Voice*, 289). Cather also liked to "score," becoming delighted when she bought St. Gaudens's *Familiar Letters* and Ellen Terry's autobiography (O'Brien, *The Emerging Voice*, 290).

65. For example, McClure did not like "The Enchanted Bluff" (Woodress, *A Literary Life*, 205).

66. Sarah Orne Jewett to Willa Cather, 19 December 1908, rpt. in James Woodress, *A Literary Life*, 203–4.

67. Willa Cather to McClure, LOVE, photocopy.

68. Woodress, *A Literary Life*, 289.

69. Ibid.

70. Bohlke, *Willa Cather in Person*, 8.

71. Cather, *Alexander's Bridge*, 103.

72. Cather to S. S. McClure, 12 June 1912, LOVE, photocopy.

73. Bohlke, *Willa Cather in Person*, 12–13.

74. In his old age, S. S. McClure came to depend upon Cather and other loyal friends for money to live on.

75. Woodress, *A Literary Life*, 226.

76. Cather, *WP*, 157; *Nebraska State Journal* (26 May 1895).

77. Cather, *Willa Cather's Collected Short Fiction, 1892–1912* (Lincoln: University of Nebraska Press, 1965), 98 (hereafter cited as *WCSF*).

78. Reported in Woodress, *A Literary Life*, 289.

79. See Evelyn Haller, "Behind the Singer Tower: Willa Cather and Flaubert," *Modern Fiction Studies* 36, no. 1 (Spring 1990), 41.

80. Cather, *WCSF*, 87.

81. Ibid., 85.

82. Ibid., 86.

83. Ibid., 89.

84. Ibid.

85. Letter to Robert U. Johnson, 22 October 1911, rpt. in Woodress, *A Literary Life*, 215.

86. Haller, "Behind the Singer Tower," 48.

87. Cather, *WCSF*, 66.

89. Harvey Swados, ed. *Years of Conscience: The Muckrakers; An Anthology of Reform Journalism* (Cleveland, Ohio: World Publishing, 1962), 369.

90. Bohlke, *Willa Cather in Person*, 8.

91. Kipling's work, published in 1894–95, was entitled *The Jungle Book*.

92. Reported in Bohlke, *Willa Cather in Person*, 15; *Lincoln Daily Star*, 24 October 1915.

93. Cather had mentioned that, during her early New York years, a critic had commented that no one ever wanted to hear about Nebraska (*Willa Cather on Writing*, 97).

Bibliography

Alcott, Louisa May. *Little Women*. Edited with an introduction by Elaine Showalter. New York: Penguin, 1989.

Alger, Horatio. *Ragged Dick, or, Street Life in New York*. 1868. New York: Penguin, 1985.

Allen, James Lane. *Summer in Arcady: A Tale of Nature*. New York: MacMillan, 1896.

Ammons, Elizabeth. *Conflicting Stories: American Women Writers and the Turn into the Twentieth Century*. New York: Oxford University Press, 1991.

Baltz, Lewis. *Landscape: Theory*. New York: Lustrum, 1980.

Bannister, Robert C. *Ray Stannard Baker: The Mind and Thought of a Progressive*. New Haven, Conn.: Yale University Press, 1966.

Bates, Herbert. *The Odyssey of Homer*. School Ed. New York: Harper, 1929.

Baym, Nina. *Woman's Fiction: A Guide to Fiction by and about Women in America, 1820–70*. 2d ed. Urbana: University Illinois Press, 1993.

Belasco, David. *Girl of the Golden West*. 1911. Introduction by Katherine D. Newman. Boston: Gregg Press, 1978.

Bennett, Mildred J. "How Willa Cather Chose Her Names" *Names* 10, no. 1 (March 1962): 29–37.

———. "Willa Cather in Pittsburgh." *Prairie Schooner* 33 (Spring 1959): 64–76.

———. *The World of Willa Cather*. Lincoln: University of Nebraska Press, 1961.

Benson, Peter. "Willa Cather at *Home Monthly*." *Biography* 4, no. 3 (Summer 1981): 227–48.

Blackwell, Elizabeth. *Pioneering Work in Opening the Medical Profession to Women*. 1895. New York: Source Books, 1970.

Blair, Karen. "Club Movement." In *Oxford Companion to Women's Writing in the United States*. Eds. Linda Wagner-Martin and Cathy Davidson. New York: Oxford University Press, 1994.

Bohlke, L. Brent. *Willa Cather in Person: Interviews, Speeches, and Letters*. Lincoln: University of Nebraska Press, 1986.

Bold, Christine. *Selling the West: Popular Western Fiction, 1860–1960*. Bloomington: Indiana University Press, 1987.

Borus, Daniel H. *Writing Realism: Howells, James, and Norris in the Mass Market*. Chapel Hill: University of North Carolina Press, 1989.

Boynton, H. W. Review of *A Lost Lady*. *Independent* 111 (27 October 1923): 198–99.

Butcher, Fanny. *Many Lives—One Love*. New York: Harper, 1972.

Byrne, Kathleen, and Richard C. Snyder. *Chrysalis: Willa Cather in Pittsburgh: 1896–1906*. Pittsburgh: Historical Society of Western Pennsylvania, 1980.

Cather, Willa. *Alexander's Bridge*. 1912. Introduction by Sharon O'Brien. New York: Meridian, 1988.

———. *April Twilights*. 1903. Edited with introduction by Bernice Slote. Lincoln: University of Nebraska Press, 1962.

———. *The Kingdom of Art: Willa Cather's First Principles and Critical Statements, 1893–1896*. [KA]. Edited by Bernice Slote. Lincoln, Nebraska: University of Nebraska Press, 1966

———. *A Lost Lady*. 1923. New York: Random House, 1972.

———. *My Ántonia*. 1918. Cambridge, MA.: Houghton, 1954.

———. "The Novel Démeublé." *On Writing: Critical Studies of Writing as an Art*. Foreword by Stephen Tennant. 1920. Lincoln: University of Nebraska Press, 1988. 33–43.

———. *On Writing: Critical Studies of Writing as an Art*. Forward by Stephen Tennant. 1920. Lincoln: University of Nebraska Press, 1988.

———. *O Pioneers!* 1913. Introduction by Blanche H. Gelfant. New York: Penguin, 1989.

———. *Song of the Lark*. 1915. Introduction by Sharon O'Brien. New York: Penguin, 1991.

———. *The Troll Garden*. New York: McClure, Philips, 1905.

———. *Willa Cather in Person: Interviews, Speeches, and Letters*. Edited by L. Brent Bohlke. Lincoln: University of Nebraska Press, 1986.

———. *Willa Cather's Collected Short Fiction: 1892–1912* [*WCSF*]. Introduction by Mildred J. Bennett, edited by Marilyn Arnold. Lincoln: University of Nebraska Press, 1965.

———. *The World and the Parish: Willa Cather's Articles and Reviews* [*WP*]. 2 vols. Edited by William Curtin. Lincoln: University of Nebraska Press, 1970.

———, and Georgine Milmine. *The Life of Mary Baker G. Eddy and the History of Christian Science*. 1909. Introduction and afterword by David Stouck. Lincoln: University of Nebraska Press, 1993.

Cochrane [Seaman], Elizabeth [pseud. Nellie Bly]. "Ten Days in a Mad House; *or, Nellie Bly's Experience on Blackwell's Island*." New York: Munro, 1887

Cowper, K. "Realism of To-Day." *Littel's Living Age* 201 (5 March 1894): 292–9.

Crane, Stephen. *Maggie, A Girl of the Streets (A Story of New York)*. Edited by Thomas A. Gullason. New York: Norton, 1979.

Curtin, William, ed. *The World and the Parish: Willa Cather's Articles and Reviews, 1892–1912* [*WP*]. By Willa Cather. 2 vols. Lincoln: University of Nebraska Press, 1970.

Davidson, Cathy. *Revolution and the Word: The Rise of the Novel in America*. New York: Oxford, 1986.

Donovan, Josephine. "Jewett and Swedenborg." *American Literature* 65, no. 4 (December 1993):31–50.

Dumas, Alexandre, *fils*. *Camille*. Translated by Sir Edmond Gosse. 1848. New York: New American Library, 1984.

Du Maurier, George. *Trilby*. 1894. Edited by Richard Kelly. Boston: Twayne, 1983.

Edel, Leon. *Henry James*. 5 vols. Philadelphia: Lippencott, 1953–1972.

Edwards, J. B. Review of *A Lost Lady*. *Sewanee Review* 31 (October/November 1923): 510–11.

Elson, Ruth Miller. *Myths and Mores in American Best Sellers, 1865–1965*. Modern American History Series. Edited by Robert E. Burke and Frank Friedel. New York: Garland, 1985.

"English Realism and Romance." *Littel's Living Age* 192 (January–March 1892):131–145.

Falcone, Joan Stevenson. "The Bonds of Womanhood: Sisterhood in Chicago Women Writers—The Voice of Elia Wilkinson Peattie." Diss. Illinois State University, 1992.

Fetterley, Judith. "*My Ántonia:* Jim Burden and the Dilemma of the Lesbian Writer." In *Lesbian Texts and Contexts: Radical Revision*. Edited by Karla Jay and Joanne Glasgow, 145–63. New York: New York University Press, 1990.

Flowers, Benjamin O. "The Monthly Magazines in the Grip of Privileged Wealth." *Arena* 41 (January 1909): 106.

Ford, James L. *The Wooing of Folly*. New York: Appleton, 1906.

Forty, Adrian. *Objects of Desire*. New York: Pantheon, 1986.

Frederic, Harold. *The Damnation of Theron Ware*. 1896. Edited by Everett Carter. Cambridge, MA: Belknap, 1960.

Geary, Susan. "The Domestic Novel as a Commercial Commodity: Making a Best Seller in the 1850s." *Papers of the Bibliographical Society of America* 70 (1976): 365–93.

Gelfant, Blanche. "'What Was It . . . ?': The Secret of Family Accord in *One of Ours.*"*Modern Fiction Studies* 36, no. 1 (Spring 1990): 61–78.

———. Introduction. *O Pioneers!*. By Willa Cather. New York: Penguin, 1989.

Gioia, Dana. "Business and Poetry." *Hudson Review* 36, no. 1 (Spring 1983): 147–71.

Graff, Gerald, and Michael Warner, eds. *The Origins of Literary Study in America: A Documentary Anthology*. New York: Routledge, 1989.

Griffing, Dale. Telephone interview. 31 July, 1994.

Haller, Evelyn. "Behind the Singer Tower: Willa Cather and Flaubert." *Modern Fiction Studies* 36, no. 1 (Spring 1990): 39–56.

Hapgood, Hutchins. "The Spirit of Labor." In *Years of Conscience: An Anthology of Reform Journalism*. Edited by Harvey Swados, 193–94. New York: World, 1962.

Hauptmann, Gerhard. *The Sunken Bell: A Fairy Play in Five Acts*. Translated with an introduction by Charles Henry Metzer. New York: Doubleday, 1906.

Hawkins, Anthony Hope [pseud. Anthony Hope]. *Prisoner of Zenda*. New York: Holt, 1894.

———. "Willa Cather in Pittsburgh." *New Colophon* 3 (1950): 198–207.

Hopkins, Mary Alden. "The Newark Factory Fire." *McClure's* 36 (April 1911): 663–72.

Horowitz, Helen Lefkowitz. *Campus Life: Undergraduate Cultures from the End of the Eighteenth Century to the Present*. New York: Knopf, 1987.

Irwin, Will. "The American Newspaper." In *Years of Conscience: An Anthology of Reform Journalism*. Edited by Harvey Swados, 369–76. New York: World, 1962.

Jacobson, Marcia. *Being a Boy Again: Autobiography and the American Boy Book*. Tuscaloosa: University of Alabama Press, 1994.

Jakes, John. *Great Women Reporters*. New York: Putnam's, 1969.

James, Henry. *Partial Portraits*. New York: Scribner's, 1887.

Jeffrey, Kirk. "The Family as Utopian Retreat from the City: The Nineteenth-Century Contribution." In *The Family, Communes, and Utopian Societies.* Edited by Sallie TeSelle, 21–41. New York: Harper, 1972.

Kittle, William. "The Making of Public Opinion." *Arena* 41 (July 1909):433–50.

Kobrey, Sidney. *The Yellow Press and Gilded-Age Journalism.* Tallahassee: Florida State University Press, 1964.

Laity, Cassandra. "H.D. and A.C. Swinburne: Decadence and Sapphic Modernism." In *Lesbian Texts and Contexts: Radical Revisions.* Edited by Karla Jay and Joanne Glasgow, 217–40. New York: New York University Press, 1990.

Lee, Hermione. *Double Lives.* New York: Pantheon, 1989.

Leubke, Frederick C. *Immigrants and Politics: The Germans of Nebraska, 1880–1900.* Lincoln: University of Nebraska Press, 1969.

Lewis, Edith. *Willa Cather Living: A Personal Record.* New York: Knopf, 1953.

Lewis, Michael. *The Culture of Inequality.* Amherst: University of Massachusetts Press, 1978.

Marovitz, Sanford C. "Bridging the Continent with Romantic Western Realism." In *The American Literary West.* Edited by Richard Etulain, 17–28. Manhattan, KS: Sunflower University Press, 1980.

McFall, Frances Elizabeth [pseud. Sarah Grand]. *The Heavenly Twins.* Introduction by Carol A. Senf. 1893. Ann Arbor: University of Michigan Press, 1992.

McLuhan, Marshall. *Understanding Media: The Extensions of Man.* New York: McGraw-Hill, 1965.

Meltzer, Charles Henry. Translation with an introduction. *The Sunken Bell: A Fairy Play in Five Acts.* By Gerhard Hauptmann. 1899. New York: Doubleday, 1906.

Morris, Clara. *Stage Confidences: Talks about Players and Play Acting.* Boston: Lothrop, 1902.

Mott, Frank Luther. *American Journalism [J].* Rev. ed. New York: MacMillan, 1950.

———. *A History of American Magazines, 1885–1905 [M].* 4 vols. Cambridge, MA: Belknap, 1938–57.

Newman, Katharine D. Introduction. *The Girl of the Golden West.* By David Belasco. 1911. Boston: Gregg, 1978.

O'Brien, Sharon. Introduction. *Alexander's Bridge.* By Willa Cather. New York: Meridian, 1988.

———. *Willa Cather: The Emerging Voice.* New York: Oxford University Press, 1987.

O'Dell, George C. D. *Annals of the New York Stage.* 14 vols. New York: Columbia University Press, 1945.

Olsen, Tillie. *Silences.* New York: Delacorte Press, 1978.

John Palmer. *Rudyard Kipling.* London, Nisbet, 1918.

Parsons, Theophilus. *Outlines of the Religion and Philosophy of Swedenborg.* Boston: Roberts, 1876.

Pulos Arthur J. *American Design Ethic: A History of Industrial Design to 1940.* Boston: Massachusetts Institute of Technology, 1983.

Regier, Cornelius C. *The Era of the Muckrakers.* 2d ed. Gloucester, MA: Peter Smith, 1957.

Review of *A Lost Lady. Independent* 111:198.

Review of *A Lost Lady. Sewanee Review* 31 (October/November 1923): 510–11.

Riedesel, Arthur J. *The Story of the Nebraska Press Association, 1873–1973.* Lincoln: Nebraska Press Association, 1973.

Riis, Jacob. *How the Other Half Lives: Studies amoung the Tenements of New York.* 1890. Edited by Sam Bass Warner, Jr. Cambridge: Harvard, 1970.

———. *Out of Mulberry Street: Stories of Tenement Life in New York City.* New York: Century, 1898.

Rippey, Barbara. Telephone interview. 1 August 1994.

Robertson, Nan. *The Girls on the Balcony: Women, Men, and the* New York Times. New York: Random House, 1992.

Romines, Ann. *The Home Plot: Women, Writing, and Domestic Ritual.* Amherst: University Massachusetts Press, 1992.

Rosowski, Susan J., ed. *Approaches to Teaching* My Ántonia. Approaches to Teaching World Literature. Series Editor Joseph Gibaldi. New York: Modern Language Association, 1989.

Rutledge, Kathy. Personal Interview. 28 July 1994.

Schaefer, Herman. *Nineteenth-Century Modern.* New York: Praeger, 1970.

Schwind, Jean. "Teaching the Illustrations in *My Ántonia.*" In *Approaches to Teaching* My Ántonia. Edited by Susan J. Rosowski. Approaches to Teaching World Literature. Series ed. Joseph Gibaldi, 163–69. New York: MLA, 1989.

Seibel, George. "Miss Willa Cather from Nebraska." *New Colophon* 2, no. 7 (September 1949): 195–208.

Sergeant, Elizabeth Shepley. *Willa Cather: A Memoir.* Philadelphia: Lippincott, 1953.

Sherman, Lucius. *Analytics of Literature: A Manual for the Objective Study of English Prose and Poetry.* Boston: Ginn, 1893.

Shiveley, James, ed. *Writings from Willa Cather's Campus Years.* Lincoln: University of Nebraska Press, 1950.

Slote, Bernice, ed. *The Kingdom of Art: Willa Cather's First Principles and Critical Statements, 1893–1896.* Lincoln: University of Nebraska Press, 1966.

———. "Willa Cather and Stephen Crane." *The Serif* 6 No. 4 (1969):3–15.

Southwick, Helen Cather. "Willa Cather, Early Years, Trial and Error." *The Colophon* 3 (1939): 92.

Stevens, Betty. Telephone interview. 31 July 1994.

Stouck, David. "Willa Cather and the Life of Mary Baker Eddy." *American Literature* (May 1982): 288–94.

———. Introduction and afterword. *The Life of Mary Baker Eddy and the History of Christian Science.* By Willa Cather and Georgine Milmine. Lincoln: University of Nebraska Press, 1993.

Stovall, James Glenn. "S. S. McClure." *Dictionary of Literary Biography.* 180 vols. to date. Detroit: Gale Research, 1990.Vol. 91, 216–225.

Stowe, Harriet Beecher. *Pink and White Tyranny.* Boston: Roberts, 1871.

Swados, Harvey, ed. *Years of Conscience: The Muckrakers; an Anthology of Reform Journalism.* Cleveland, Ohio: World Publishing, 1962.

Takaki, Ronald. *Iron Cages: Race and Culture in Nineteenth-Century America.* New York: Knopf, 1979.

Tarbell, Ida. "The History of Standard Oil." *McClure's* 20 (November 1902): 248–60.

———. "The History of Standard Oil." *McClure's* 23 (June 1904): 660–72.

———. *All in a Day's Work: An Autobiography*. New York: MacMillan, 1939.

Wagner-Martin, Linda. "Willa Cather: Reassessment and Rediscovery." *Contemporary Literature* 30, no. 3 (Fall 1988): 444–47.

———. *The Modern American Novel, 1914–1945: A Critical History*. Twayne's Critical History of the Novel. Boston: Twayne, 1990.

Wasserman, Loretta. *Willa Cather: A Study of the Short Fiction*. Boston: Twayne, 1991.

Wenger, Robert E. "The Anti-Saloon League in Nebraska Politics, 1898–1910." *Nebraska History* 52, no. 3 (Fall 1971): 267–92.

Wharton, Edith. *A Backward Glance*. New York: Appleton, 1934.

Wilbur, Sibyl. *The Life of Mary Baker G. Eddy*. 1907. Boston: Christian Science Publishing Society, 1913.

Wilhite, Anne L. Wiegman. "Sixty-Five Years Till Victory: A History of Woman Suffrage in Nebraska." *Nebraska History* 49, no. 2 (Summer 1968): 149–63.

Wilson, Garff B. *Three Hundred Years of American Drama and Theatre: From* Ye Bare and Ye Cubb *to* Hair. Englewood Cliffs, NJ: Prentice-Hall, 1973.

Woodress, James. *Willa Cather: A Literary Life*. Lincoln: University of Nebraska Press, 1987.

Woodward, Helen. *The Lady Persuaders*. New York: Obolensky, 1960.

WPA. *Printing Comes to Lincoln*. 1940.

Ziff, Larzer. *The American 1890s: The Life and Times of a Lost Generation*. New York: Viking, 1966.

Index

The names of magazines are grouped under the heading Magazines; likewise specific newspaper titles may be found under the heading Newspapers. All works, fiction and nonfiction, by Willa Cather appear under the heading Cather, Willa.

165